The Hurting Game

By Nathan Gottlieb

The Hurting Game

Published by: Endless String
Published: August 2012
ISBN: 978-0-9858533-1-0

This is for Fred,
the original one and only.

Robert Johnstreet,
who made this book possible.

Bobby and Jess,
who showed me the way.

And my son, Alex, light of my life.

What matters in court isn't the truth. It's which side presents the best illusion of truth.

—Fred from Jersey

Justice is a word politicians use when they're picking your pocket. It's a word people in law enforcement exploit to further their careers, even when they know they're probably sending someone that isn't guilty to prison. It's a lousy world. Justice is where you find it."

—Fred from Jersey

Chapter 1

Las Vegas. The Last Hurrah

Danny Cullen perched on the edge of the press row seat closest to Julio Babbas' corner, clenching his pen so hard he could have snapped it. It had been a brutal war from the opening bell, and Julio was taking the worst of it. Eleventh round, felt like the fiftieth, and the clock was winding down in super slow motion. Julio's face was all bruised and bloody, his right eye completely closed. He was fighting blind on that side and couldn't see the brutal left hooks that were bashing in his face. The ref should have stopped the brawl in the ninth, but Julio would've killed him for that.

Cullen was supposed to be taking notes for his post-fight report, but he'd stopped long ago. His reporter's objectivity was shot to shit. You don't watch your best friend get bludgeoned by a guy with anvils for fists and scribble a few lousy notes to fatten a thousand-word column. The gut-wrenching reality was that nothing short of a last-round knockout by Julio would allow him to keep his middleweight belt.

Mercifully, the bell finally rang. The blood-thirsty crowd was still on its feet screaming and cheering as Julio walked on wobbly legs to his corner. He glanced down at Cullen and smiled. What the hell? How could he flash a grin at a time like this? Didn't he know what all the warm bodies in the MGM Grand had already concluded? His butchered face would be down for the count as soon as the next anvil struck him. He was going to lose his title.

Cullen leaned closer so he could hear what trainer, Ryan McAlary, said.

"Helluva way to make a living, isn't it?"

Julio nodded.

"Listen to me!" the trainer said. "Remember the first day Danny brought you to my gym and you were gassed after a few minutes of sparring with me? Then Danny yelled he'd ship your ass back to Colombia if you didn't keep fighting, and you got so angry you found another gear and almost knocked me down. Find that gear now!"

The bell rang for the last round. Julio stood up. He almost lost his balance before grabbing the ropes to help keep him up. He glanced back at Cullen with the same crazy smile as before. Maybe the fighter already had brain damage?

Cullen didn't know, nor did he ask later where Julio went during those final seconds in the corner, but whatever he found inside made him attack his opponent like a man possessed, connecting with enough power shots to knock down a wall. It was as savage an assault as Cullen had ever seen. Julio kept pounding his opponent until the guy plunged face down on the mat, out cold. After the ref raised Julio's hand in victory, the exhausted victor dragged himself to the corner, pointed at Cullen, and smiled. And then winked! Cullen shook his head in disbelief. By now he was drained of feeling, unable to make sense of what he had just witnessed. The crowd was roaring. The MGM Grand shook. Hell, it seemed like all of Las Vegas had felt an earthquake as Julio raised both arms in triumph. McAlary embraced his fighter, as much hugging him as to keep him from falling. Cullen left his seat and pushed his way near Julio and McAlary, his two best friends.

"Don't know where that came from," Julio said.

"That's the beauty of it, isn't it?" McAlary replied.

***

After the fight, Julio insisted against all logic that they go dancing at Raven, his wife Cassandra's favorite club. Cullen suggested that a hospital for a brain scan would be a better destination, but Julio didn't lose arguments any more than he did fights. The music at the club was blasting at ear-shattering levels. Smoke machines were pumping enough white stuff to make it seem like they were dancing in a burning building. Out on the floor, Cullen felt like a pinball as Ecstasy-fueled dancers bumped him around. It was worse than being back at the Grand. At least in the arena, you were given a minute break between rounds to gather your senses.

On the ride to Julio's house, the fighter put on a Colombian alternative rock group, turned up the volume to the max, and sang along. This fight Cullen won. He popped out the CD and threatened to throw it out the window. Julio relented and drove his Mercedes SL the rest of the way to his Spanish-style split-level without speaking.

They pulled up in the driveway just as a thunderstorm with bad intentions split the sky with a dazzling bolt of lightning. Raindrops the size of quarters pelted the windshield. The majesty of the rare desert storm seemed to Cullen a perfect welcome home to the still-reigning king of the middleweight division. Cassandra stepped out of the car and opened a large umbrella, then motioned for them to get under it. Cullen did, but Julio just stood there in the rain. Then he raised his arms and face skyward and let the water pound him about the same way his opponent had been hitting him in the ring.

"Come under the umbrella!" Cassandra shouted.

"I want to feel the rain."

"Well, have a good time. I'm going inside."

Cullen wasn't big on getting drenched, but he stayed there with Julio while Cassandra hustled over to the house and went inside. "So you survive twelve rounds of a near massacre," he said, "and now you're going to die of pneumonia? Come on, *Perro*. Let's get out of the rain."

Julio lowered his arms, looked at Cullen, and flashed that same enigmatic smile he had before the last round. "You know why I grinned at you in the corner?"

"Not a clue."

"I saw in your face you thought I was gonna lose. After all we've been through, you lost faith.

That made me determined to let you know don't ever count Julio Babbas out. Truth is, *Carnal*, I had my doubts, too, but seeing that fear in your eyes gave me a shot of adrenalin. No way in hell was you gonna be right and me wrong. That just wasn't gonna happen."

"*Tu es mas loco in todo el mundo*," Cullen said.

"*Si, mon.*"

"Okay, now that I believe in you again—can we get our butts inside?"

"Why? Don't you like the rain? Rain is a good thing. It makes the grass grow, the flowers bloom and—"

"And it creates floods that drown idiots like us."

Julio laughed as they trotted over to the house and hurried inside.

"Take those wet shoes and socks off!" Cassandra called from the kitchen.

She was rinsing plates and silverware and putting them in the dishwasher when they walked in looking like two drenched, shaggy dogs. When Julio walked over and hugged her from behind, she pushed him away.

"You're getting me wet," she said. "Get out of those clothes before you hug me."

Julio took two bottles of Tecate from the refrigerator and handed one to Cullen. Then he turned to Cassandra. "Did you enjoy the fight, *querida?*"

Cassandra gave him a sour look. "What sane person would enjoy watching something like that?"

"The fans did."

"That's because they're animals like you. The more blood, the more they cheer."

"What I want to know," Cullen said, "is after the beating you took, how you had the energy to dance at the club."

"I popped a tab of Ecstasy."

"Since when do you do drugs?" Cullen said.

The fighter laughed. "Just kidding. Who needs Ecstasy when you're the Latino Spider-Man?"

"Okay, Spider-Man," Cassandra butted in, "I want you and Danny to get out of my hair while I finish up. Go into the den after you change clothes. I'll join you when I'm done."

They went to Julio's workout room first, where he dug up a couple clean sweat suits and pairs of white socks. They stripped off their soggy clothes, hung them across the Nautilus machines and slipped on the dry ones. Still shivering, they went into the den, where Julio fired up the gas fireplace and they stood there drinking in the warmth of the flames. When the chill had left their bones, they plopped onto the leather couch, put their stocking feet up on the coffee table, and sipped their beers. Cullen glanced at the black drapes pulled closed over a sliding glass door leading to the backyard. The drapes belonged in a funeral home, but no matter how hard Cullen and Cassandra had lobbied for a warmer color, Julio had a thing for black, and that was that.

Cullen took his cell phone out of the fresh sweat pants and looked for messages. Finding none of any importance, he left the cell on a table next to the couch.

Julio suddenly seemed subdued, face troubled.

"What's wrong?" Cullen said.

"Nothing."

"Don't be telling me nothing, *Perro*. You just won a big fight, made a ton of money. Remind me again where I discovered you."

"In a shitty club fight at a hotel ballroom in Venezuela."

"And who was it who saw something special in you and brought you back to Vegas to train with McAlary?"

"You, *Carnal*."

"So have you forgotten where you came from?"

"Not a day goes by when I don't think about that. If you hadn't brought me to America to train with Ryan, I'd still be on the streets of Colombia. Or dead or in jail."

"So then why aren't you happy? What's going on?"

"Just tired, I guess."

Cullen frowned. Julio always told him everything. "What are you hiding from me?"

"I have some things on my mind, that's all."

"Like what?"

Julio said nothing, just stared off at the drapes.

It happened fast. A man holding a gun stepped out from behind the drapes. He was dressed head to toe in black, and a ski mask covered his face. The gun made a spitting sound; then a hole appeared in Julio's forehead. Cullen opened his mouth to say something. Nothing came out. The gunman slid the door aside and disappeared into the night. Julio slumped over onto Cullen's lap, eyes open, not seeing.

Cullen's heart was beating out of control, mind racing. *This can't be happening. Gotta get help. Maybe chase the guy. No, can't leave Julio like this. So much blood.* He couldn't stand seeing it, so he pressed the palm of his hand hard against Julio's forehead to try and hold back the flow.

"Don't die on me, *Perro*! Hang in there!"

He grabbed his cell phone with his free hand just as Cassandra walked in carrying a bottle of beer.

"What's wrong with Julio?"

"Shot! Gotta get help!"

"Shot? What do you mean?"

He removed his hand to let her see.

"OH MY GOD! OH MY GOD!"

The beer dropped from her hand and shattered on the floor. She rushed over and knelt by Julio. The room filled with a wailing sound. Cullen's hand shook as he punched in 911.

Las Vegas Nine-One-One, what's your emergency?

"My friend just got shot! He's bleeding badly! Send an ambulance!"

What's the exact location of your emergency?

"What?"

Where are you located?

"Julio Babbas' house. Hurry!"

I need your address.

"Spring Mountain Road."

What's the house number?

"I don't fucking know! I just come here all the time!"

Is there someone with you who can tell me?

He looked at Cassandra. She was still screaming. "What's your house number, Cassandra?"

She didn't respond. Cullen removed his bloody hand from the forehead and shoved it into Julio's back pocket. He took out Julio's wallet and found his driver's license.

"One eighty-six! Hurry before he dies!"

The nightmare had begun.

***

Cullen sat on the couch in his apartment drinking a can of beer. The lights were off. It felt better in the dark. A bunch of crushed cans littered the coffee table. His sweatshirt was still damp with blood. More of it was caked on his hands. He should change the shirt and wash his hands, but the blood was all that was left of Julio.

He had stayed at the house until the last detective finished questioning him. Then he and Cassandra hugged for a long time, just standing there, holding on for dear life…lost life. Cassandra's sister finally took her away as the cops brought in a body bag. Cullen had shuddered, seeing it. Two cops had lifted Julio and started to place him in the bag, but the one holding the blood-soaked head lost his grip and Julio's head banged on the floor. Remembering, Cullen winced. The cop muttered something and picked Julio up again, and this time they succeeded in placing him in the bag. Cullen had stared at his friend's face until the zipper closed over it. They took away the bag. Alone in the den, he looked at the open sliding door and could still see the gunman dashing off into the night. The black drapes trembled now in the breeze.

Rain had started riding the wind into the den, so Cullen got up, closed the door, and made sure it was locked. As if it mattered. Nothing mattered anymore. Julio was dead. A cop walked in and told him it was time to seal off the house. It felt like his legs were made of wood as he let the cop escort him to the front door. There he stopped and looked back at the living room. This place would never be the same. Neither would his life. Not without Julio.

The cops had offered to drive him home, but he'd wanted to be alone, away from all the questions he didn't want to answer because there were no answers. He called a taxi. On the drive back to his apartment the rain was still driving hard. His eyes were as wet as the cab's windshield. He had no idea how he got home or up the stairs into his place.

Now, guzzling down the beer, Cullen crushed the can and tossed it on the pile. He couldn't stop seeing the hole in Julio's forehead. It made no sense. Everybody liked him. There had to be an explanation. Was Julio in some kind of trouble? If he was, why hadn't he told him?

Cullen closed his eyes. He tried in vain to shut everything out, but could still see the masked man with the gun, hear that awful spitting sound again and again. One second the guy was there, the next gone, almost like it never happened. Who would do this? He desperately wanted to know...*needed* to know.

Then Cullen understood what had to be done. The hole in Julio's forehead was now in his own soul. No surgeon or priest could remove it, only getting justice for Julio could. He would let the cops look for the killer, but if they failed him and the system broke down, somehow he would find the guy on his own, no matter what it took.

Chapter 2

Las Vegas. Eight months later

Detective Lew Gholston was leaning against an unmarked police car in an abandoned Flying J gas station on a remote stretch of Route 93. A Chevy Malibu with a lot of dust and miles pulled off the road and parked near him. Out of the car rolled a tall man in his mid-forties, about six-foot five and with the kind of ordinary face you'd expect to find behind a Home Depot counter or working at the post office. The only thing distinctive about him was the intense steel-blue eyes that Gholston knew from experience never missed a thing.

"I see you picked a scenic spot for our first meeting in three years," the man said. "I should've brought my camera."

They didn't shake hands.

"I can't be seen with you, Boff," Gholston said.

"Why? We're old friends."

"We were never friends."

"Don't you believe in bonds forged in combat?"

"Not when I lose," Gholston said. "I'll get to the point. I want to make this as quick and painless as possible. I have someone who's looking for a private investigator. I recommended you."

"What'd the mutt do? A murder involving a sex scandal would be great. I haven't crushed a juicy homicide case in a while."

"The person didn't commit a crime."

"It's a civil suit?" Boff said.

"No."

"Look, I really enjoy playing Twenty Questions with you, but I didn't bring sunscreen and I burn easily. What's the case?"

"The person wants you to find a killer."

Boff looked surprised. "Is there a punch line coming?"

"A friend of this person was shot eight months ago, one bullet to the forehead. It was a hit."

Boff spread his arms and stepped forward. "Look at me, Gholston. Who do you see? Frank Boff. I don't FIND killers. I help defend them when they get caught."

"You put a lot of drug dealers in jail when you were in the DEA."

"Ancient history."

"It'll come back, like riding a bicycle."

Boff shook his head. "You've got the wrong man for this. Even if I found the killer, my first impulse would be to ask for a retainer."

Gholston said nothing.

"Did you have a brain fart when you picked me for this job? You had to know I'd turn you down."

Gholston said nothing.

"Well, it was certainly nice seeing you. Let's do it again in another three years." Boff turned to go.

"I'm calling in a favor."

That stopped Boff in his tracks. He turned around frowning. "Don't do this to me, Lew. I was just hired by a rich mope accused of running an interstate Ponzi scheme allegedly preying on elderly women. The case could go on for months. I could pay off my mortgage with the money. How could you ask me to drop it?"

Gholston said nothing.

"Aw, hell, who's the stiff?"

Chapter 3

Cullen spotted the same blue Acura with two people in the front seat that had been there since he left his apartment. This was the third time in a week the damn car had been following him. He wasn't spooked, just pissed. It was time to get rid of these jerks.

Hitting the brakes, he did a swift U-turn and gunned his Camry. Before he could reach the Acura, however, the driver made a hard, screeching right turn and sped off. Cullen took the turn the same way, went into a skid, got the car straightened out, and floored the pedal. Not only did he not like being crowded, he *hated* being ignored.

He was closing the gap when a light ahead turned red. The Acura blew through it. Cullen was reckless, but not that crazy. He slowed down a bit, saw a small hole in the cross traffic and shot into it, causing a fast-approaching SUV to swerve badly, hop the curb, and come to a halt just before hitting a tree. *Shit.* Cullen knew he couldn't leave the scene. As the Acura disappeared in the distance, he banged his fist on the dashboard, violating one of boxing's most important rules: never hit anybody or anything with your bare hands. His hand started to feel sore, but not half as sore as he was. He swung his car around and drove back to the intersection.

The driver was out of his car and circling the vehicle, apparently looking for damage. Cullen was relieved to see the man didn't appear to be hurt.

Several pedestrians had stopped to look.

This wasn't going to be pleasant. Cullen left his car and walked over. The driver's face was contorted with rage. Cullen didn't blame him. He had been really stupid. "Any damage?" Cullen said.

The guy turned at him. "You almost got me killed, asshole! What the hell were you trying to do?"

"I'm really sorry. Somebody has been following me and—"

"I don't want to hear your goddamn excuses."

"I understand completely. If there's any damage, I'll pay for it."

"There isn't."

"Are you all right?"

"Yes. No thanks to you. I could fake whiplash, but it's not worth the trouble."

Cullen felt crummy. He pulled a twenty out of his wallet and handed it to him. "Buy a couple six packs, buddy."

It sounded lame the moment it came out of his mouth. The driver crumpled the bill and threw it in his face. "Screw you."

Brushing by Cullen, the guy got back into the SUV and backed it off the curb. The pedestrians were staring at Cullen.

This is starting out as a great day. First I lose the Acura, now I've got people looking at me like I'm a moron.

He couldn't think of a thing to say to salvage his dignity. He glanced down at the twenty. It was the only cash he had. He needed it for lunch. He scooped up the bill, quickly stuffed it in his pocket, and headed back to his car.

At the precinct, he parked his car in a spot reserved for police vehicles and flipped down his sun visor to display his PRESS credential. Now that he was boxing professionally, he didn't write more than a couple columns a month, but it was enough to keep his status as a reporter. He put a chain holding a plastic-enclosed ID around his neck and stepped out of the car. He was a couple inches over six feet with a handsome face marred by a slightly crooked nose, a going away present from an ex-girlfriend who'd been a kickboxer.

The precinct had a cold look to it, all blocky cement and glass and about as friendly as the cops inside, most of whom were sick of seeing him. He couldn't have cared less. It wasn't his fault they hadn't been able to find Julio's killer. He had given them their chance. Now it was his job.

The desk sergeant frowned at Cullen when he walked in. No surprise there.

"He's having lunch. Don't disturb him."

"Cheese crackers aren't lunch."

The trick to getting by the Gestapo was to move fast. Cullen breezed past the sergeant's desk before he could say anything else and hustled down the steps to the basement. By now he knew exactly how many stairs there were and the number of strides it took to walk the corridor to the door of the Unsolved Bureau. Not many people could say that, but then who would want to?

When Cullen had first started coming to Unsolved, he had always knocked on the door to announce himself. He'd quickly learned that doing so gave Gholston time to rush to the door and lock it. Now he just opened the door and stepped in.

He guessed there were more depressing places than the Unsolved Bureau, but he was hard pressed to think of one. The file cabinets were filled with dead people. The basement office had no windows, and the only light came from harsh fluorescents overhead. Even though smoking was against the rules, Cullen could smell Gholston's stale tobacco in the air. There were three desks in the room, only one of which was occupied. Sergeant Gholston was opening a package of Cheetos cheddar-cheese crackers as he studied a case file. There were three more packages on his desk. Cullen wasn't sure if Gholston really liked those things or if it was just that they were the only crackers in the vending machine on the basement level. The machine on the first floor had more variety, but that required climbing stairs.

Gholston didn't even look up. "Eating. Go away."

"Just checking to see if—"

"No new leads. No new suspects. Same story I tell you every time. The case is so cold I'd have to defrost it before handling."

Gholston was approaching fifty with badly thinning hair and a body no health club had ever abused. Other than his obsession for solving cold cases—which he was quite good at—he had no discernible interests. That was the only thing Cullen had in common with him. Outside of boxing, he didn't spend much time in the so-called real world, either. Movies, clubs, parties didn't interest him. Even if they did, he never had the energy after a double-workout day. He guessed it wasn't normal to go through life like that, but then nobody said boxers were dealing with a full deck.

"Hate to bug you, Lew."

Gholston still didn't look up. "Like hell."

"But today's the anniversary of Julio winning his first championship."

"So go to church and light a candle."

"You know, sometimes you're as cold as your cases."

Gholston gave him one of his stony looks. He had a variety of get-lost looks, but by now Cullen was immune to them. Once he stepped through that door, Gholston knew he was stuck with him.

"I work with dead people." The sergeant addressed his cheese crackers. "If I took every victim in need of justice to heart, it would kill me. Much as I admired Babbas, he's just another body. Cut to the chase, Cullen."

"Can I see the list of people Homicide questioned?"

"Again? Why?"

"Maybe something will click this time."

Gholston let out a weary sigh and walked over to a row of old file cabinets. He tried to slide one open, but it caught halfway, and he slammed it with his palm until it came free, then thumbed through folders. He pulled one out and handed it to Cullen. It was fat and heavy. Cullen probably knew half of it by heart, but it kept him connected to Julio, so he liked looking at it. He sat down at one of the empty desks and began leafing through. Even though he had read the thing cover to cover countless times, he was still convinced there must be something he'd missed, a hidden clue that would one day reveal itself. Wishful thinking, but it beat having no hope. He looked through the folder until he found the list of names Homicide had questioned. He knew who they all were by now, but just to irritate Gholston, he said, "Who's Edgar Santiago?"

"Didn't I tell you that last week?"

"I don't remember."

"Santiago was Julio's parish priest. Now are you done with their folder?"

"Ten more minutes." A thought occurred to Cullen. "You just said *their* folder. Isn't it yours now?"

"No, it's *theirs*. When we get a new case from Homicide, we do our own investigation, write a report, and keep it in a separate folder, *our* folder."

"For chrissake!" Cullen slammed the folder shut. "All this time you never told me there was a second folder?"

"You didn't ask."

He felt like lashing into Gholston but knew the sergeant would see that as a victory. "Okay, can I see *your* folder?" He made his voice sound calm.

"We've found nothing new."

"I believe you. I'd still like to look."

Gholston let out another weary sigh, went to the cabinet, and brought back a much thinner folder.

Cullen opened it with growing excitement. *These* pages he didn't know by heart. He plowed in with growing expectations that were quickly deflated. Gholston was right. No new angle he'd investigated had yielded anything remotely of substance. It was the same problem. For six months, four detectives had been assigned full time to the murder, yet they hadn't found a single clue, not one motive. One Homicide detective said it was that rare case in which a murder seemed to begin and end at the crime scene. Facing a heavier than usual workload, Homicide reluctantly sent it to Gholston, who had a history of cracking the coldest ones.

The list of people Gholston had questioned was mostly the same, but three were new.

"Who's David Briggs?" Cullen said.

"Bartender at a pub Julio went to."

"Why'd you talk to him?"

"Sometimes people say things to bartenders they wouldn't tell anyone else."

"What'd you find out?"

"It's in the folder. Look for it."

"Come on. I'm going to be late for my workout."

"Cullen, my heart bleeds. The bartender told me when Babbas came alone, he liked to check out the babes."

"Gee, what a revelation. Julio was human."

"Sit with them and buy them drinks."

"That's important because?"

"If he was a womanizer, there might've been a jealous boyfriend or husband."

"Julio was totally faithful to his wife."

"Yeah, well, nothing developed on that."

Cullen looked at the file again. "Bernard Greenstein?"

"He's the councilman for the sixth ward where Babbas lived. Politicians sometimes know their constituents' secrets." Gholston swallowed, opened another package of cheese crackers. "I took a swing and struck out."

"Okay, what about Yitzhak Soliman?"

Gholston swiveled his chair to face Cullen with another pet look: exasperation. "Let me ask you something. Do you know *anybody* in this town outside of boxing?"

"About as many as you know who aren't dead."

The cop shook his head. "If you weren't so hung up on boxing and Babbas' murder, you might pay attention to the drug problem we have and write something about it in that rag you occasionally work for. Soliman is the head of the Israeli mob that controls most of the Ecstasy trade here. A multi-million dollar business. His only rival is a Colombian named Humberto Arango. Who you also probably never heard of. Right now, they're waging a war. My fondest hope is they wipe each other out."

"Julio wasn't involved in drugs. Why talk to Soliman?"

"If a hit was ordered in this town, Soliman might know. If it was a rival, he'd be only too happy to tell me. He's also a big fan of boxing, so I figured he might've heard about Babbas being in some sort of trouble. It was just a shot in the dark."

Cullen nodded. "What was your gut feeling about him?"

"Didn't have one either way. Although he did say something curious."

"Which was?"

"Well sometimes I like to provoke people…."

"I never would've guessed."

"So I asked him point blank, 'Did you kill Julio Babbas?' I knew he wasn't going to tell the truth, but sometimes a person's face gives away things if you catch them off guard. Soliman said, 'Why would I do that?' I found that a curious answer."

"Because?"

"Cullen, did *you* kill Julio?"

"What, are you fucking crazy?"

"See my point?"

Cullen nodded. "Most people would've simply said no. Soliman asked why. What was your follow-up question?"

"'I don't know why. You tell me.' He said, 'I can't think of a single reason.' Then his cell rang. He walked away to answer it and didn't come back."

"A non-denial denial. What'd you do next?"

Gholston finished another cheese cracker. "Went to a diner, had cheese Danish and coffee, then drove back to the precinct and put the folder away."

"You didn't investigate any further?"

"Look, there could've been a dozen reasons why he didn't just say no, prime being he wanted to bust my balls."

"Still, you should've—"

"Hey! Don't you tell me how to do my job. I have over a hundred cases in those cabinets. Sometimes I think I hear them crying out to me for help. I'm not going to waste time on a ball-breaking mobster unless I have a concrete reason to. And I didn't." Gholston swiveled his chair and picked up another file.

The sergeant was probably right, Cullen thought, but what the hell, he hadn't had anything new to look into for weeks. "Who should I talk to in Narcotics about Soliman?"

"Lt. Harris is in charge. He's a prick, but he's your prick because he doesn't let anyone else in the department talk to you poison pens."

Cullen turned to go. "If I brought a real sandwich next time, would it make you more pleasant?"

"You want me to be pleasant? Don't make any more next times." Gholston raised his left arm. "Keep the left up, kid."

Lt. Vince Harris was at his desk talking on the phone when Cullen walked in. They had passed each other in the halls a few times, but had never actually spoken. Like most people around here, Harris knew Cullen was a nuisance and didn't look pleased to see him. There was one other guy in the room, a heavyset detective who glanced over, then went back to his work.

"I understand where you're coming from," Harris said into the phone, loud enough to make sure Cullen heard. "One of the bottom feeders from the press is here. Let me get rid of him and call you back." Harris hung up. He was in his forties, fit and strong with slate eyes.

Cullen gave him the best smile he had. "How's it going, Lieutenant?"

"Did you read the sign on the door? It says Narcotics, not Homicide or Unsolved. I know nothing about Julio Babbas."

"Yitzhak Soliman?"

"Wonderful human being."

"Gholston interviewed him. I'm curious if anything was ever mentioned to you in Julio's case about drugs."

"It was Homicide's case. I don't pay attention to other departments' cases unless they ask me."

"Did Homicide ask you for help?"

"No. End of discussion. Have a nice life." Harris turned his chair so his back was to Cullen and picked up the phone.

Cullen didn't like being dismissed like that, but for now he'd let it go. "Good talking to you, Lieutenant. You have a pleasant day."

Chapter 4

Cullen was eating his usual low-fat breakfast of poached eggs on dry toast when a UPS package arrived with no return address on the brown paper wrapping. Inside, he found a pair of his running shoes and a note attached to the laces made from newspaper headline cutouts:

STAY AWAY FROM THIS
YOU WILL BE MUCH EASIER
TO KILL THAN BABBAS

Cullen crumpled the wrapping and threw it hard across the room, then he called Gholston. "Lew, I just got a package with a death threat tied to one of my sneakers. Somebody fucking broke into my apartment."

So what do you want me to do?

"Duh. You know, maybe check it for fingerprints. Whatever the hell it is you cops do."

I got my hands full already.

"How can you take this so lightly? It could be an important clue in solving Julio's case."

Gholston sighed. *Read me the note.*

Cullen read him the note.

Gholston sighed again. *Okay*, he said, *bring the box down the next time you come by to pester me. I'll have Forensics look at it. Don't expect anything to come of it. If this guy was good enough to kill Babbas and not leave a single clue, Forensics won't find anything*. He hung up.

Cullen put the box in a plastic supermarket bag

and set it aside. Most people would have been unnerved by such a note, but he didn't scare easily. The upside, he told himself, was he must be onto something if they were trying to scare him off. The downside was they might actually kill him.

On his way to the gym, he made a quick stop at the *Review-Journal* to check for phone messages and glance at his email. Mostly, he did it just to show his face. It made him feel less guilty about forcing his editor to let him write only a couple columns a month. He had been a boxing writer at the newspaper since he was eighteen, a job he had gotten only because he was the son of a famous champion. That was the reason he knew the editor wouldn't fire him. A few reporters nodded to him, but most avoided his eyes. Around here, he was considered a prima donna. Ignoring them, he fired up his computer and went to the message center. There were the usual crappy press releases from boxing promoters and invitations to press conferences he had no intention of going to. Not much else.

McAlary's gym was in the garage of his house in a nice middle-class neighborhood. From the street you wouldn't know it was there. As Cullen parked his car, a dusty-looking Malibu pulled up behind him and out stepped a goofy-looking, tall man in funky plaid shorts and blue Knicks jersey.

"Danny Cullen?"

"That's me."

"Frank Boff. Got a minute?"

"Actually I don't. I'm late.

"I'm a private investigator looking into the murder of Julio Babbas."

Cullen's curiosity nearly got the best of him, but late was late. "My session'll be done in an hour. Can you come back?"

"No problem. I'll pop over to a Dunkin' Donuts."

Cullen was ten minutes late. He knew what was facing him. McAlary was a stickler for rules, so he was going to be put through a more brutal session than usual. It was a no-frills gym with a quality ring and a variety of bags, all hanging in front of a wall of floor-length mirrors. The other walls were filled with fight posters and photos, many of McAlary in his day, some of Cullen and his trainer's other fighter, Miguel Trillo. A large space was devoted to Julio. As usual, the heat was stifling and the air smelled of body odor. This may have been the only gym in Las Vegas where the family washer and dryer were tucked in a back corner beside the water heater.

McAlary was working out on the speed bag. In his prime, he had been a three-time welterweight champion and Olympic silver medalist from Ireland. At thirty-six, he still looked fit enough to fight. His wife Kate was in the ring watching Trillo practice new moves. She'd been her husband's manager and Julio's, and now was Cullen's. In a sport dominated almost exclusively by men, she had a hard-earned reputation for being tough in negotiations and fiercely protective of her fighters.

"You're late," McAlary said. "Go change."

Cullen ducked behind a wall partition into what passed for a locker room: a sweat-stained bench, a closet-sized bathroom, and a few beat-up old lockers, including Julio's. It still had his name tag on it and a combination lock. Cullen had mixed feelings about the locker. Once in awhile he could pretend Julio was alive and was about to walk into the gym, but mostly it just reminded him that his friend was dead. Julio had taped a quote from Jack Dempsey on the locker: *A champion is someone who gets up when he can't.*

Cullen's father had been like that. No matter how many times you knocked Dan Cullen down, he always got up and attacked you. He had lost fights during his career, but no one had ever been able to knock him out. Dan Sr. had been a world champion in three weight divisions and a first ballot Hall of Fame inductee. Cullen remembered the first time his father had let him carry his championship belt on the ceremonial walk to the ring. The MGM Grand had been packed with screaming fans that night. Cullen was eight and could barely breathe as he walked side-by-side with his father toward the ring. It had made him feel special.

His father had been a powerful presence in his life. Asked to choose between God and Dad, Cullen would have taken his old man any day. Of course he had wanted to follow in his footsteps and be a boxer, but his father was having none of that. He said boxing was a tough sport with too many people out to exploit you. Cullen protested, but once Dad made up his mind, there was no changing it. Cullen's burning desire to box just smoldered somewhere in his psyche.

And the urge had come back strong the day his father died of a rare blood disease, just forty-three years old. Cullen was fifteen at the time. He felt angry at a world that had taken his father without asking him. He wanted desperately to start boxing to punch out the pain, but he still couldn't bring himself to defy his father's wishes. The death had devastated both him and his mother. She had married Dan Sr. right out of high school and known no other man. After his burial, she took to drinking heavily and barely left the house anymore except to buy more booze and crummy frozen dinners for the two of them. Living in that house felt like being in a funeral home, worse than Gholston's morgue. When he tried to get her to talk about Dad, she just walked away. Most days, she sat around and got sloppy drunk while listening to soppy Irish ballads. Cullen and his mother had never really been close, at least not like he was with his father.

That's why it didn't come as a shock when she announced out of nowhere one day that she was moving back to Ireland, where she had been born and still had a lot of relatives. She'd packed up all his clothes and dumped him with Aunt Aileen, his father's sister. He couldn't say Aileen treated him badly, but she wasn't one to show feelings, so he felt terribly alone, and his mother's once-a-week calls from Ireland did little to cheer him up. Mostly, they just made small talk. She asked if he was doing his homework and treating his aunt with respect, shit like that, and he gave the same mechanical answers. As time passed the calls became more infrequent, and eventually there were none, just a greeting card with a twenty-dollar Euro inside at Christmas, Easter, and on his birthday. He stashed those Euros in his closet and forgot about them.

Cullen's whole identity had been wrapped up in being his father's son. Without him, he hadn't known who he was until Julio came along and filled the void. And then Julio's murder had tipped Cullen over the edge. Now he had no father or mother and he had also lost his closest friend. He felt depressed and angry at the same time. Maybe it was the anger that saved him from sinking to a place he might not have come back from. After getting into a couple bar brawls and being hostile with everyone who crossed his path, he finally ignored his father's wishes and showed up at McAlary's gym, asking if he could train.

He was twenty-five when he started, old by boxing standards, but not unheard of. It didn't hurt that he had inherited his father's rugged build and indomitable will, or that watching his dad train all those years had given him a pretty good grasp of the technique and discipline needed to become a boxer. Seven months later, after fighting almost every two weeks, Cullen was unbeaten in twelve bouts and was going to make his television debut on Showtime's series for young fighters, *ShoBox*.

A shout from McAlary brought him back to the present. He quickly tied his boxing shoes, tapped the Dempsey quote with his fist, and hustled out into the gym.

For two hours in the sweltering heat, McAlary pushed him to the limits of his endurance. As usual, being punished triggered Cullen's temper. He waited for a chance to get even. It came when they were working in the ring with the punch mitts. Cullen purposely missed the mitts at one point and slammed a shot into McAlary's chin. He knew it was stupid, because McAlary would only make him pay for this latest "accidental" miss with an extra fifteen minutes on the mitts, but he felt better for having done it.

The tall guy was back, leaning against his Malibu with a coffee container. Dressed the way he was, he didn't look to Cullen like much of an investigator.

"How was your workout?" he asked. "My name's Boff."

Cullen nodded. "Tough. I got hammered by my trainer."

"You any good?"

"I'm undefeated."

"That's pretty good. Mind a few questions?"

"Sure. First, can I ask why if you're a private investigator you're dressed like that?"

Boff grinned. "I'm undercover."

"Passing as what?"

"A basketball junkie who never grew up."

"How does that help you find Julio's killer?"

"It doesn't. Before I came here, I was trying to teach my uncoachable son rebounding tricks in our driveway."

That made Cullen grin. "Okay. Fire away."

"As I said before, I'm looking into the murder of Babbas."

"So you asked a bunch of people about him, and they all said you should talk to me."

"That's correct. But I already knew that."

"Then why didn't you come to me first?" Cullen said.

"I wanted to cover other bases before I went to the source, which apparently is you."

Cullen nodded. "Who's your client?"

"I'm not at liberty to say."

"Can I guess?"

"Sure. Knock yourself out. I won't tell you, and I'm an excellent poker player, so you won't be able to read my face."

"Forget I asked."

"I already did." Boff took a hefty drink from the cup. "How many months have you been looking for Babbas' killer?"

"You know how long. What's your point?"

"You haven't had much luck, as I understand."

"I've had leads."

"None of which were worth a shit," Boff said.

"Hey, pal, if you think you can do better, go ahead and run into the same walls I did."

Boff pushed off his car. "Ask around about me," he said in a lazy voice. "Check with the police.

Then we'll renew this conversation." He turned to go.

One of Cullen's failings was being addictively curious. He should have just let the jerk take off. On the chance he might've discovered something about Julio's murder, however, he said, "Okay, hot shot, you want to talk to me, buy me lunch."

Chapter 5

Cullen took Boff to Franny's Diner, a truck stop on Boulder Highway. Drivers were zipping by, heading downtown to lose their money on the one-armed bandits and at the tables.

Franny's Diner had one paved parking lot in front and a larger dirt one in back to accommodate the truckers who made up the bulk of her trade. Cullen waved to a couple regulars and then led Boff to a booth. To make the truckers feel at home, Franny had decorated her walls with photos of eighteen-wheelers, highway signs, nearby motels, and one grainy blow-up shot of the diner on its grand opening twenty years ago.

Boff looked around. "Good choice." He opened the menu. "I love diners. How's the food here?"

"The meatloaf's great. So is the turkey platter. For dessert, try the key lime pie."

Boff closed the menu. "Sounds good to me."

A plump young waitress came over with a bread basket. "Hey, champ, heard you got a big TV fight. Congrats."

Cullen smiled at her. "Thanks. It's right here in town, so if you and Franny want to come, I'll leave tickets."

"Cool. Okay, you'll take your usual meatloaf, no gravy or butter on the mashed potatoes. And the gentleman?"

"I'll also take the meatloaf," said Boff, "but with loads of gravy and butter, key lime pie, and iced tea. Extra potatoes if you can sneak some on the plate without the cook noticing."

"The cook is my mother, Franny. I'm Terry."

"Oops."

Terry smiled. "Don't worry. Mom will be glad to pile on the spuds. She thinks people don't eat enough because they all want to look like Paris Hilton."

"I would need massive liposuction to look like her, never mind the cosmetic adjustments."

Terry laughed and left.

"I've got to make a phone call," Cullen said. "The signal in here is weak, so I'm going outside."

"Be my guest," Boff replied. "I'll butter up some of this fine-looking bread while you're gone."

Something told Cullen this guy wasn't a goofball, no matter how he dressed. In the parking lot he took out his cell and faced the diner so he could keep an eye on Boff, who was eating a roll and watching him back. Cullen called the department and asked to be connected to Detective Epps, one of the few cops who liked him, a fight fan, naturally.

This is Detective Epps, how may I help you?

"It's Danny."

Hey, champ. How's training?

"Real good."

Don't forget to keep that left up.

"Will do."

So, said the detective, *are you still gonna talk to the little people when you become a Showtime star?*

"I need info."

Two tickets ringside.

"You got it."

What do you want to know?

"You ever hear of a private investigator named Frank Boff?"

The phone went silent. Epps's voice was cool when he finally spoke. *Yeah, I know Boff. Everybody in the department does. Ex-DEA. Makes his living now helping lawyers defend scumbags.*

"He any good at it?"

Let's put it this way, Epps said. *If a detective has worked months on a righteous case and sees the courtroom door open and Boff walks in, chances are he knows he can get up and leave because his case is going to get blown to shit. Boff has helped crush more airtight cases than anybody I know. Worse, he makes so many veteran cops look like rank amateurs, if he walked into headquarters today, I couldn't guarantee his safety. Around here we call him Darth Vader.* He paused. *So why the interest?*

"He's going to be asking me questions about Julio."

If he does, promise when he gets under your skin you won't beat on him. I'd hate to see you facing an assault rap with your TV fight coming up.

Cullen grinned to himself. "I won't rattle. I'm like my father."

Your father never went up against anyone like Boff. If he doesn't get under your skin, you're not human.

Epps hung up. Cullen had a feeling this wasn't

going to be a pleasant lunch. He went in and sat back down in the booth. Boff had polished off over half the bread basket, leaving almost nothing left for him—not that he wanted any—but it said something about the guy.

"So what did Detective Epps tell you about me?"

"How do you know—?"

"You should've turned your back on me. I can read lips. One of my many talents. I'm guessing he told you I'm a morally-challenged dirtbag with no respect for justice."

Cullen nodded. "You help defend the worst criminals and get them off."

"Alleged criminals, and the proper term is acquitted. I'm sure he also told you I'm quite good at it."

"Doesn't it bother you cops that hate you?"

"The more cops that hate me, the better the job I'm doing. Basically, I'll defend any criminal—except child molesters and rapists out of respect for my wife—as long as their checks don't bounce."

Terry brought over iced tea for Boff, Diet Coke for Cullen, and left.

"Look, kid," Boff said after taking a drink. "Everything you're going to hear about me is tied to my job. That's only one side. I live in the suburbs with my wife, barbecue on the deck, watch sitcoms on TV, and dote over my children. In many ways, I'm your typical Joe. Now that I've put my cards on the table, can I ask you some questions?

"You left one card in the deck," Cullen said.

"Who hired you?"

"If I told you that, I'd be breaking a confidentiality agreement and could lose my license. I like to think of my license as an ATM machine. Thanks to a world filled with indicted felons, it keeps spitting out cash which enables me to buy things for my lovely wife and my two spoiled kids, who, by the way, don't like me very much, either."

"Why? Are you a shitty father?"

"I'm a terrific father."

"Then why don't they like you?"

"My cases are often high profile and get me on TV and in the newspapers. When I'm helping defend an especially notorious felon, my kids get harassed at school. One teacher even made my daughter Sharon move to a desk in the back of the class when he found out I was her father. My kids are ashamed of me. But of course that doesn't prevent them from taking my money. Next year Sharon's going to a college that will cost me forty thou a year. When I tell her murderers and drug dealers will be paying for her education, she gives me a dirty look and walks away. Such is life."

Cullen smiled at this. "If you can't reveal your client, can you at least tell me why you of all people were hired?"

The food arrived, and Boff dove right in. He cut off a big piece of meat loaf with his fork, dipped it in the mashed potatoes, and shoveled it home. Cullen wasn't going to eat until he got his answer.

"You're right," Boff told him. "This is good."

"Why were you hired?"

"Obviously, it's not my usual job, but I was pretty good at chasing down bad guys when I was in the DEA. In fact I was one of the best the agency ever had. So while this kind of righteous job will tarnish my reputation on the Dark Side, the generous retainer I got will help soothe my pain."

"If you were such an ace in the DEA, why'd you leave?"

Boff's eyes went cold. "I lost respect for law enforcement. Let's move on."

"No problem. If it upsets you to talk about it, I figure you got in some kind of trouble and were canned."

Boff said nothing, just sipped his iced tea and kept eating.

"Does your client have new evidence he wants you to explore?" Cullen said.

"Nope."

"Have you found any decent leads?"

"I have leads. Whether they're any good remains to be seen."

If this character was as good as Epps said, Cullen thought as he finally took a bite, then it might be worth teaming up, unappealing as that would be. "I'll swap leads with you," he said. "Maybe we can work together."

"Why would I want to do that? Your leads have obviously been losers."

Terry returned with a pitcher of iced tea and topped off Boff's glass. "How's the meatloaf, sir?"

"Terrific as advertised. Please call me Frank."

Terry looked at Cullen's plate. He had barely touched it. "Anything wrong with the meatloaf, champ?"

"It's fine. I'm just a little annoyed at something."

Boff looked up. "He means me," he said with his mouth full. "I apparently have of a way of irritating people, although I really don't know why."

"You seem fine to me," she said, "and I'm a good judge of character. Like my mom. Danny's probably just on the rag." She frowned at Cullen and left.

"Is it my turn yet to ask a question?" Boff said.

"Go ahead. I'll try to be as candid as you are."

"Did your friend have any enemies or owe money to bookies? Did he fool around with women besides his wife or do drugs? Anything you can think of that might've put him at risk?"

"That's three questions. Julio had no enemies and was well liked by everyone. He didn't gamble, cheat, or use drugs."

"Which raises a red flag for me."

"Why?"

"Because he's dead. Obviously, somebody had a different opinion of him than you, which means Babbas did things he kept from you. I'd call it a secret life, but that sounds so melodramatic."

Cullen shoved his plate away. "Julio kept nothing from me. You don't know what you're talking about."

"As long as you keep on believing that, you'll

continue to spin your wheels."

"There's no evidence Julio led some kind of 'secret life,' as you call it."

"None you in your very limited capacity as an investigator have discovered," Boff said. "I, on the other hand, know from experience that people don't get killed in the manner in which your friend did without making an enemy or two. It was an execution, a contract hit. So Babbas was into something he didn't want you to know about, meaning he wasn't too proud of it."

Damn, the jerk was making sense, although Cullen found it hard to believe Julio had hidden things from him. He tried again. "If you don't want to work with me, why'd you agree to go to lunch?"

"Why I usually go to lunch. I was hungry. Plus I figured I might as well pump you on the slim chance you had something worthwhile to tell me, which so far you haven't."

"I think you're bullshitting," Cullen said. "You want to work with me."

"Really? That's amusing. Why would I want a partner who makes his living punching people in the face?"

"Because I know more about Julio than anybody. Even his wife. The kind of stuff it'll take you weeks or months to find out."

"The longer it takes, the better off I am," Boff said, reaching for another piece of bread. "I get paid by the hour, and very handsomely, I might add. That's why I may be the last private investigator in the civilized world still using dial-up to surf the net.

It makes no sense to do research in an hour when I can stretch it to two."

Detective Epps was right. Boff was getting under his skin, and he felt like punching him. This guy may be good, but he wasn't good for him, not with a big fight coming up. Cullen let out a breath. "Forget about partnering with me. I can't have any more distractions than I already do. I can tell you're a major headache."

"I've been called worse."

Cullen studied Boff's face. It was impossible to read. He didn't buy his excuse for going to lunch. "I sense you're holding something back," he said. "Tell me what it is now or I'm out of here."

Boff stared at him a moment with his steel blue eyes. "Much as I'd like to finish this wonderful lunch and never set eyes on you again, I can't."

"Why not?"

"It's a bit complicated, but I'll try explaining it to you in terms even a boxer with no college education can understand. My client went to Lew Gholston for help in finding an investigator. He recommended me."

"How do you know Lew?"

"We crossed paths once when he was in Homicide. Apparently he's worried about you. He says you might be asking questions about someone who doesn't like people snooping into his business."

Soliman.

"So," Boff continued, "he asked me to keep an eye on you while I find Babbas' killer for my client."

"Lew isn't paying your fee. Why would you agree to do something you obviously don't want to?"

Boff made him wait for an answer while he sliced off another big piece of meatloaf, loaded it with mashed potatoes, and stuffed his face. Then he sipped on his ice tea. He was taking his time and watching Cullen getting more impatient.

"A few years ago," he finally said, "I experienced a rare lapse in judgment and did something for which my license could've been revoked. Gholston was going to be a hero among his peers and turn me in to the state licensing board. On her own, my wife Jenny went to his house to speak with him. Jenny's the type of person everybody falls in love with. Kind, gentle, just as sweet as can be. Yeah, I know, you're wondering why she'd marry a guy like me. The answer is we were high school sweethearts, and when we got married I was in the DEA and a patriotic guy committed to ridding the world of bad guys. That changed, of course, but by then she'd learned to love me for my good side and ignore what she considers my somewhat less admirable qualities."

Boff took another sip of iced tea.

"Jenny told Gholston I was the only means of support for our family because she was out of work at the time, and if I lost my license, it was unlikely I could hold another job for long because I tend to be overbearing and rub people the wrong way. She brought him a cake she'd made. Jenny could be a pastry chef, she's that good. Long story short, Gholston took pity on her and the kids and didn't drop a dime on me. In the world I work in, that means I owed him a favor. Which turns out to be the Babbas case and you. This is also Gholston's way of punishing me for crushing one of his cases in court. He knows I'll hate every minute working with an amateur."

Terry brought Boff's slice of key lime pie. He asked for the check and paid it.

"Thank you, Frank." She turned to Cullen. "Danny, your friend is such a nice man, I hope you bring him back again." She smiled at Boff and left.

Despite what Gholston thought, Cullen said to himself, he didn't need someone watching over him. He was a fighter. He could handle himself. He looked at Boff. "I'll spare you the pain of working with me. I have no intention of being around someone like you. Thanks for the lunch, although I can't say it was pleasant." He got up to go.

Boff reached out, nearly touched his arm. "Sit down a moment. Let me explain something to you."

Cullen had a feeling getting rid of Boff wasn't going to be so easy. Against his better judgment, he sat.

"Okay," Boff said, "you don't want to work with me and I don't want to work with you. Trouble is, I'm obligated to, as I just said."

"That's your problem."

Boff smiled. "Unfortunately it's yours, too. I'm an extremely persistent man. Count on me being around and watching you. We may even talk from time to time."

"Like hell we will."

"Do you know what I was most known for in the DEA?"

"Annoying people?"

"My tenacity. They called me Bulldog Boff. Once I sank my teeth into something, as the saying goes, I didn't let go. I was something of a legend for that. Keep that in mind when you think you can get rid of me."

"This is not going to happen. No way."

"Look, I'll make you a deal. I'll try to stay away from you as much as possible. In return I want some info."

"About what?" Cullen said.

"Take me back to the last couple of weeks before your friend was killed. Tell me as much as you can remember."

"I can remember everything."

"I'm listening.

After the fight, did you and Julio go anywhere, or straight home?"

"We hit a club and took turns dancing with his wife, Cassandra. Julio was like a dynamo on the floor. I asked him later how he had the energy after fighting twelve brutal rounds. He said he'd taken a tab of Ecstasy. But when I questioned him about that, he told me he'd just been kidding."

"Did you believe him?"

"Of course. I'd never seen *Perro* do drugs."

"*Perro*?"

"Julio."

Boff nodded. "Where did you go after the club?"

"His house. Cassandra had some dishes to clean up. Julio and I grabbed beers and went into the den. We sat on the couch. Then…." He looked away for a moment. Talking about it now was as bad as the night it happened.

"Then what?" Boff's voice was marginally gentler.

"This guy stepped out from behind drapes covering a sliding door. He was wearing a ski mask and had a gun. He shot Julio in the forehead, opened the door, and ran off."

"How big was he?"

"Maybe six feet. I think he was well built."

"Anything unusual about him stick in your mind?"

"Nothing I can recall. I was real focused on Julio."

"Did the killer point his gun at you?"

"No. He just shot Julio and left."

"I find it curious he'd leave you as a witness."

"With the mask on," Cullen said, "I couldn't identify him in a million years, not even his voice because he never said a word."

"Where was the wife?"

"In the kitchen. She didn't hear the shot. The police said he used a silencer."

"Did he leave a spent casing on the floor?"

"I heard the cops talk about that. Apparently he didn't."

"That means he was probably using a revolver. They don't automatically eject casings."

"Why's that important?"

"It helps to know anything about the murder weapon."

Cullen shifted in his seat. "Okay, I've told you all I know. Now I'm done talking to you. I've got to get some rest for my second training session."

Boff insisted on following Cullen back to his apartment. "Gholston wants me to check for bugs," he said. "He thinks it's possible somebody planted some."

"No, thanks."

Cullen got in his car and headed home. It didn't really surprise him that Bulldog Boff followed. Fuck it. Let him. He wasn't getting into his apartment. When Cullen parked near his building, Boff pulled into a space behind him. They both got out.

"Why the hell can't you take no for an answer?"

"It's not in my nature."

"Well, you aren't going to search my apartment." Cullen started up the stairs to the second floor. He didn't have to look back to know Boff was right behind. At his door, Cullen turned around.

"What is it you don't understand? No means no. If you don't leave, I'm going to punch you out."

"No, you won't."

"Says you."

"No, says the laws of the State of Nevada. You're a professional boxer, which means your hands are registered weapons. Hit me, and you'll be charged with assault with a deadly weapon."

Cullen raised his hands, lowered them. "You've got an answer for everything."

"The day I don't, I'll retire and take up golf."

"There isn't a chance in hell I'm letting you into my apartment. Get lost."

"Son, I can do it now and you can be rid of me, or I can come back later when you're training and pick that Mickey Mouse lock you have and do it then. One way or another, I'm going to do what Gholston asked. The choice is yours."

"If you break into my apartment, I'll call the police."

This made Boff smile. "There won't be a single clue I was there. I'm very good at getting in and out of places undetected."

And this is the price he paid, Cullen told himself, for letting his curiosity get the best of him. Next time he'd be smarter, which is what he'd said the last time he was this stupid. Well, he sure as hell didn't want this jerk nosing around inside his apartment when he wasn't home, so he admitted defeat and led the way in.

"Do it fast and get your ass out."

Boff seemed to know exactly where to look. He found bugs inside the living room and bedroom phones. There were more in the overhead lights in the kitchen and bathroom, under the couch, and inside the one suit he owned. Cullen felt violated. Boff left all the bugs in place and told him to follow him outside so they could talk.

"It would take me just a few minutes to remove them, but I don't think you should."

"Why not?"

"They'll just put new ones in. This way, you can let them hear what you want them to hear."

"Whatever."

Boff pulled out his wallet and handed him a business card.

"Call me when you need me."

"I won't."

Cullen tried to give the card back. Boff wouldn't take it. "Listen to me. You're working on something involving some really bad people. Think of Michael Corleone in a vindictive mood, and you won't have scratched the surface. This is not Xbox. If you get killed, you don't get to play a new game." He reached over and closed Cullen's fingers around the card. "Keep the card."

Cullen stuck the card in front of Boff's face and dropped it on the steps.

"Well," said Boff, "you can always look me up in the phone book. Meanwhile, I've got to run. I'm working the Dark Side the rest of the day."

"What's with this Dark Side? You mean like in *Star Wars*?"

"Sort of, but instead of Imperial Storm Troopers, I deal with mobsters, drug dealers and various other unsavory people I've helped keep out of jail. By the way, the windows in your bathroom and bedroom are unlocked. I suggest you lock them. A sixth-grader could kick in your front door. Install a double cylinder deadbolt with keyholes on both sides. At night, make sure all your curtains are closed and the shades pulled. If I tell you much more, it'll cost you a fee."

With a cordial nod, Boff went down the stairs to his car. Cullen walked inside and slammed the door. That old devil curiosity drew him to the window, and he watched as Boff popped his trunk, took out a label-free aerosol can, and sprayed both his license plates with a clear liquid. What the hell was that about? This guy was screwy. Then Boff got in his car and drove away.

The only trace left of him was that damn card littering his steps. Cullen went out and picked it up. He glanced at what was written under Boff's name and job title: *When all else fails, see me.*

In the kitchen, Cullen dumped the card in the garbage pail, then got a wooden spoon and shoved it down deep so he wouldn't have to see it. He grabbed a bottle of Gatorade and tub of low-fat cottage cheese to make up for the lunch Boff had ruined and took them into the living room. Like the rest of the apartment, it lacked personality. He had bought all the furniture on one trip to IKEA because that was the path of least resistance.

There were two photo albums on his coffee table. One had pictures of his father and newspaper clippings about his fights. The other was basically the same thing, except all the photos were of Julio. As he ate the cottage cheese, Cullen tried to figure out who had hired Boff. Cassandra came to mind, but she felt he was too obsessed with Julio's case and was always trying to get him to drop it. He ran down the list of possible names. None seemed right. Frustrated, he picked up the phone and dialed.

Unsolved, Detective Gholston.

"It's me, Danny."

Oh, Christ. What now?

"I want to know who hired Boff."

I can't tell you.

"Why not?"

I was asked not to. I honor my word.

"Is this person a relative or a friend?"

Don't waste my time with questions I'm not going to answer, Cullen. I'm hanging up.

"Wait! Can I trust Boff?"

I wouldn't.

"Then why'd you dump him on me?"

So you'd stop bothering me. Which apparently was wishful thinking.

"Why can't I trust him?"

Gholston laughed. *You mean besides the fact he has no morals or scruples? Let me tell you a quick story, then I'm getting off. Boff once took a case in which a nun was accused of killing her crippled elderly mother by pushing her out a third-story window. Boff orchestrated the defense for the nun's lawyer. He had the nun claim the mother committed suicide by climbing out the window, and the nun had tried desperately to pull her back in. It took all of Boff's powers to convince the jury a woman confined to a wheelchair with very limited mobility in her legs was able to climb on top of a cedar chest in front of the window and had the strength to pull herself through. Boff discovered the mother had a history of psychological problems. He dug up two highly-respected psychiatrists who testified the mother was textbook suicidal.*

"The jury bought that?"

Hook, line and sinker. Boff was so convincing, the dead mother herself would've believed him. Gholston hung up.

Cullen picked up Julio's album to take his mind off Boff. His favorite shot was one of Julio in Venezuela smoking a cigarette on the way to the ring. That's where it had all begun.

Chapter 6

Venezuela. Three Years Earlier

Cullen had been vacationing on the Islas Los Roques in the Caribbean, a half-hour plane ride from Caracas, when he discovered Julio. He was at the hotel bar when the bartender told him the World Boxing Association was holding a benefit boxing show in the city of Turmero, about forty miles east of Caracas.

The fights were the next night, so Cullen booked a flight to Caracas the next day, then rented a car and drove to Turmero. The event was being staged in the ballroom of a hotel. Maybe two hundred people were there. The boxers in the first two matches were not very good, and Cullen's interest started to wander. He looked at the program. The third fight looked like a mismatch, another bore. One boxer, a Colombian named Julio Babbas, had an undistinguished 10–4 record, although Cullen noted all ten victories came by way of knockout. Babbas' opponent was an unbeaten local favorite, Alberto Lara, who seemed to be well-regarded.

His initial impression of Babbas was not positive. He came down the aisle from the locker room smoking a cigarette. Cullen had never seen a fighter do that, so he took a shot with his camera. Babbas crushed the butt out against the side of the ring before climbing through the ropes. In place of a traditional robe, he wore a soiled grey sweatshirt. When he took it off, Cullen could see that he was powerfully built but had a gut and love handles. In contrast, his opponent looked dead fit and danced around the ring showing off his fancy footwork and quick hands.

Babbas looked so out of shape that Cullen figured one round, tops, and it would be over. He was right about the round, wrong about who he thought would win. When the bell rang, Lara came out bobbing and weaving as Babbas stalked him flat-footed. Lara hit him with a quick combo and then danced away. Cullen noticed that Babbas kept his right hand cocked by his head like a hammer. After a minute of Lara sticking and moving without getting hit back, the crowd grew restless and began chanting his name. *Lara, Lara, Lara.* Lara's machismo kicked in. He moved straight at Babbas, obviously intent on taking him out. And just as he got within range, Babbas flashed that right hand so fast Cullen barely saw it. Neither did Lara. He went down flat on his back and didn't move. While the ref quickly examined him, then signaled that the fight was over and called for the ring physician, Babbas went back to his corner. The corner man put a lit cigarette in Babbas' mouth and helped him take the gloves off. Babbas didn't even wait for the official announcement. He left the ring and headed away.

Cullen dropped his program and ran after him, catching him just before he went into the locker room. He had taken enough Spanish in high school to invite Babbas out for a beer. Babbas asked if he was a manager.

"No," he said, "but my father was the great champion Dan Cullen. I write for a big newspaper in Las Vegas and know all the important managers and trainers."

That inspired Babbas to agree to a drink in the hotel bar. He ordered a double tequila on the rocks, Cullen a light beer.

"In your four losses," Cullen asked, "were you ever knocked out?"

"No. Never been down. Even in the street, they hit me over the head with whiskey bottles, I don't fall. When I'm hurt, it makes me fight harder. I only lost those four fights because my opponents danced around like fairies and won on points."

Something about Babbas intrigued him. He took a room with two beds at the hotel. The next day he found a gym, paid a small fee, and borrowed mitts to see what skills Babbas had besides the thunder in his right hand. Babbas was awkward and weak on fundamentals, but he made up for it with exceptionally fast hands and stinging blows to the mitts. He reminded Cullen of a raw version of his father.

"If you come back to Las Vegas with me," he told the fighter, "I can get you a trainer."

Babbas didn't have much to return to in Colombia, so he agreed to go. When their flight touched down, Cullen took him directly to his apartment. He laid sheets, pillow, and a blanket on his couch.

"*Mi casa es su casa.*"

The next morning, he bought Babbas some good boxing gloves and took him to McAlary's gym. McAlary, who had only recently started training other fighters, was doing stomach crunches when they walked in. Kate spotted them and walked over.

Cullen introduced Babbas and briefly told her about Turmero and the workout on the mitts. "I want Ryan to train him," he told her. "I'll pay for it."

Sizing Babbas up, Kate looked skeptical, to say the least. "He's out of shape and his fingers and teeth are stained yellow," she said. "Did you explain to him no smoking or drinking or Ryan won't work with him?"

"Yes."

She took another look at the fighter and shook her head. "I don't know. Ryan'll have to spar with him to see what he's got."

They waited until McAlary was done with his crunches before bringing him over.

"Danny found him in a boxing circus," Kate said. "Lots of luck."

Where Kate saw a guy in bad shape with toxic habits, McAlary undoubtedly recognized someone to whom the streets had not been kind. Cullen knew that in Belfast during the Troubles, many of McAlary's schoolmates had quit boxing and taken to the street life. Boxing had kept McAlary from doing the same thing, and that saved his life. He agreed to spar with the Colombian.

"Tell him to get changed," McAlary said.

A few minutes later, Babbas came out from behind the wall partition and climbed into the ring.

Kate pulled Cullen aside. “Why’d you do this?”

“Watch and you’ll see.”

She shrugged and said “Ding” to start the round.

Babbas came forward, flat-footed, and McAlary immediately let his hands fly, landing some heavy shots, but the Colombian didn’t back up. Babbas flashed his big right. McAlary slipped the punch with his head and countered with two body shots. Frustration showing in his face, Babbas threw a four-punch combo, which McAlary picked off with his gloves.

Babbas was already sucking for air. Cullen knew McAlary would take advantage and attack again.

Kate was watching closely, too. “The guy doesn’t know how to box, no basics, nothing,” she said.

Cullen shook his head. “My father once told me, ‘Boxing any man can learn. Heart and the will to win at any cost you can’t teach.’”

She turned to go. “I see no point in watching this. I have laundry to do.”

He touched her arm. “Please watch. I want you to manage him.”

She laughed at what she obviously considered an absurd notion, but she stayed.

“Work the body, stop head-hunting,” Cullen called out in Spanish.

Babbas threw several wild body shots, two landed, the second of which made McAlary wince and momentarily back up. But the flurry of punches had clearly cost Babbas what was left of his energy reserve. McAlary started throwing hard combos. Babbas didn't have the energy to hit back.

"Toast," Kate said. She started to go.

Again he touched her arm. He shouted at the ring, "Beat him. Or you go back to Colombia!"

Later Babbas would tell him those words had brought back a flood of painful memories and filled him with anger. McAlary had immediately symbolized the streets. Hell would freeze over before he'd go back to them.

This time, when McAlary moved in, Babbas pushed him off hard and filled the space created between them with a flurry of powerful punches. Several broke through McAlary's gloves and snapped his head back. Fighting purely on adrenalin, Babbas drove McAlary to the ropes, where he staggered him with a thunderous overhand right. Nearly spent, Babbas used everything he had left for a right hook that caught McAlary on the ribs and must have felt like the kick of a mule.

McAlary groaned and stumbled backwards, clearly hurt. A stunned Kate, fearing for her husband, hastily sounded the "bell."

Bent over with exhaustion, Babbas looked at Cullen. "I will not go back to Colombia!"

McAlary must have sensed what he was saying. He smiled. "Tell him to show up tomorrow morning at eight, and we'll begin with some light road work."

Kate smiled, too. "Looks like you found us a

fighter.”

Chapter 7

Cullen couldn't say he was surprised to see Bulldog Boff was in his car outside the gym when he came out from his morning workout.

"Didn't we make a deal you'd stay away from me as much as possible?" he said.

"Yes, and I will," Boff returned, "but I'm heading over to the Dark Side. You seemed curious about it, so I thought I'd give you a glimpse into my world."

"I've seen enough of your world. No, thanks."

"Don't be pigheaded. Come along. You might even learn something from the master to help you in your own futile investigation."

Cullen had four hours to kill before his late afternoon session. Seeing how this big-shot investigator operated beat watching *The Young and the Restless.* He walked around to the passenger side and got in.

"This doesn't mean I'm working with you."

"I understand perfectly."

"The Dark Side consists of many different places for me," Boff said as he drove. "One is northeast Las Vegas. It's the worst neighborhood in the city. Most people who aren't criminals, bums, or drug addicts steer clear of it." He gave that a brief smile. "To me, it's like a second home." He opened his CD case, took one out, and slid it in. "This is Jerry Lee Lewis. You're going to love it." And he turned the volume up high and sang along.

Cullen popped the CD out.

"What kind of crap is that?"

"Fifties Golden Oldies. It's all I listen to."

"Play it when you're not with me."

"Your loss."

Boff said nothing more until they reached northeast Las Vegas. Then he pulled over by a pawn shop with two large caricatures painted on the front windows. One was a chimp saying, NEED SOME FAST CASH? The other was a donkey: ECONOMY KICKING YOUR ASS?

"Why are we stopping here?" Cullen asked. "You gonna pawn something?"

"No. I just want to drink in the atmosphere. If you had an experienced eye—which you don't—you'd notice there are junkies out in force. Two drug peddlers and a fence selling watches out of a briefcase."

Cullen spotted the guy with the watches, but couldn't pick out the others. They all looked like bums. The area could be a street scene in a post-apocalyptic film. There were abandoned cars with tires and body parts missing, the streets and sidewalks were filthy, and a lot of storefronts were boarded up.

"This place is depressing," he said.

"Not to me. In a world where nothing seems to stay the same, I take comfort knowing this neighborhood is still the armpit of the city."

A black Lincoln Town Car slowed down alongside Boff's car. A man at the passenger side window nodded to him. The car moved on.

"Mobsters. Most know me because I've helped them in court at one time or another."

"And you're proud of that?" Cullen said.

"You bet." Boff put the Malibu in gear and drove seemingly at random.

"We here just to sightsee?" Cullen asked. "Or are you looking for someone?"

"Him." Boff pointed to a Hispanic man about thirty dressed in ragged clothes. He was standing in the recessed entrance to an apartment building smoking a cigarette. Boff beeped his horn and rolled down the window.

"Hi, Kiko, long time, no see."

"Go away, Boff. If I'm seen with you, it'll blow my cover."

"Meet me where we talked last time." Boff pulled away.

"What do you want with a homeless man?"

"Watch and you'll see."

Boff drove a few blocks and parked by an alley strewn with garbage. They got out. There was another bum sleeping in the alley on a piece of cardboard. His possessions were tied in a bundle roped around his waist. Boff used his foot to nudge him awake.

"Wassup?"

Boff handed him a five dollar bill. "Go buy a Cadillac."

As the bum pocketed the cash and walked off, Boff started down the alley, Cullen right behind him. It ended at a cement wall covered with Day-

Glo graffiti laced with obscenities. Kiko came into view at the top of the alley. He looked left and right, apparently to see who was around, then hurried over. The stench coming off him made Cullen's stomach churn. He smelled like a dumpster.

"Who's this dude?" Kiko asked.

"He's my nephew. I'm teaching him the business."

Kiko glanced back toward the street. "Man, I'm trying to make a living. What you bugging me for?"

"Who're you snitching for now?"

"Does it matter?"

"Not really. I just need some info."

"Show me the green. Fifty bucks."

Boff took a twenty out of his wallet and handed it to him. "Keep the change.'

Kiko frowned but pocketed it.

"When's the last time you took a shower?" Boff said. "You smell worse than autopsies I've witnessed."

"Once a week is all I do. I'm undercover. I gotta look *and* smell the part."

Boff took a package of Kleenex out of his pocket. He stuffed a sheet in each nostril and handed the package to Cullen, who gladly did the same.

"Ask what you came to ask and then go," Kiko said.

"Yitzhak Soliman and Humberto Arango. You know who they are, right?"

"'Course I do. You think I'm stupid?"

"Yes, but that's neither here nor there. How

about Julio Babbas?"

"The boxer? Took a bullet."

"Ever hear Babbas' name mentioned in the same sentence with either Soliman or Arango?"

Kiko said nothing.

"I take it you have."

"Not for twenty bucks."

"You want to up the stakes?" Boff said.

"Now you be talking."

"Okay, here's the deal. You tell me what you've heard, and I promise not to tell my good friend Luis Rodriguez what you do for a living."

Kiko suddenly looked scared. "You'd do that?"

"Sure. No skin off my back if Luis chops you up and feeds you to his pit bulls."

Kiko glanced behind him again. "I heard Babbas and Arango in the same sentence."

"Were there other words in the sentence? Like drugs for example?"

"Not exactly drugs. What I'm told, Babbas and Arango went way back. Arango had Babbas down to his villa in Panama a few times, so they musta been tight."

Boff leaned in. "What about Soliman?"

"I don't know jack shit about the Jew, except he deals Ecstasy. I never heard his name connected to Babbas."

Boff took out a ten dollar bill. "Give the twenty back. Ten's all that was worth."

"Over my dead body."

"As I mentioned, that can be arranged."

"Motherfucker!" Kiko exchanged the twenty for

the ten.

"When I was in the DEA," Buff said, "do you know what the life expectancy was for a snitch?"

"Don't know, don't care."

"Six months. A few lasted a year. I suggest you look for a new line of work. I hear Taco Bell is hiring. Make sure you take a shower before filling out an application."

Boff started to walk away. Cullen was only too happy to join him. That guy was ripe.

"Hey, Boff!" Kiko called after them. "I got some advice for you, too. The life expectancy of someone who messes with Arango or Soliman, that's less than six months. Especially Soliman. He's one bad dude. You oughta keep your distance from him."

Boff turned. "I thought you didn't know anything about Soliman."

"I don't. It's just what everybody says."

"Thanks for the advice. Remember to take that shower. Good luck at Taco Bell."

"Fuck you, asshole!"

They resumed walking.

"I've got a feeling Kiko knows more about Soliman than he told us," Boff said.

"Why?"

"Just a hunch. I thought it odd that he warned me off Arango and Soliman. It isn't like I wouldn't already know to be careful around those guys. The fact that Kiko volunteered it out of nowhere raises a red flag for me."

"Meaning what?"

"Not sure yet. Have to give it some thought."

They got in the Malibu. It felt to Cullen like the stench from that guy was still on his clothes. He opened a window.

Boff started the engine. "Bet you had no idea Saint Julio was involved with a Colombian mobster."

"I'm not taking the word of some bum. I can't see Julio being friends with a drug lord."

"Unless he led a secret life."

"Don't start that shit again."

Boff put the car in gear, and they left northeast Las Vegas and headed toward the mountainous area at the southern end of the valley.

"Who're we going to see now?" Cullen asked.

"A dear old friend."

"I hope he doesn't smell as bad as the last one."

"The only odors coming off this man are money, power, and expensive cologne."

Boff pulled up at the gates to a large estate. There was a guard station next to the wrought iron gates. Inside, a man was watching a small TV. He turned it off, came out, and swung open the gates.

"Hey, Frank," he said, "what's the good word?"

"Crime's up."

The guard was around forty-five with very pale skin.

"When did you get out of jail?" Boff asked him.

"Four months ago. Dante lets me stay in a nice cottage on the grounds. He gave me this job."

"Dante takes care of his people. He always paid me well." Boff glanced around. "Business must be good. This is quite a spread he has here."

A stone and mortar wall six-feet high surrounded three acres of manicured lawn plus shrubs and trees. About a dozen sprinklers were on. The mansion itself was a pink, multi-level stucco, lit up even during the day by floodlights.

"Dante ain't in trouble, is he?" the guard said.

"This is a friendly visit."

"No offense, but I've heard Death makes a friendly visit before he takes you."

"That's a new one. I like that." With a nod to the guard, Boff drove up a long gravel road to a circular driveway in front of the mansion. There was a center island thick with flowers. They got out of the car and were met by two muscular men wearing golf shirts and slacks.

"Monzi and Laterza, I haven't seen you guys in…how long?"

"Not long enough," Monzi said.

They shook hands with Boff.

"Who's the kid?" Laterza said.

"Name's Danny. He's retarded and lives in a shelter. Doesn't get out much, so I take him with me once in a while."

One of the men smiled. "Sort of like a big brother."

"Yes. I try to give back to society whenever I can."

"That'll be the day."

"So when are you two jokers going to get in some trouble? I can always use the business."

"We're law abiding citizens," Laterza said.

"I'm sure you are, but just in case you slip up, take my business card." Boff handed each of them one of his cards. "I'm here to see Dante," he said.

"He knows you're coming?" Monzi asked.

"I wanted to surprise him."

"Do we need to frisk you?"

"I haven't carried since the DEA. And I'm much too smart to wear a wire."

"What about the kid?"

"He's clean."

"Go around back. Dante's in the hot tub."

They found Dante Ferretti naked in a huge, pool-side hot tub with three buxom young women, also in the buff. He was a fat man in his late fifties with a thick head of dyed brown hair. They were drinking champagne from flutes. A magnum of Dom Perignon sat in a big silver bucket on top of a cart with an open pool umbrella over it. An old man was attending it. The geezer had to be pushing ninety, Cullen thought. The view of the valley was spectacular.

Ferretti looked up at his visitors. "Whatever they say I did, I didn't do it. I'd stand and shake your hand, but you might faint seeing the size of my schlong right now."

"No problem," Boff replied. He pulled up a beach chair. So did Cullen.

"What'd the kid get indicted for?" Ferretti said.

"He's not a felon," Boff said. "This's Danny. He's a college student writing a paper on real life private investigators, as opposed to the bogus ones you see on TV and in the movies."

"Well, kid, you picked the right guy. Frank's the best there is."

"He came highly recommended by the police," Cullen said.

Ferretti laughed. "I'm sure."

"Can I ask what you do for a living?" Cullen said. "This place is amazing."

"Tell him, Frank. I don't like to brag."

"Dante takes care of the New York Colombo Family's gambling and prostitution interests in Las Vegas."

Ferretti nodded. "Frank helped defend me a few years back on a RICO charge. That's a fancy word for racketeering. Nobody thought I'd beat the rap, but he helped my lawyer poke holes in the prosecutor's case, and I walked. Like I said, he's the best."

"Can I include you in my college paper?"

"I'd rather you didn't. So, Frank, how's your wife?"

"Wonderful as always."

"Never could figure out what she sees in a stunad like you. You must have some charm that eludes me."

"She's just a better judge of character."

Ferretti laughed hard and his champagne spilled into the swirling water. The old man brought over the magnum and refilled his glass.

"You want some bubbly, Frank?"

"Iced tea would be great. Danny's a recovering alcoholic. He'll take tea, too."

Ferretti nodded at the old man, who walked over to a wet bar by the pool and poured two tall glasses of iced tea with lemon.

"I know I ain't in trouble, or my lawyers would've called me," Ferretti said. "So what brings you to my humble abode?"

The old man gave Boff and Cullen the tea and went back to the cart.

Boff took a long drink. "You've heard of Julio Babbas, right?"

"Sure. Bad break he caught."

"Do you know if he had a gambling monkey?"

"If he did, I never heard about it, and there isn't much about gambling here that gets by me. Especially if it concerns a celebrity. What I did hear was he had some kind of connection to that Colombian garbage, Humberto Arango, but I couldn't tell you if he was a user." Boff winked at Cullen. "To my knowledge, I never heard anybody say anything bad about the kid."

"That's what bothers me," Boff said. "The guy supposedly had no enemies, didn't cheat on his wife, and now you're telling me he didn't owe money, either. So why'd he get whacked?"

"He could've been paid to throw a big fight and didn't. But that's something I would've heard about." Ferretti sipped his champagne. "What's your interest in Babbas? He's dead. You can't make money defending him."

"It's a little embarrassing" Boff said. "Do you have to know?"

"No, I don't have to know, but you've got me

curious."

"I was hired to find his killer."

"That's a good one. You're almost as big a bullshit artist as me."

"I wish I was lying."

"You're serious? This is way out of character for you. Does this mean you're switching sides?"

Boff took another drink. Cullen was just holding his glass. "And lose all my good friends like you?" Boff said. "Absolutely not. This is strictly a one-shot deal. I'm hoping for old time's sake you can keep this to yourself and not spread the word among our mutual friends."

"Sure. Scout's honor." Ferretti burst out laughing. His wine spilled again. He turned to the old man.

"What's with this champagne, Venero? It keeps spilling."

"I'm sorry. It must be the glass. I'll get you a different kind." He headed for the wet bar.

"Venero used to work for Bugsy Siegel, can you believe that? As a hitman, no less. That old man knows where all the bodies are buried and tells great stories. Life was better for guys like me back then."

"Bugsy Siegel got murdered. You're still alive."

Ferretti tapped one of the girls' head three times with his knuckles. "Knock on wood." Then he stood to stretch his legs. He had a prick as big as a stallion.

"You missed your calling," Boff said. "You could've had a lucrative career in porn flicks. Like

Long Dong Silver."

"Don't think I never considered it when I was young, but I'm glad I didn't. A lot of those guys got AIDS and died."

"Can you have your people ask around about Babbas?"

"Consider it done. Where can I reach you if I find out anything?"

Boff put the iced tea down, took out his wallet, and handed his card to Ferretti.

"How'd you and your college buddy like to take my girlfriends inside and clean your pipes before you leave?"

Boff shook his head. "I've never cheated on my wife, and Danny's impotent from all the drinking he did. Thanks, anyway."

"If a man doesn't cheat on his wife, he can never be a real man."

"I believe what Don Corleone said to the Sinatra character was, 'a man who cheats on his wife can never be a real man.' Something like that."

"Well, I don't know a single married guy who doesn't."

"That's because all you hang out with are riff-raff like yourself. Thanks again, Dante."

"Good luck with your college paper, kid."

They started walking away.

"Hey, Frank," the mobster called, "if you catch the killer, you can be like those lawyers who chase ambulances. Offer to defend him on the spot." His laughter followed them all the way to the car.

Chapter 8

What he'd heard on the Dark Side made it hard for Cullen to concentrate during his afternoon session. Rumors repeated by a snitch and mobster didn't add up to proof Julio was involved with Arango, but it was hard to completely ignore.

Leaving the gym, he drove to the *Review-Journal* office to look for stories about Soliman in the computerized archives. He noticed his friendly blue Acura was back. He wasn't in the mood to chase it again, so he opened his window, stuck his hand out, and gave it the finger. The Acura driver didn't get the hint and stayed with him until he got to the newspaper office, then he turned off.

If Soliman had something to do with Julio's death, Cullen wanted to know everything he could about him. He found some articles covering the last few months of the war he and Arango were waging, but there were very few older stories. There wasn't a single photo of him. Given that the Ecstasy trade is one of those problems Las Vegans don't want the tourists to know about, it probably wasn't hard for Soliman to fly under the radar.

Before coming to Las Vegas, Cullen read, Soliman had apparently been a key lieutenant in the Israeli mob the DEA had nicknamed the Jerusalem Network. One report said Soliman had been in charge of making sure the Ecstasy produced in mob-owned labs in Belgium found its way to America. Four years ago, after a long investigation by the Israeli attorney general, Soliman and a dozen other Network members had been thrown out of the country as undesirables. Soliman had come to Las Vegas with several of the men and set up his Ecstasy trade. A couple of the reports speculated that Soliman had severed his ties with the Belgian suppliers and taken advantage of the rapidly-growing Canadian Ecstasy industry, which eliminated the need for transport across the Atlantic. To sell his drug, he cut deals with dance and strip club owners. Besides the club people, probably the only Las Vegans who knew much about him were members of Lt. Harris' narcotics squad, who weren't allowed to speak to the media.

Frustrated, Cullen printed out what little he had, put it into a folder, and shut down the computer.

***

Yitzhak Soliman stood outside a chop shop on an East Las Vegas street lined with warehouses and factories. The buildings were all dark. Six of Soliman's men, including Zev, his oldest friend, were with him.

"It'd be safer if you waited in your car, Yitzhak."

"I'm fine here."

Soliman was a broad-shouldered man in his forties who had the look of an athlete, rangy and fit. He wore creased black jeans, a light blue cashmere sweater, and a gold Star of David on a gold chain around his neck. His face was commanding—a prominent jaw with a brown beard, an unusually broad forehead, and close-cropped hair. He had on sunglasses with metal frames and gray reflecting lenses, which he wore day and night when around his men so they couldn't see his eyes and get an idea about what he was thinking.

"The Koreans should've been here by now," Soliman said.

"I know."

Except for Zev, his men considered him a cold man. Soliman used words economically, often saying nothing, in fact, when they expected him to speak. His silences made his men nervous. Only with his family did he reveal anything of himself. His wife and kids found him a loving man, except for those times when his fierce temper got the best of him. At those times, Soliman invariably went into his weight room and pumped iron until the anger was gone. But when Arango had ambushed and killed his son David, Soliman knew lifting weights was not going to cut it. He ordered his men to break into the apartment of one of Arango's top soldiers, grab him out of bed, and take him to an abandoned warehouse, where they stripped him, hung him by his wrists from a wooden beam, and doused his body with gasoline. Soliman beat him to death with a tire iron, then set him on fire. The charred body was chopped up, stuffed in a box, and mailed to Arango.

That had made Soliman feel better, but he still knew there would be no satisfaction until he took an axe to the Colombian.

Six blocks away, a Hyundai Sonata was moving at a good clip. Its Korean driver, Kim, looked down at his watch and frowned. He was late. He was about thirty, with long unruly hair and a flat nose. On the passenger side sat a much larger man named Choi, who was asleep and snoring. Kim could have kicked himself for thinking they'd had time for a quick pit stop at Denny's. The restaurant had been busy, service slow, and now he'd have to deal with Soliman in one of his black moods.

Kim ejected the CD of K-pop singer Hyori Lee from his player. The last thing he needed was to show up late with music blasting. Suddenly he heard a siren behind him. Choi woke up fast and looked back. A Crown Victoria with red bubble light on its roof was bearing down on them, flashing its high beams.

"Pull over and stay calm!" Choi said.

Choi slid up one leg of his jeans and released the strap on his ankle holster, then covered the gun again. The Crown Vic stopped about twenty feet behind them and the driver got out and walked over. He was a Hispanic with a holstered gun clipped to his belt. Kim's mouth felt incredibly dry. If they looked in his trunk, he was as good as dead. The cop tapped on the window with his ring finger.

Kim rolled it down. "I'm sorry if I was speeding, officer. My mother was rushed to the hospital and—"

The Hispanic drew a Beretta and shot him in the head. Choi went for his ankle gun but never reached it. The shooter pumped three bullets into his back, and the big Korean slumped over. Reaching through the window, the Hispanic popped the trunk. A second man got out of the Crown Vic and walked over.

"Pedro, you sure the big one's dead?"

"Close to it. If he ain't already."

"Just in case…." The second Hispanic took out a Smith & Wesson 9 mm and shot Choi twice in the head. Then they lifted the Sonata's trunk and found the four suitcases. Pedro used a pocket knife to pry open the lock on one. There were dozens of clear plastic bags filled with blue and brown Ecstasy pills. He closed the suitcase and took it and a second one back to their car. The other guy grabbed the remaining two. After dumping them in the trunk, Pedro removed the bubble light, and they got back in the Crown Vic. Pedro killed the high beams and they drove away.

"How much is the shipment worth, Pedro?"

"I'm guessing street value would be close to six million."

"*Ay, caramba*, we should head for Mexico and live large."

"If we did, we wouldn't live at all. Arango would find us."

When Soliman heard the shots, he raced for his Lexus and jumped in. Two of his men got in back, the rest piled into Lev's BMW, and they sped in the direction the shots had come from. When he reached the Sonata, Soliman slammed his brakes and stepped out of the car. Zev hustled over right behind him, but the other men stayed by the cars, apparently wary of getting too close to their hot-headed boss. There was no question, the driver and other man were dead, but Soliman shot each of them twice anyway, just to vent.

He and Zev walked back to the trunk. His Ecstasy shipment was gone.

"Arango," he muttered.

"Maybe the Koreans at the Canadian lab cut a deal with him," Zev offered.

"No. They'd be too afraid of me to try something like that."

Soliman walked a few steps toward his men. "Somebody here must be a rat. How else could Arango have known when the shipment was coming?"

Soliman took off his sunglasses and stared at each man for a few seconds. They all squirmed under his gaze. Then he turned to Zev. He had known Zev since they were kids playing in the streets of Tel Aviv and had been best man at his wedding. Soliman took a step toward him and made a show of sniffing the air, as if he'd just detected an odor.

Zev suddenly looked uneasy. "Yitzhak, surely you don't think it was me."

Soliman had no idea if any of his men had betrayed him, or which one it could possibly be, but somebody had to pay for this. In choosing Zev, he would send a powerful message to the others that nobody who betrayed him was safe. Soliman circled his childhood friend, still sniffing.

"What is that odor coming off you?"

Zev said nothing.

Suddenly a powerful arm wrapped around his neck and a knife slashed across his throat. Zev staggered forward, clutching his bloody neck. Soliman pumped four shots into Zev's back with his Glock 22. As Zev crumpled to the ground, Soliman glared at the other men again. They would fear him now more than ever.

He knelt by Zev, put his mouth to his ear. "I'll see your wife and children are taken care of, old friend."

Turning his back on the men, he got back in the Lexus and drove off, leaving them to dispose of the mess.

Chapter 9

Boff stopped for an Egg McMuffin at a McDonalds, then drove back to northeast Las Vegas. He parked his car by a tattoo parlor where a couple heavily-inked bikers were polishing the chrome on their Harleys. He walked over to them.

"Luis Rodriguez is a friend of mine," he said. "I'm going inside to see him. Do you guys mind watching my car for me? I wouldn't want it stolen or taken to a chop shop."

One biker glanced at the car in question. "Who'd steal that piece of crap?" he said.

"Probably nobody. I'm just sentimentally attached to it. My wife gave it to me as a birthday present."

"When did that bomb last see the inside of a car wash?"

"Why pay ten bucks? I just wait for it to rain, put on my raincoat and galoshes, and soap the car down in the driveway. Don't even need to hose it off." He took out his wallet and handed each biker a twenty-dollar bill. The bikers tucked them into vest pockets.

"Just don't be too long," one said.

Boff stepped away, then turned. "By the way, I have a terrific collection of Fifties music in my car, if you want to listen."

"What's that? Like the Rolling Stones and the Beatles?"

Boff shook his head. "Buddy Holly and the

Crickets. The Teddy Bears. Richie Valens. Jerry Lee Lewis."

The bikers made faces.

"Man," the other one said, "you just go do your business with Luis. Your car will be here when you get back."

Boff headed for the entrance. A colorful sign painted on the window said *Kreative Khaos Tattoo & Piercing*. Two men in their twenties were leaning against the window next to the door. They stepped in front of the door and blocked Boff.

"You got business inside?" one asked.

"I'm Frank Boff. Luis is expecting me."

The guy took out his cell, made a call. "Do you know a big white dude named Boff?" He apparently heard what he wanted to hear. He hung up. "We still have to frisk you."

They patted him down; then stepped aside and Boff went inside. The shop smelled strongly of incense, and its walls were covered with framed tattoo stencils. He spotted the artist washing his hands in a sink. He was a round-faced Hispanic in his forties wearing an unbuttoned Hawaiian shirt and cargo shorts. He had multiple piercings, and there didn't appear to be an inch of exposed body where you could slap down another tattoo.

"How's business, Ruben?"

"*No hablo ingles*," he said, smiling

A client was sitting on a stool stripped to the waist. He had an exotic floral design on half his back and was reading an *Astonishing X-Men* comic.

"What's with the honor guard outside?" Boff

said.

"Luis heard somebody might be trying to muscle in on his business. He doesn't expect trouble, but you never know."

"Who'd be stupid enough to try and move Luis out?"

"Like I said, it's just some buzz on the street. Nothing specific."

Boff nodded. "Is he in his office?"

"Pumping iron and training his pit bull downstairs. They've been starving the dog for days to make him meaner for a fight. Watch out he don't take a chunk out of your big white ass."

"Dogs love me."

"Nobody loves you except your wife. If you want a tattoo today, I can make one special for you. The scales of justice with a big lump of coal on your side."

"I'm afraid of needles, but thanks, anyway." Boff opened a door in the back and headed down to the basement. The room was hot and humid and had weights, benches, a couple Nautilus machines, and a treadmill, currently occupied by a very lean pit bull terrier running under the watchful eye of a trainer.

"That's Panchito," said a muscular man with dreadlocks in his mid-thirties doing curls with heavy weights. "He's the best bull I got."

The dog appeared to slow down, so the trainer standing next to the treadmill lashed him with the kind of leather strop old-school barbers use to sharpen razors. The bull sped up.

"I see you take good care of him," Boff said.

Rodriguez began to grunt and strain. He did four more reps, then dropped the heavy barbell onto the mat. His long dreadlocks were dripping beads of sweat. "I *am* taking good care of him. If I don't make him mean enough, he could get himself killed."

"He'd probably benefit more from a raw steak and nice home with kids who love him."

"That dog lives to fight. He'd roll over and die if you put him out to pasture with some bratty kids." Rodriguez toweled his sweaty face. "After his fight I'll feed him." He turned to the trainer. "Run him a few more minutes. Then put the heavy chains around his neck."

"Does he get a shot today?"

"Yes."

"How do the chains help him?" Boff asked.

"They increase muscle mass in his neck. Shots are steroids. These dogs train harder than boxers. Panchito has incredible endurance and the ability to withstand pain. Once he went an hour in a fight. The other dog dropped dead of a heart attack. Panchito was pissed off because he wasn't done fighting, so he savaged the dog's neck and face. Is he special, or what?"

"He'd have made a great pet for Jeffrey Dahmer."

Rodriguez shrugged and pointed across the room. "Sit down, Frank."

Boff parked himself on a weight bench.

Rodriguez opened a small refrigerator, grabbed a Coke and a power drink, tossed the soda to Boff and sat on a nearby bench. “You ever see a dog fight, Frank?”

“In the DEA. We were going after a dealer who staged them.”

“How’d you like it?”

“It was interesting up until the point the dealer sniffed out we were Feds and sent a couple of his dogs on a search and destroy mission.”

“You guys musta run your asses off.”

“We pulled our forty-fives and shot them dead. I haven’t been big on running since I tore up my knee playing college basketball.”

“Same old Frank.” Rodriguez glanced at the dog again, then took a pull on his power drink. “What can I do for you?”

“Julio Babbas and Humberto Arango. I hear they were friends.”

“You could say that. The story I heard was Babbas knew Arango when he was a street kid in Medellin. Three or four times a year, Arango and his crew would drive in truckloads of food for the poor. Babbas helped him distribute it. When Arango moved to Las Vegas, Babbas by then was a boxing champion. He and Babbas became *amigos*.”

“Social or business?”

Rodriguez seemed reluctant to talk. “I’m not looking for any trouble with Arango,” he said. “Our businesses don’t conflict. I don’t sell Ecstasy, he doesn’t traffic in H.”

“You know you can trust me.”

“Only if I’m paying you.”

“Give me a buck.”

Rodriguez walked over to a pair of jeans hanging on a hook. He pulled out a wallet, grabbed a crisp new dollar, and gave it to him.

"Now that I have your retainer," Boff said, "everything you tell me is confidential."

"You always get what you want, don't you."

"I win more than I lose."

Rodriguez took another swig of his drink. "You know about the little war Arango and Soliman are having, right?"

"Yes."

"When Arango first got here, he found it hard to recruit club owners. So he stole a page from Soliman's playbook and began using celebrities and athletes to introduce his people to owners. By doing that, he was able to muscle in on Soliman's trade." Rodriguez paused. "As for Babbas' involvement, use your imagination."

"He helped his old friend out."

"You said that, not me."

The trainer stopped the treadmill and wrapped the chains around the dog's neck before restarting the machine.

"Any idea who killed him, Luis?"

Another pause. "Even if I knew, which I don't, I wouldn't tell you that."

"What *can* you tell me?"

Rodriguez hesitated. "Two weeks after Babbas was offed, a dance club that was one of Soliman's best money-makers burnt to the ground. Some of Arango's men were spotted there earlier in the night. The cops said it was arson. I'm guessing it was payback for Babbas."

"By payback, I presume you mean Soliman killed Babbas."

"I don't know if he did. Just guessing.

Rodriguez got up, then lay down on another bench. He grabbed hold of a barbell with very large weights and pushed it off its stand and up over his chest.

"Spot for me, Frank."

"Not on your life. The heaviest weight I lift is my five-liter box of Almaden Chablis."

"Jacobo, come here."

The trainer whacked the dog with the strop to make sure he kept running. Then he walked over and took up the spotter's position. Rodriguez started his reps.

"How much weight?" Boff asked.

"Three hundred-sixty." Rodriguez began grunting under the strain. When he'd done eight reps, he handed the barbell off to the trainer, sat up and turned back to Boff.

"I don't know why you're nosing around in Arango's business," he said, "and I don't want to find out. Just be careful. You're an important man in our community. If you get whacked, there's going to be a lot of indicted felons in mourning."

"It's always nice to know there are people out there who care about me." Boff glanced at the dog. "Just curious. What's the beast like to eat?"

"White men around six-feet five."

"Nice seeing you again, Luis."

Chapter 10

Cullen got a call from Boff just before he left for his morning session. He let it go to voicemail and then listened to it:

Soliman is someone an amateur like you doesn't want to mess with, said Boff's voice. *If you suspect him, let me check it out for you. Arango is another man you should steer clear of. I'm sure Gholston told you what's going on between them. You don't want to get caught in the middle. Call me when you get this message.*

He deleted it and headed for the door.

While Cullen shadowboxed, he thought about the one question that had bugged him most since the beginning. Why hadn't the cops been able to find a single clue about the killer? There were no fingerprints, no foot marks in the rain-soaked grass. None of the neighbors had reported seeing a man dressed in black or a strange car parked on the street. It was like he was a phantom. The cops said the guy had to be a real pro. Without the hitman, Homicide's chance of tying anyone to the murder had been handicapped from the beginning.

When no answer came, Cullen shifted his mind into his *Godfather* movie mode. That film and its sequels were his all-time favorites. What he liked most about Don Corleone and Michael was the power they wielded and that they were untouchable by the system. Toward the end of his twenty minutes of shadowboxing, he was replaying the scene from *The Godfather Part II,* where Michael's house in his Nevada complex is attacked by assassins and his men are searching the floodlit grounds. Suddenly a door opened in Cullen's brain. Michael's soldiers found the would-be assassins dead in a water drain. The men who had tried to kill him had been eliminated by whoever had sent them. That way, nobody could tie the shooters to them.

Boff was back outside the gym, leaning against his Malibu and eating a thick burrito. There was a Taco Bell bag on the roof of his car, along with a king-size soda.

Cullen stopped as soon as he saw him. "What are you doing here again?"

"I left you a message. You didn't have the courtesy to call back, so I thought I'd drop by and tell you what I found out."

"I'm not interested."

"Sure you are. Want a bean burrito?"

Boff stuffed down the last of the one he was eating, pulled out another large one from the bag, and held it out. Cullen headed for his car.

Boff called after him. "Aren't you the least bit curious what I have to say?"

He was, but didn't want to let Boff make himself a daily distraction. He got in his car and started the engine.

"Keep spinning those wheels!"

Cullen glanced in his rearview mirror. Boff was still there, eating the second burrito. He knew the guy was manipulating him by playing on his curiosity. He should just ignore him.

He threw the car in reverse. "Okay, what is it? Make it fast."

Boff glanced at his watch. "Sorry. It's too late now. You lost your window of opportunity. I have something important to do. Maybe I'll get back to you later if I find the time." He went around to the driver's side of the Malibu and got in.

"You asshole! You're really not going to tell me now?"

Boff started his engine. "Have a nice day."

Cullen was still angry when he got home. He slammed his front door shut and went into the kitchen. Using rubber gloves, he dug through his garbage pail until he found Boff's business card, now stained with slimy French dressing. He washed it off in the sink, then removed the gloves and took out his phone. It rang four times before Boff picked up.

"You know what you are, Boff? You're—"

What? I can't hear you! You're breaking up!

"I said do you know what you—"

Still breaking up! I think my battery's dying!

The line went dead. Cullen felt like throwing his phone against the wall.

After a quick shower, he changed into clean sweats, grabbed the box with the note and the sneakers, and drove to the *Review-Journal* office again. If Julio's killer had been eliminated, there might be a story about it. He limited his search to the two weeks after Julio was killed. If they were going to get rid of the hitman, it would probably be done quickly to make sure the cops didn't get to him first. He found three killings in the archive. One was at a poker game in a bar near the airport. Two guys got into a heated argument. One was carrying and blew the other away. A second man had been shot to death by police after a high-speed chase. The last was found lying in a dumpster. There was no wallet or any form of identification on him. He printed a copy of the third story and left.

Minutes later, Cullen walked into Unsolved armed with a steak sandwich for Gholston along with the box with his sneakers.

"I brought you lunch," he said.

"I ate already. Go away." Gholston brushed cracker crumbs off his desk into a waste basket.

"I got you a steak sandwich at Chicago Joe's. Cost twelve bucks."

"Did you bring ketchup?"

"Shit. I forgot."

"I eat steak sandwiches with lots of ketchup."

"I'll run to the grocery store down the street and get some." He turned to go.

Gholston smiled. "Stay put, ace. Lucky for you, I keep a stash for moments like this." He opened a desk drawer and brought out a handful of little Heinz ketchup packages.

"Where should I put the box?" Cullen asked.

"My garbage pail would be the best place. Barring that, dump it on top my file cabinet. I'll get it to Forensics later."

Cullen set the box down as instructed.

"Where's the wrapping the box came with?" Gholston asked, opening the sandwich and examining it carefully.

"Why?"

"The handwriting on it would be something Forensics would look at."

"I put in my building's recycle bin."

Gholston shook his head. "Amateur Hour." He started spreading ketchup on the sandwich. "Okay, what is it you want to know that I can't possibly help you with?"

Cullen laid the printout of the dumpster murder on Gholston's desk.

"This one of yours?"

Ignoring the printout, the cop took a healthy bite of the sandwich. Ketchup squirted out and landed on the printout. He ran a finger over the blob and sucked it off. "Waste not, want not."

Cullen waited. The trick was not letting Gholston get to him.

"Good sandwich," the cop finally said. "But I wouldn't pay twelve bucks for it."

"You didn't. I did. Now how about looking at the printout?"

Gholston put the sandwich down, kept chewing, and picked up the printout with greasy fingers. "Yeah, I remember this one. Stiff turned out to be a hitman. Bobby Pearce. Fitting ending."

A hitman! Now he was getting somewhere. "Who killed him?"

"Homicide couldn't find out, so they gave him

to me."

"You come up with any new leads?"

"Nope."

"Could you show me his folders?"

Gholston burped. He spoke with his mouth full. "Not much to look at. Pearce worked this town for a few years. Everybody I spoke to said he was a primo asshole but apparently good at what he did. Then a bum found him in the dumpster. End of story. Why the interest?"

"He was killed six days after Julio."

"So?"

"I was thinking if somebody hired him to kill Julio...."

"Hit men rarely get eliminated by a contractor. It would discourage others from working for them. Pearce probably just finally pissed off the wrong guy and was dumped where he belonged. In the garbage."

"I'm sure you're right, but humor me."

"Been doing that since you walked in."

"Can I see his folders?"

"You want me to interrupt my fine free lunch to hunt through my cabinets?"

"Tell me where to look."

"You'll screw everything up." Gholston tried to slide one of the cabinet doors open, but it wouldn't budge. He gave it a whack. It still didn't move. Cullen was sure Gholston could have requisitioned new cabinets, but suspected he got pleasure out of banging these around. Finally Gholston wedged a screwdriver in the cabinet and yanked hard. It came free. He took out a thin folder and handed it to Cullen.

"Just one?"

"What little I found wasn't worth putting in a second folder. I just tucked my notes in the back of Homicide's. Hitmen are not a high priority here."

Cullen opened the folder and stared at the photos of the body in a dumpster. The guy was wearing a muscle shirt and appeared to be in his forties, but it was hard to tell with so many flies around his face. He seemed well built, like the man in the ski mask. Cullen flipped through more shots. Then he scanned the report for anything that could tie him to Julio or the Israelis. Nothing. In the back of the folder were Gholston's notes. His handwriting was impossible to read. He gave the file back.

"Who'd he work for?" Cullen asked.

"Use your head. How would I know? If I did, I would've arrested the contractor."

"Then why do you say he was a hitman?"

"You hear someone's name mentioned in the same sentence as 'murder' enough times, you can connect the dots. Unfortunately, there weren't enough dots for Homicide to tie him to any hits."

"How do I find out more about him?"

"Go to Artie Stark's Gym."

"Why?"

"Before Pearce took up killing for a living, he satisfied his urge to hurt people by boxing. Stark trained him."

"Is Stark still there?"

Gholston shook his head. "He moved to Woodlawn Cemetery. Had a heart attack while porking a male hooker. His assistant, Eddie Haymon, operates the gym now on South 4th Street. What I hear, Haymon used to run with Pearce." He poured some coffee from a Thermos. "Knock yourself out, kid."

***

Artie Stark's gym was in a converted warehouse on a rundown street with shuttered factories, garbage strewn lots, a diner that had to be over fifty years old, and a check-cashing place. Cullen went inside. It was a classic old-world gym, but dirtier than most with a heavy odor of sweat mixed with mold and dust. The usual suspects were working out. Cullen didn't recognize any of them, but he spotted an older man showing a heavyweight with love handles the size of watermelons how to work the double-end bag. Then somebody yelled from the bathroom, "Hey, Eddie, the shitter's backed up again!"

The man with the heavyweight said, "Fuck you want me to do?"

The man came out, adjusting his pants. "Like maybe, you know, get a plumber in here. You can afford it, all the money I pay you."

"Use the plunger."

"Why me? It's your gym."

"You took the dump."

Grinning, Cullen headed over toward Haymon.

He was a stocky man with an ex-boxer's face that had caught too many punches. "Eddie," he said, offering his hand, "I'm—"

"Danny Cullen. Seen you fight a couple times. You're good. Never be your father, though."

Cullen nodded. "He was special. Just like Julio Babbas."

"You got that right. So what brings you to my gym?"

"Bobby Pearce."

Haymon turned to the heavyweight. "Do your neck exercises."

"Aw, man, I hate that crap. Why I need it?"

"To help cushion all the blows you take in your fat puss."

That settled, Haymon led Cullen to an office without a door in the rear of the gym. He stopped in his tracks when he saw a mouse on his desk, nibbling at the remains of a sandwich, and pulled a switchblade out of his pocket. He threw it at the mouse. It missed and stuck in the back of his desk chair.

"Fucking little prick. I almost squashed his ass a couple days ago with a barbell. Ending up denting my floor."

"Do you have traps set?"

"There's no sport in that. I want to kill him myself and see him die." Haymon took the blade out of his chair and sat down. "Okay, shoot."

"You hung with Pearce, right?"

"I did when he boxed. Then he found another profession, which I didn't like so much. After that, maybe I ran into him two, three times a year. When he got killed, I figured somebody just got tired of his act. Pearce could be a real dipshit."

"Any idea who might have killed him?"

"Ask the cops."

"They don't know. Don't care."

Haymon rubbed his scarred, meaty hands. "Bobby wasn't the nicest guy," he said after a minute, "but he was a good drinking partner and a loyal friend. You needed cash or a favor, he delivered. I asked around after he was killed."

"What'd you find out?"

"There was some talk about drugs and gambling. Nothing specific. It was just a feeling I got. One thing I know is Bobby wasn't dealing or using. He was strictly a booze guy. As for gambling, well, he did like the ponies."

"Did he work for the mob?"

"You make a living the way he did, it's inevitable."

"Which one?"

"I imagine whoever had the green," Haymon said. "Wops, Mexicans, Chinese."

"Israelis?"

Haymon didn't answer.

"Is that what you heard, the Israelis?"

"Look," Haymon said, "I hope you go on to win glory and riches in the ring. This crummy gym's all I got, so I mind my own business. That's all I got to say." He stood up and walked back into his gym.

Chapter 11

Boff's car was parked in front of Cullen's apartment building when he got home, but the guy himself was nowhere to be seen. Cullen went up the steps and opened his door. Boff was sitting on his couch, eating from a big bag of Wise potato chips.

"How the hell did you get in here?"

"I'm very good with locks."

"Get out!"

"Is that any way to speak to a guest?"

"You weren't invited, and you're spilling crumbs all over the couch. In case you haven't noticed, I keep a clean apartment."

Boff brushed the crumbs off the couch onto the rug. "I'll run the vacuum for you before I leave. I'm quite the domestic one at home."

"Make this quick."

Boff put his feet up on the coffee table. "You have any soda that isn't diet? There wasn't any in your refrigerator."

"No. Get your feet off my coffee table."

Boff shrugged and swung his legs down. "What have you learned? Not that I put much stock in anything you dig up."

Cullen put his gym bag down. He went into the kitchen and returned with a Diet Coke.

"Where's mine?"

"You just said you didn't want diet soda."

"No, what I said is I prefer real soda. I'll drink diet if that's all you have."

Cullen made no move to get him one so Boff got up and fetched it himself. "You're a terrible host," he said.

"Good. Don't come again. Now if you'll shut up, I'll tell you what I found out."

"Wait a second."

Boff went over to Cullen's CD collection, glanced at the titles. "No Fifties rock?"

"Before my time."

He pulled out a CD. "I believe Bach died in the eighteenth century. Unless you've been reincarnated, he was way before your time."

"I like classical. It relaxes me after a workout. I don't like, 'Be bop a Lula she's my baby.'"

"Gene Vincent. Nineteen fifty-six. Great song." Boff took the Bach CD out of its case. "The last time I listened to this crappy music, I was working for a philharmonic orchestra conductor accused of stabbing his lead cellist after the musician screwed up a concert. Every time I met with the defendant at his house, he had this classical garbage on. The things I do for money." Shaking his head, he inserted the CD, turned the volume up loud.

"Are you deaf?"

Boff walked over. "Remember your bug problem?" Then he told Cullen to sit close to near him on the couch so they could hear each other.

"You want some chips?" he asked when they were seated and listening to a *Goldberg Variation.* He pulled a big handful out of the bag. Several spilled onto the rug.

"I don't eat potato chips," Cullen said in a sullen

voice.

"Everybody eats potato chips."

"Not boxers trying to make weight."

"I guess that's why I didn't find anything worth munching on in your kitchen and had to run out and buy these. Normally I get generic chips, but my client is paying so I splurged for Wise. I'm curious about something. Why do you have six different pairs of sneakers?"

"You looked in my bedroom?"

"I had time to kill, so I took the lay of the land."

"Shithead."

Boff stuffed more chips into his mouth. "Relax. I didn't find any porno magazines or girls undies, if that's what you're worried about."

"The only thing I'm worried about is getting rid of you as quickly as possible."

"So tell me what you found out."

"A hitman named Bobby Pearce might've killed Julio and then was eliminated by the Israelis, who hired him."

"Impressive. Proof?"

"I don't have it yet."

"Meaning you're guessing. So let me guess. Pearce is residing in Gholston's morgue."

"Yeah."

"Sounds like a dead end to me."

"What'd you come up with that's any better?" Cullen asked.

"I got a third confirmation your Saint Julio was involved with Arango."

"Another mobster or smelly snitch?"

"Drug dealer. He told me Saint Julio knew Arango from when he was a street kid in Colombia. Arango used to bring food into the ghetto a few times a year. That's where your amigo met him. My source also said Saint Julio was introducing Arango to club owners so he could find outlets to sell his Ecstasy.

"No way. Julio hated drugs."

"I'm sure he did, but he was a macho Latino and went back a long way with Arango. And while Ecstasy can be a very harmful drug, most people think it's like pot, a recreational thing. So I don't think it would've bothered your friend's conscience much."

Cullen frowned. In just a few days Boff had apparently discovered important stuff about Julio he didn't know. "What else did you find out?"

"Two weeks after he was killed, one of the most popular dance clubs selling Soliman's Ecstasy burnt to the ground. Some of Arango's men were seen hanging around earlier."

"This relates to Julio how?"

"One possibility is the Israelis found out he was helping Arango and whacked him to set an example for other boxers and athletes. Viewed that way, torching the club could be seen as payback."

"That's it? You could've told me all this crap on the phone without breaking into my apartment."

Boff leaned close enough to breathe potato-chip breath on Cullen. "Your phone's bugged. Remember?"

"So next time, call on my cell. I'll give you the

friggin' number. Only use it if you have something solid." Cullen pulled a card out of his wallet.

"Forget it," Boff said. "I could make one call to the Dark Side and have your cell tapped today. A cell phone is never secure from tapping. It operates using radio waves, which are easily intercepted with a radio receiver. By simply acquiring the right decryption software, anyone can tap a cell phone in a non-invasive manner."

He got up and picked up the half-empty potato chip bag. "I've gotta run now. My wife is cooking cider-braised pork loin with cabbage and fingerling potatoes. I don't want to be late because my inconsiderate teenage son will eat all the potatoes just to spite me." He headed for the door with his bag of chips.

"Wait! You didn't vacuum my rug."

Boff looked at the floor by the couch. "You know, you're absolutely right." He walked out and left the door wide open.

Chapter 12

Boff was about seven blocks from his house in Henderson when he noticed he'd picked up a tail. Two men in a blue Acura had stayed with him after he'd made four turns. The last thing he wanted to do was bring a tail home to share his braised pork dinner and endanger his family, so he drove past his house and took a circuitous route to Henry's American Grill. Going in, he noticed the Acura pulling over down the block.

It was early for the dinner crowd and the restaurant was relatively empty. He was greeted by Annie, the hostess.

"Hi, Mr. Boff. It's nice to see you again."

"How's your zoo?"

"The two dogs are doing great. One of the cats had a fever, but he's okay now."

"What about the cockatoo, the gerbil, and the hamsters?"

"All fine. Here for an early dinner?"

"I just want to speak to Hector. Can I go back?"

"Sure."

He walked to the kitchen entrance, stepped aside to let a waiter go in through the swinging door, then followed him.

Hector was a huge man, maybe three hundred pounds of muscle and fat. His head was shaved and his thick arms had crude prison tattoos. He had learned to cook in Nevada State Prison. Boff helped spring him on appeal and find him this job. Seeing his visitor, Hector broke into a smile.

"Hungry, Frank? I can whip up your favorite tuna melt." He had just dumped an industrial-size can of white-meat tuna into a big bowl. He added a jar of mayonnaise and started mashing it with his bare hands.

Boff took a closer look. "Do all restaurants mix tuna like that?"

"Don't know. I just find it a bitch mashing this much tuna with a large spoon or a fork. But I wash my hands first, especially if I've taken a big dump like I did awhile ago. For you, I'll open a small can and mix it with a fork."

"Thanks, but my wife's cooking dinner. I need a favor."

"You name it."

"Are you busy now?"

"Nah. We don't fill up for another hour. Whatcha need?"

After a brief conversation, Boff left the restaurant and sat in his car. In a couple minutes, Hector came down a narrow alley next to the restaurant carrying a plastic bucket filled with used oil from the French fry maker. It was black as tar. When he reached the pavement, he started waddling toward the blue Acura. Just as he was coming close, he appeared to trip. The bucket flew into the windshield, covering it with smelly grease. The Acura's front doors sprang open. Two men in suits jumped out.

"Fucking mamzer!" the driver said. "Look what you did!"

"It was an accident, sir. I'm sorry."

Boff started his engine and revved it loud. They got back in their car. The driver turned on the ignition and ran the wipers. All the blades did was swish the grease back and forth. Boff did a U-turn and drove past them, waving as he went by.

His cell rang a couple minutes later.

"I got the license plate." Hector gave him the number.

"Thanks, Hector. You did a great job."

"No problem. That was fun. The driver had some kind of foreign accent. He called me a mamzer. What's that?

"Jewish term for bastard."

Who were those guys?"

"Mobsters, I believe."

"I thought mob guys loved you."

"Apparently these don't. Can you describe them for me?"

"I didn't get a good look at the dude on the passenger side, but the driver had these strange eyes. Like different colors. I think one was brown and the other milky gray."

"Anything else?"

"He was missing a nice chunk of his right earlobe."

Boff had a hacker friend run the plates. They were stolen. No surprise there. Then he called a towing company and gave them the Acura's location. He said to tell the guys in the Acura there wouldn't be a charge. Frank Boff had treated.

Next, he drove past his house four times to make sure there was no other surveillance. Satisfied that there wasn't, he got out of his car at the foot of the driveway and removed his son Steven's BMX bicycle, sprawled as usual in the middle of it. Then he pulled in next to his wife's Taurus. The house was a split level colonial that would fit nicely on any suburban street in America without being noticed. There were a backboard and a basket affixed to the front of the garage. The Mexican gardener had mowed the lawn and trimmed the hedges that day. Boff would have preferred that his son did the work because the gardener was expensive, but the first time he forced Steven to do it, the kid butchered the hedges so badly Boff had to call in a pro just to fix the damage. Walking toward the front door, he kicked aside a skate board from the slate walkway. He half suspected his son always left it there in hopes he'd step on it one day, fall and break his neck. The front door was unlocked. He was met in the living room by his wife, a slender, attractive woman. He liked it that Jenny wore her auburn hair the same style she had as prom queen, sleek with long, fringed bangs. She gave him a kiss.

"I wouldn't let Steven eat until you got here. He never leaves you any potatoes."

"Did I tell you I love you?"

"Not since this morning."

Boff hugged her. "Do me a favor, honey. Keep the doors locked when I'm not here."

"Are we in some kind of danger?"

"Unlikely. I'd just feel better if you locked them." He followed Jenny into the kitchen. The braised pork smelled heavenly. The table was set for three.

"Who's the missing plate?" he asked.

"Sharon. She's decided to become a vegetarian. She's eating at her girlfriend's house. She said Diane's parents are vegans, whatever that means."

"Why'd Sharon become a vegetarian?"

Jenny picked up a pot on the stove. "Do I have to tell you?"

"Yes."

"She said watching you eat huge portions of red meat has begun to sicken her."

A big-boned lanky kid around fifteen came bounding down the stairs. "About time you showed, Boff," he said. "I'm starving."

Steven had called his father Boff instead of Dad since he was little. He had picked it up from Sharon. Although he wished his kids would call him Dad, he sure as hell wasn't going to let them know.

"Nice to see you, too, Steven."

"Wish I could say the same, Boff."

Steven sat at the table and reached for the bread basket. Jenny slapped his hand away. "Not until your father says grace."

Boff didn't believe in God, but he said the prayer in order to please his wife, a devout Catholic.

"Amen," Jenny said. "Is locking the door connected to the latest criminal you're defending?" she asked.

Steven looked up. "What's this about locking

doors?"

"Your father thinks we might be in some kind of danger."

"A very slight chance."

"Can I get a gun?"

"No, you cannot."

"I could protect Mom."

"If you handled a gun like you did the hedge trimmer, you'd wind up shooting either her or yourself."

"Thanks for the vote of confidence." The boy helped himself to some potatoes. "So who's the scumbag you're defending now?"

"Language, Steven," Jenny said. "I told you not to use that word at the dinner table."

"What should I call them then? Dirtbags? Slimeballs? Or how about I just label them by the crime they committed, like murderer or drug dealer or—"

"That's enough!" said his mother.

Steven smirked at his father as Jenny went to the refrigerator, took out her husband's box of Almaden Chablis, and brought it to the table.

"Hate to disappoint you, son, but I'm not defending an alleged criminal. I've been hired to find a killer."

Steven laughed derisively. "That'll be the day."

Boff shrugged. Steven only dwelt on the negative when it came to him.

Jenny started carving up the pork. "Is that true, Frank? Are you on the right side of the law this time?"

“Yes.”

“I’m so glad. I can’t wait to tell Father Nolan. He’s been very concerned lately you won’t be able to join me in heaven because of the line of work you’re in.”

Steven laughed out loud. “Boff in heaven? There goes the neighborhood.”

The phone rang. Jenny picked up.

“Boff residence.... Yes he is. We’re having dinner. Can he call you back....I see. Hold on.” Frowning, she cupped her hand over the receiver. “He said it was urgent.”

“Who is it?”

“He didn’t give his name, but he has some kind of accent, maybe Middle Eastern.

He got up and took the phone. “Your windshield cleaned yet?”

There was a pause at the other end. “I understand your daughter Sharon is at her friend’s house. A lovely girl you have. It would be a shame if anything happened to her.”

Boff hung up, took out a card from his wallet, and dialed. “This is Frank Boff. I’d like to speak to Dante.”

“Honey, what did the man on the phone say?”

“He wanted to thank me for something I did.”

What’s up, Frank? Ferretti asked.

“I need a big favor.”

Shoot.

“I’d like a twenty-four/seven parked in front of my house and a tail following my kids to and from school.”

Jenny and Steven exchanged worried glances.

What's this about? Ferretti asked.

"I'll tell you later."

Okay. I can also send Monzi or Laterza to sleep in your living room.

"That's not necessary, but thanks. How soon can you do this?"

They're on their way.

Jenny and Steven stared at Boff, waiting for him to tell them what was going on, but he only sat down and poured Chablis from the plastic spout. Swirling it in the glass he sniffed the cheap wine like a connoisseur before sipping.

"Are you in some kind of trouble?"

After another sip, he put the glass down and stared at his son. "This is what happens when you work *against* the scumbags."

Chapter 13

Although Boff didn't let his family see his anger, he was seething. As soon as supper was over, he called Ferretti from his basement office and explained why he needed guards. Then he asked for one more favor. Three hours later Ferretti called back and told him to come around to his place.

Boff took a side road inside the fence around the estate that led to one of three guest cottages fronting a fountain encircled by marble. He parked and got out. Monzi and Laterza were waiting for him.

"I hope you're not offended by naked men," Monzi said.

Boff smiled. "Saw plenty in the shower after basketball practice."

Inside, there was a naked guy gagged and tied to a chair, colorful knit yarmulke on his head. One of his eyes was brown, the other milky gray. A chunk of his right ear lobe was missing.

Ferretti looked up. "Yarmulke's a nice touch, don't you think?" he said.

"Where'd you find him?"

"At a cocktail bar the Jew boys hang out at. I had one of my hot tub girlies come on to him. She invited him back to her apartment. Poor guy never did get laid."

"Now he looks fucked."

"We're just waiting for my surgeon to arrive. Want a drink?"

"Cola."

Ferretti tossed him a can of Pepsi from a refrigerator behind the bar. "So is this the fuck was tailing you?"

"Yes. Take off his gag. I want to hear him speak."

Laterza removed the gag.

"You cocksuckers! Touch me, and Soliman will ram his fist up your asses!"

It was the one who had called his house. Boff knelt down in front of him. "Are you that stupid to think you could get away with threatening the family of Frank Boff?"

"Fuck you!"

The door opened. In walked the old man, Venero, wearing a green hospital gown and carrying a doctor's black bag. He took a pair of surgical gloves out of it and slipped them on; then a white cloth that he spread on a small table. He lined up surgical instruments neatly on it.

"Who the fuck is this?" the Israeli said, clearly panicky. "What are you going to do?"

"Is Venero any good at this?" Boff asked.

Ferretti shrugged. "He used to be. Now, who knows? His hands shake a little and sometimes the scalpel doesn't always cut where he intends, but he likes his work. I believe in using men who take pleasure in their jobs."

The Israeli tried frantically to wriggle out of the ropes.

Boff stood up and looked down at him again. "You have my word Mr. Ferretti will set you free right now if you tell me what I want."

"Bullshit!"

"My word is my bond. The reality is I want you to go back and tell Soliman what happens when you mess with me."

"Yitzhak will go after you and these greaseballs with everything he's got!"

"Soliman's a drop of piss in the bucket, Jew boy," Ferretti said. "I have an army. He's got a platoon."

"What I want to know," Boff said calmly, "is where Soliman gets his drug supply in Canada."

"Fuck you."

"Wrong answer." Boff turned to Venero. "See if you can help him find the right one."

Venero picked up a scalpel, held it high, and let the light glint off it. He frowned. "I missed a blood spot." After wiping the blade on his gown, he walked over to the Israeli.

"Get this old fart away from me!"

"How do you feel about him calling you an old fart?" Boff asked.

The old man paused. "It makes Venero angry. The last person who did, I sliced the skin off his face with a steak knife."

Urine began flowing down the Israeli's leg.

"You're going to lick that floor clean after I'm done with you," Ferretti said.

Boff turned to Venero again. "Do you notice how one ear is different than the other?"

"Must've been a bad surgeon."

"Can you make both ears match?"

"I can try. I forgot my eyeglasses, but I think I can see okay."

The Israeli tried to meld into the wall behind him. "Get him the fuck away from me!"

"I'll ask you again. Who's Soliman's Canadian supplier?"

"I don't know."

Venero took a chair and sat close to the Israeli. He grabbed the ear without a slice missing. The Israeli shook his head violently and yanked free.

"If you don't sit still," Venero told him, "I can't be responsible for a botched job."

Ferretti pointed a finger at Monzi. He went over to the Israeli and grabbed his ear hard enough to pull it out of his head. The Israeli screamed and tried in vain to shake free of Monzi's grip.

"Last chance," Boff said.

"I don't know where the fuck it comes from!"

Boff turned to Ferretti. "I'm going to step outside now. I wouldn't want to witness a possible crime and endanger my license."

"Go ahead."

He left the cottage. A minute later, a blood-curdling scream came from inside. He walked a short distance away, took out his phone, and called his wife.

"Everything okay, honey?" he asked.

There's a black Cadillac parked out front with two men inside, she told him.

"Good."

Steven and Sharon didn't like the idea of being followed to school, but I told them it beats getting killed. They're going to hate you for this.

"They already do."

Another loud scream came from the cabin.

Frank, what was that noise?

"A bird. Is it just me, or do birds squawk louder now than when we were young?"

Jenny said nothing.

"I've got to go," he said. "Love you."

Half an hour later, Ferretti came out of the cabin. Boff was leaning against his car listening to "Silhouettes" by The Rays on his CD player. He turned down the volume.

"The guy's got balls," the mobster said. "I'll give him that. But when Venero picked up a scissor to cut them off, the Israeli suddenly remembered what he didn't know."

Ferretti handed him a slip of paper. "That's the supplier. City, street, and house number. Seems our Jew friend made a couple trips up to the lab and had the address in his wallet."

"Dante, you're the best. I'm sorry if I put you out."

"Are you kidding? That was the most fun I've had in a long time. You should've seen Venero work. The old man must've watched that movie, *Reservoir Dogs.* The one where Michael Madsen dances with the knife before cutting up the cop?" Boff nodded. "We put Italian opera on. Venero loves opera. He sang along while he worked."

"Sorry I missed that. Do me one more favor. Don't let this putz go until morning. I need some extra time before Soliman finds out I've got the address."

"What're you going to do with the information?"

"It's best you don't know."

Chapter 14

The next morning Boff called a former DEA partner assigned to the Las Vegas office and tried to set up a meeting, but Bob Ward hung up on him. Boff called back and told Ward it'd be well worth his while. Ward hung up again. When Boff got his ex-partner's voice mail the next time, he left a message: "Just remember I tried to do this as discreetly as possible."

A half hour later, he stepped into the DEA office and showed the receptionist his old agency badge.

"I'm here to see my former partner, Bob Ward."

The receptionist picked up the phone. "I'll tell him you're here."

"Please don't. I want to surprise him. He'll like that."

She hesitated. "Let me see your badge again and your driver's license." When he showed her both, she relented and said, "Okay. Go on back."

Ward was working on his computer. He looked up and frowned as Boff approached his desk. "Jesus Christ," he said. "You can't come in here. My supervisor will see us."

"I tried to save you the embarrassment by meeting somewhere else," Boff replied with a too-wide smile, but you gave me the cold shoulder. The smile changed to an exaggerated frown. "And after all those great years we had together."

"I hated every minute I was working with you,"

Ward said. "You gave me ulcers. I still have stomach problems. Which your presence here is making worse." He picked up a bottle of Maalox sitting on his desk and chugged some down.

Boff sat on a corner of his desk. A few of the agents who knew him were staring, but not smiling. He waved to them, and they went back to their computers.

"Make this fast," Ward muttered, then, "Oh crap! My SAC just saw us. Now I'm in deep shit."

"Relax. Dickhead Lasker is going to promote you after the gift I give you."

"Yeah, to head up the Alaska bureau. Lasker has hated your guts ever since you helped that dealer Luis Rodriguez beat a drug rap that would've put him away for life. Lasker had personally overseen that operation. You made him look like an idiot in court."

Boff nodded. "Well he is an idiot, and that's what I'm supposed to do. Given the incompetence level of most cops and Feds, it isn't really that hard."

"All the years you and I worked our butts off to get scumbags like Rodriguez in jail, and now you help turn them free? You're a disgrace."

"Stop being a drama queen. Tell me something. What happened when we'd put a bad guy away?" Ward said nothing, so Boff continued in a level voice. "Another one took his place. The system's useless. If you'd sent Rodriguez to prison, within days somebody else would've been running his operation. It's like trying to stop roaches once you have an infestation."

Ward shook his head. "So we just let the drug dealers go on killing kids with the poison they sell?"

"I can see this is going nowhere."

"Yeah. Say what you came to say and go."

Boff got off the desk. "How do you feel about Yitzhak Soliman?"

"Take a fucking guess."

"Considering he's operating the biggest drug operation in Las Vegas right under your nose, and you haven't been able to do a thing to stop him, I'd say you don't have warm fuzzy feelings about him."

"Headquarters thinks we're a joke out here because of Soliman. Nobody in our office has gotten a promotion in two years."

"Then today's your lucky day," Boff said. "I expect an apology from you." He took out the slip of paper Ferretti had given him and laid it carefully on the desk.

Ward picked it up. "What's this?"

"The address in Canada where Soliman gets his Ecstasy. He'll find another supplier, but it'll take time to set up the connection. Lost time is lost money. Big money."

"Why are you doing this?"

"He threatened my family."

"So this is on the level?"

"Absolutely."

"Does Soliman know you have the address?"

"He just found out a little while ago."

"Then we'd better move fast."

"I only ask one thing in return."

Ward nodded. He was expecting this. "Is this going to be painful?"

"Actually, you might get as much pleasure out of this as I will. After I walk out, dickhead will call you into his office. Let him ream your ass for as long as he wants. Then look properly humbled and hand him the slip of paper. Tell him what it is and say, 'Frank gave it to me.' Let me know what his face looked like after getting the biggest break of his miserable career compliments of Frank Boff." He slid off the desk and started to go.

"When I said I hated all those years partnered with you," Ward called after him, "that wasn't true."

"Thanks."

"It was just the majority of them."

Boff headed across the office with a bounce in his step.

On the way home, he stopped at a Dunkin' Donuts. He was wondering why Soliman had put a tail on him. How would the Israeli even know he suspected he was involved in the murder of Babbas? Unless…. Boff grabbed his coffee and drove back to northeast Las Vegas. He found Kiko and then waited by the alley wall for him.

"Man, what you back here for?" the snitch asked. "I already done told you all I know."

"I'm curious who you're snitching for."

"You said you didn't care."

"Now I do. Who is it?"

"I can't be telling you that. It's confidential."

Boff took out his phone and started to dial.

"Wait! Who you calling?"

"Luis Rodriguez."

"Stop! I'll tell you what you want to know. I'm working for Soliman."

Boff put his phone back in his pocket. "Why would he want a snitch in this neighborhood?"

Kiko took a step backward. "I told you who I'm working for. Isn't that enough?"

"Unfortunately for you, it isn't. If you don't want to end up as dog food for Luis' pit bulls, answer the question."

"This stays between us, right?"

"Cross my heart and hope to die."

Kiko hesitated. "Oh, man, I can't be telling you this."

"Sure you can. It'll be worse if you don't."

"Soliman wants to expand his operation and sell H here."

"That makes no sense," Boff said. "This is Hispanic territory. A Jew couldn't operate here."

"Soliman is going to use a Latino to front the business. A guy he can control." He looked behind him. "Now I gotta go before anyone sees us."

"One last thing, Kiko. Did you tell Soliman I was asking questions about him and Babbas?"

"That's my job."

Kiko headed for the sidewalk, then stopped and looked back. "That shit I just told you is confidential, right?"

"Your secret will go with me to my grave."

Kiko hustled off.

As soon as he was gone, Boff dialed his cell. “Luis, Frank. I’ve got some information for you about a snitch named Kiko and Yitzhak Soliman.”

Chapter 15

As curious as Cullen was to know if Boff had found out anything else, he wasn't about to call him. He'd probably pull that dead battery shit again.

"Stop daydreaming and get over here," McAlary yelled at him.

McAlary had driven him out to Sam Boyd Stadium near the UNLV campus to run sprints on the football field. There were a bunch of cheerleaders practicing summersaults on the sidelines

"I don't see the friggin' point in these friggin' sprints," Cullen protested. "I don't run in the ring. Stamina is what I need."

"When you throw a bunch of punches rapidly, do you ever get winded?"

"Sure. Everybody does."

McAlary nodded. "Throwing punches like that is a form of sprint. So you need sprint stamina. Now get your butt over to the goal line." When Cullen was where he wanted him, the trainer barked, "Go!"

Cullen raced to the fifty yard line, turned around and ran back. "Ten seconds," the trainer said. "Then go again."

McAlary made him do this for half an hour. Lungs on fire, Cullen bent over, gasping for air. McAlary started to walk away.

"Where're you going?" Cullen gasped.

"You have to jog back to the gym. See you there."

"I can't run all the way now. My legs are shot."

McAlary gave him a sunny smile. "You'd be surprised what you can do when you dig down deep. Have a nice run."

It was about five miles to the gym, the sun was unbearably strong, and Cullen's arms and face were sunburned when he reached the gym. He barely had enough strength to open the door and walk in. Kate was holding Trillo's legs while he did sit-ups. Cullen nodded at her, then glared at McAlary and headed for the locker area to change.

"Where do you think you're going?" McAlary said. "You're not done."

"Oh, come on! I'm exhausted."

"When you feel like this in the ring, does the referee give you a timeout?"

Cullen sneered at his trainer, who said, "Do the popcorn drill. Then you can go home."

Cullen put his gloves on, then McAlary stood behind a heavy bag and held it for him. Kate had a lap counter. Cullen started hitting it in his usual fashion until McAlary said, "Popcorn!" This was the signal for him to let fly with as many punches as fast as he could for three minutes, sort of like a popcorn popper bursting kernels. When he finished, his arm hurt just from raising it to wipe the sweat from his eyes.

"How did he do?" McAlary asked his wife.

"Three hundred and eighty punches."

"Good. Not great, but good. I want you up to four-fifty by the fight."

Cullen was still having a hard time believing Julio had been helping Arango sell his Ecstasy, so he decided to do some checking on his own. When he walked out of the gym, he saw Bulldog Boff in his Malibu, Fifties rock blasting. Cullen walked past him to his own car.

"Where're you off to?" Boff called over the music.

Cullen started his engine and drove off fast. Boff followed fast. Cullen tried to lose him by making some abrupt turns, but Boff was more experienced at this than he was. He gave up and drove straight to the dance club, parked, and got out.

So did Boff. "A little early to go dancing, don't you think?"

Ignoring him, Cullen walked into Raven. Boff was right behind. It felt strange being in the big club without all the crazy dancers, noise, and smoke. The club staff was getting things ready for the evening. A bartender came by carrying a case of wine. Spotting Cullen, he paused and greeted him.

"Hey, my favorite rum and Coke."

"How's the acting business, Tommy?"

"I did a deodorant commercial and got a call-back for a Mamet play."

"Great. Mike around?"

"In his office talking with some mobster."

"How do you know he's a mobster?"

"I'm a bartender. I read people. This particular guy, I actually happen to know about. He's an Israeli. Johnny Black on the rocks." Tommy glanced at Boff, who was still standing by the door, looking around. "Who's your friend?"

"He's not with me," Cullen said.

Boff came forward. "I'm his bodyguard," he said.

The bartender looked back at Cullen. "Are you in some kind of trouble, Danny?"

"No. The guy's a boxing groupie. I can't get rid of him."

The bartender shrugged. "Keep the left up, man."

Cullen took a seat at one of the bars that had a view into owner Mike Guerrini's glass-enclosed office. Guerrini was talking to a man in a suit. When Boff sat right next to him, Cullen got up and moved three seats away.

Boff followed him. "I gather you don't believe what I found out about Julio."

"You don't mind if I do some investigating of my own, do you?"

"Go right ahead. You're not going to find out anything I didn't already tell you."

A little while later, when the Israeli came out and left, Cullen walked over to the office. Boff was right behind him.

Guerrini stood up to shake his hand. "I heard you're going to be on Showtime," he said. "Who's the victim?"

"Jesse Tucker. He's undefeated in thirteen fights, has good power, fast hands, and a better-than-average chin."

Guerrini went into a crouch, threw a few hooks.

"Work the body, break him down."

"That's the plan," Cullen said. "Can we talk?"

"Sure. Take a seat." The night club owner looked at Boff. "Who's your friend?"

"I'm Frank Boff, Danny's publicist."

"Ignore him, okay?"

"No problem."

"You know I'm nosy," Cullen said, "so I'm going to ask who the sinister-looking guy was."

Guerrini hesitated. "An Israeli business man."

"That's not the answer I was hoping for. Someone told me Julio was introducing the Colombians to club owners to help them sell their Ecstasy."

"That would be me," Boff interjected.

"So anything you can tell me about that or the guy who just left will be appreciated," Cullen said.

Guerrini hesitated. "You know what the Israelis do for a living in this town, right?"

"Yes."

"Then I'm not revealing any secrets. The guy wanted to cut a deal with me."

"Did you?"

Guerrini shook his head. "You know me better than that. I teach my kids to stay away from drugs. Is there Ecstasy on my dance floor? Sure. Did the dancers get it from my employees? No. These kids club-hop. They hit one that sells before coming here. Nothing I can do about that. Occasionally, some punk tries to deal on the floor or in the bathroom. We got cameras. The punk's out."

"Did Julio try to sell you on the Colombians?"

Guerrini shook his head again, but this time he glanced at Boff. "No. But middleweight champ Floyd Raymond came to me a week ago on behalf of the Israelis. FYI, Jamaal Prince is also helping the Israelis, and Manuel Medina is with the Colombians."

As soon as they were outside the club again, Boff stopped Cullen. "I gather we're going to go talk to this Raymond," he said. "If he's helping the Israelis, he might know if Julio was doing the same for Arango. It's a waste of time, really, because I already told you he was. But you seem to delight in the pointless. Lead the way."

Cullen drove to the gym where Raymond trained and walked in, his "bodyguard" right behind him. They both leaned against a back wall. Cullen knew Raymond was a rugged fighter with a nasty streak that usually turned dirty in the ring. Right now, he was beating up on a sparring partner, turning what should have been a useful training session into one of his infamous gym wars. Blood was coming out of the sparring partner's nose and his left eye was bruised and puffy. Raymond's trainer had apparently just decided it was time to step in.

"Okay, Floyd, that's it."

The partner ripped off his head gear and threw it across the ring. "Last fucking time I spar with this dickhead!"

Raymond smiled. "Pay this has-been his money. Get me someone tougher."

"In my prime, I eat you for lunch." The fighter

took cash from the trainer, gave Raymond the finger, and stormed off to the locker room.

The trainer turned to his champion. "Floyd, I'm running out of sparring partners. You should be perfecting the fight plan we worked on, not back-alley brawling."

"It's my nature, what can I say?" Raymond spotted Cullen. "What the fuck are you doing in my gym?"

"Just wondering if we could talk."

"I ain't got shit to say to you."

"I do something to piss you off?"

"Last fight, you wrote in the newspaper my gloves looked skinned. The boxing commission investigated. They found nothing, but I still ended up with a lot of unnecessary hassle and bad pub on the Web. Get out!"

Cullen did not move. "How about we cut a deal? You need a good sparring partner, I need information. I'll go a couple rounds with you if you agree to talk with me."

Raymond smiled. "Get the rookie gloves."

Cullen knew he shouldn't be doing this with his Showtime fight coming up, but he really wanted to ask Raymond about Julio. He let the trainer wrap his hands and put on gloves and head gear.

Boff walked over. "I must say this is a novel way to get information out of someone. This is not in the investigator's manual."

Ignoring him, Cullen climbed into the ring. When the trainer sounded the bell, he used a crisp jab to keep Raymond at a distance, then circled away from his power hand. But as he often did, he forgot to keep his left up. Raymond made him pay by firing a hard right that stung Cullen's cheek, then, apparently encouraged by Cullen's sloppy defense, Raymond came forward aggressively. He got inside and landed a short right to Cullen's jaw, then hooked him twice to the body. Cullen knew this was only going to get worse. He had to end it fast, so he decided to use Julio's favorite neutralizer, left hook to the liver.

He waited until Raymond threw a wide looping right that left his right side exposed. Cullen put everything he had into the hook. It landed near Raymond's liver and had the desired effect. Raymond's legs wobbled, his eyes got glassy.

The trainer rushed over and got between them before Cullen could follow up. "That's it!"

"I was just warming up," Raymond said without conviction.

"You're done for the day. Now touch gloves."

"Okay. No sweat. Maybe I'll move up to super middleweight when this rookie earns the right to fight me."

Raymond stepped forward like he was going to touch gloves, but instead, he suckered Cullen with a hard right that caught him flush under the left eye. As Cullen charged back to retaliate, the trainer grabbed him in a bear hug.

Raymond smiled. "Okay, chump. Now we can talk."

He surprised Cullen by leading him and Boff around the corner to a sidewalk juice bar attached to a vegan restaurant. They sat on stools. Raymond ordered carrot juice, Cullen, papaya.

"What about you, sir?" the counter woman asked Boff.

"Do you have root beer?"

"Sorry. This is a juice bar."

"Then I might as well be adventurous." He looked at the chalked menu board. "I'll take a mango passion smoothie."

Cullen looked at Raymond. "I figured you for a beer guy, Floyd."

"Don't drink, smoke, or do drugs. Health food fanatic. Your body is your temple, yada, yada, yada."

Cullen sipped his papaya. "If you don't like drugs, then what're you doing helping peddle Ecstasy?"

"Is this for the newspaper?"

"No. It's about Julio."

"You're still beating that dead horse?"

Cullen let the jab ride. "I know you're introducing the Israelis to club owners."

"BFD. Your soul mate Julio was doing same for the Colombians. He wasn't the saint everybody thought he was."

"Told you," Boff said.

Cullen frowned. Hearing it from Boff and some lowlifes was one thing, but Raymond was in a position to know. He turned back to the fighter. "If Julio was involved with the Colombians," he said, "it was only because he was old friends with Arango and did him a favor out of respect."

"Lot of respect, I'd say," Raymond shot back. "He was also recruiting other boxers for them. Like Manuel Medina." He paused and smiled. "But only when he had time free from cheating on his wife."

"No fucking way!" Cullen exclaimed.

Raymond smiled. "I can give you the names of his sweeties."

"Julio had a great marriage."

"I'm sure he did, but spics and wops, they don't think screwing around is cheating, it's recreation. Remember my wife? Samantha? Beautiful babe and great in bed. Now I'm divorced. Why? I found out she was screwing Julio. You don't believe me, talk to Samantha."

Cullen sure as hell didn't want to discuss Julio's sex life with this guy. "I bet the Israelis weren't too thrilled to find out Julio was helping the Colombians," he said. "You hear anything about that?"

Raymond stared at him a moment. "These Israelis are a nasty bunch behind their fancy suits and sunglasses," he said. "I guess you get that way, surrounded by towel heads who want to wipe you off the face of the earth. Maybe I hear things. Some of the Jews get drunk on their kosher wine, they say shit."

"Such as?"

"I'm not going into specifics. Let's just say Julio helping the Colombians didn't make him their favorite boxer." He took a long drink of carrot juice. "Use your imagination." Then he drained the glass, got up, and put a few bills on the counter. "Finish your papaya, rookie. It's good for digestion. I'd say from the look on your face you'll need help digesting what I just told you." He walked away.

"My, my," Boff said. "In addition to being pals with a mobster and helping peddle Ecstasy, Saint Julio was a swinging dick."

Cullen glared at Boff and slid off his stool.

"Before you go," Boff said, "you should be aware I did something that's going to make Soliman a very unhappy man, so be alert for trouble. Don't walk around in a fog when you're not in the gym."

"What did you do?"

"Let's just say I bit the hand that feeds him." Boff stood up. "What're you going to tell McAlary about your eye?"

"My eye?"

Boff pointed to the mirror behind the juice bar. Cullen looked at it and winced. There was a red bruise under his left eye. McAlary was going to be pissed.

Chapter 16

Yes, indeed, McAlary took one look at Cullen's eye and walked away from him.

"I'm sorry, Ryan," Cullen said. "I sparred a round with Floyd Raymond because he wouldn't talk to me about Julio unless I did."

Kate came into the gym carrying a laundry basket. "Where the hell did you get that bruise?" she asked.

"He doesn't work hard enough here," McAlary replied, "so he went to Floyd Raymond's gym and sparred with him."

Kate dropped her basket and got up in his face. "How could you be so stupid! I had to pester Showtime for a month before they went for my idea to showcase sons of great fighters. Raymond's a world champion. He could've seriously hurt you. Idiot!"

"Actually," Cullen said, "I was the one who hurt him. I buckled his knees with a left hook."

"Whooptee-doo. You try this again, you find yourself another manager." She picked up the basket and turned to her husband. "Ryan, work his butt into the ground."

On the way home, Cullen glanced behind him a few times to see if the blue Acura was following. It wasn't, but a gray van with tinted windshield had been with him for awhile. As they approached a sharp curve in the road, the van suddenly sped up and rammed his rear end, sending the car into a spin. Sliding sideways toward a big palm tree, Cullen slammed his brakes, but it didn't stop the car. Just a few feet from the tree, he managed to get it straightened out. He hopped the curb and missed the trunk by inches, and then his car plowed into a thick hedge and stopped. He turned around to look for the van. It was gone. Before backing off the curb, he called Gholston.

"A van just tried to run me off the road. I almost hit a tree."

Drive more carefully.

"What the hell is wrong with you?"

Nothing that I know of.

"How can you take this so lightly?"

You injured?

"No. But I sure as hell could've been."

Did you get the license plate?

"No."

So long. Gholston hung up.

Cullen was about to put his key into his apartment door lock when he noticed it was ajar. The first thing he thought of was Boff. He looked for the detective's car on the street, but it wasn't there. Maybe the Israelis were inside. He debated whether to go in or call the cops when the door swung open and a Hispanic dude out of *Muscle Magazine* made the decision for him.

"Inside."

Cullen looked past the guy and saw four more Hispanics in his living room.

One of them was sitting in his easy chair. “I’m Humberto Arango, an old friend of Julio.” Arango was a portly man with black hair slicked back and a lot of jewelry.

Cullen stopped at the door. “What’re you doing here?”

“I’m sure you know the answer to that. Relax. We’re on your side. We’d love to find Julio’s killer as much as you.”

Cullen wasn’t happy they had broken in, but at least now he might get some definitive answers. He walked in and sat down opposite Arango. “Julio was introducing you to club owners,” he said.

“Yes. Julio knew about friendship and respect. He wouldn’t even take money.”

Cullen wondered if he should turn on the music because of the bugs. But it could’ve been the Colombians who planted them. He didn’t feel like shouting, so he scrapped the idea.

The big thug suddenly farted loudly.

“*Ay caramba,*” Arango exclaimed. “*Que pesta!* Francisco, what did I tell you?”

“I tried to hold it in, squeezed my cheeks, too.” Francisco shrugged and smiled sheepishly.

“Stop with the chili.”

“If I don’t eat Silvia’s chili, she pouts. Then I don’t get laid.”

“Get a butt plug when you’re around me. I’m sick of smelling this every day.” Arango turned back to Cullen. “I would shoot him, but he’s very efficient at what he does.” He cleared his throat. “Ask me questions. I’ll answer what I can.”

"Did the Israelis kill Julio?"

"I believe so, just don't know for sure. At one point, I was able to convince an Israeli gang member to be my informant, but—"

"How'd you manage that, if I may ask?"

"I had someone strangle two of his sisters in Israel. He had three more brothers and sisters, so he made a wise decision and agreed to work for me. But before he could find out anything about Julio, the *pendejo* goes and screws Soliman's oldest daughter. Soliman fired him, so to speak. With a blow torch. Animal!

Cullen nodded. "Assuming the Israelis killed Julio, would they have used someone in-house or contracted outside?"

"Outside. Someone who knows nothing about their business. That way, if he got caught, he couldn't rat out whoever hired him."

"Did you check out the local hit men?"

"Most of them. All had alibis. One, I wasn't sure about, and he gave me some attitude, so I put him out of business. Probably was telling the truth, but I lost my self-control."

"Was that a guy named Pearce?"

"No," Arango said. "I didn't know of this man. You think he killed Julio?"

"There's a possibility."

"I'll check him out."

"Don't bother. He's dead." Cullen hesitated. "When Julio visited you in Panama, did he bring his wife?"

"Sometimes."

"When he came alone, did he screw around with women?"

"If he did, it meant nothing. He loved Cassandra very much."

"I've heard he cheated here in Las Vegas."

Arango frowned. "I told him I didn't approve. What's the American expression? Avoid taking shits in your own nest? Why do you want to know this?"

"I ask because while it's more likely the Israelis killed Julio, isn't it possible he did the same thing your informant did? Screwed the wrong woman?"

"I hadn't thought of that. I'll look into it."

Arango snapped his fingers at Francisco and pointed to a carrying case on the floor. Francisco opened it, took out a bottle of whiskey and a glass.

"Nineteen-year-old Saint Magdalene," Arango said. "Finest single malt in the world."

Francisco suddenly put the bottle and glass down and ran out of the room. A string of farts came floating out of the kitchen.

"Stay in there until the odor is gone!" Arango got up, poured some Scotch into a glass, sat back down, and sipped. He looked at Cullen again. "If you weren't in training, I'd invite you to touch glasses."

"I figure you're here because you want something from me."

"Yes. If you win your Showtime fight, Soliman may try to recruit you. You had a famous father, and your style of fighting is crowd-pleasing. Like Julio."

"Soliman wouldn't do that," Cullen said. "I'm sure he knows I was Julio's best friend. He also knows I've been asking questions about him."

"That would be his main reason to approach you." Arango leaned closer to Cullen. "What is it the Godfather said to Michael about enemies?"

"'Keep your friends close, but your enemies closer.' You want me to say yes to Soliman?"

"The Godfather's words can work both ways, no?"

"I'll think about it."

Francisco came back into the living room. "Sorry about that, Cullen," he said. "I opened a couple windows in there. Wait awhile before you go in."

Downing his Scotch, Arango stood up and handed Cullen a blank business card with only a phone number written on it in pencil. "If you ever need me, call."

Cullen watched them go. There was no doubt in his mind now that Julio had hidden a side of himself. Could there be more? He hoped not, but if there was, he had started down this road and was not about to stop now. The only upside was that when all the ugly details were revealed, he would likely find out who had Julio killed and why.

Chapter 17

Eating lunch at a Burger King, Boff tried to get a handle on why the DEA hadn't been able to pin a thing on Soliman. He didn't have the highest regard for the agency, but he was still puzzled. When he finished his french fries, he took out his phone and called a lawyer who had represented several drug dealers.

"Emmanuel, Frank Boff."

Hey, man. How's business?

"Great as always. Have you ever had Yitzhak Soliman as a client?"

Nope. Nobody has.

"Why's that?"

He's never been arrested and none of the clubs he sells Ecstasy at have been raided by the police.

"Is he protected?"

I can't say for sure, but everybody seems to think so. Nobody in the trade is that untouchable.

"Thanks, buddy." Boff had a pretty good idea who was shielding Soliman and where to get confirmation.

As soon as he finished his burger, he drove to Clark County Regional Justice Center on Lewis Avenue. He walked down the corridor and sat on a marble bench outside the courtroom. Court was in session. He could hear a D.A. he had bumped heads with grilling a witness.

A well-dressed man around forty carrying a briefcase approached. "Frank," he said, "what's the good word?"

"My wife looks lovelier each passing day. How about you, Epstein?"

"Could be better, I'm not complaining." He sat next to Boff on the bench and put his briefcase on the floor. "Listen, I've got this great case coming up and I might need some help on it."

"I thought you had two investigators on salary."

"Neither of them is named Frank Boff. I need someone with your talent and flair for the devious." Epstein took a small bottle of Scope out of his suit jacket, uncapped it, and swallowed a slug.

"I see you've got your drinking under control," Boff observed.

"I've had a rough day."

"What's the case about?"

"Securities fraud. It's real complicated, and my goy gumshoes are clueless when there's no blood or dead bodies. I need a Jewish *mench* like you."

"Half Jewish."

"That's right. You're also part African-American."

Boff smiled.

"You have a case in court?" Epstein said.

"No. I'm waiting for Ellen Petrie."

"That bitch? She's a second-string lawyer and overrated piece of ass."

"Overrated? I heard you came on to her in the women's room of the Catbird Lounge, and she grabbed your nuts so hard you had trouble pissing for a week."

Epstein pulled out the Scope, took another hit.

"Don't believe everything you hear. He stood up and picked up his briefcase. "I've gotta go. If you're interested in the case, give me a call."

Epstein took off just as the court doors opened and people began filing out. Boff waited until nearly everybody was gone before he went in. Attorneys for both sides were usually the last to leave. He walked to the defense table and stood there until an attractive woman in her forties wearing a Calvin Klein suit turned and saw him.

"Go away."

"Come on, Ellen. You can't still be holding the Arreola case against me."

"No? You come recommended to me because you have an incredible acquittal rate. You almost never lose. So I hire you. And what happens? The cop I'm defending doesn't walk. What was it, Boff? You have a thing against women lawyers? Did you resent me because I wouldn't sleep with you?"

"I never asked you to sleep with me."

"Then what was it?" she asked.

"Your case was a total loser. I told you from the beginning. You should've had the cop plead out like I advised, but you wanted to be a swinging dick in court. So you lost. Your fault, not mine."

Petrie snapped her briefcase shut and brushed past him. He followed her up the aisle. She stopped by the door and turned around and faced him. "Don't stalk me. There are laws against men doing that."

"Women, too. Once I defended this gal who—"

"Spare me your war stories."

"Most people are amused by them."

"Nothing about you amuses me." She looked at her watch. "You've got one minute."

"What happened to Arreola after his two years at the minimum security lockup?"

"Last I heard," she said, "he was out. As in down and out. Wife left him, he started drinking heavily, couldn't hold a job. Like I always say, take away a cop's badge and gun, most of them are bums."

"Ellen, that's pretty harsh. Even I wouldn't say that, and you know my low opinion of cops." He smiled but she didn't smile back. "Any idea where I can find him?"

"Try looking in Freedom Park. I see him sitting on a bench sometimes with his brown bag of rotgut wine. It's on the way to my office."

"Thanks, Ellen. If I wasn't married, I'd fall in love with you."

"Screw you, Boff. Go beat off in the men's room."

Boff drove to Freedom Park, an ironic name because in Las Vegas the only things that were free were the rooms and booze for high rollers, who ended up losing a lot more than the cost of the amenities at the casino tables. The park had always been an eyesore, but now it appeared to be undergoing renovation. A city crew was planting palm trees around a new pond.

Although he hadn't spotted a tail on the way, he sat in his car and studied his rear view mirror, trying to see if anybody had pulled over down the block.

He doubted that Soliman would mess with him again because of his connection to Ferretti, but it never hurts to be careful, he told himself, especially when you're going to be walking around in a wide open park.

Satisfied there was no tail, he got out and searched around for the ex-cop. Arreola wasn't sitting on any of the benches, so Boff went into the men's bathroom. It stank of overheated urine and ammonia. There was nobody at the trough and the two stalls were empty, so he walked out again and spotted a scrawny-looking woman with a bad red-orange dye job and the sickly skin of a drug user sitting on a nearby bench. He walked over and sat down beside her. Her body odor was off the chart. He inched away.

"Nice day," he said.

"Fuckin' sun shines alla time, it's hotter 'n hell, tell me something I dunno."

"I'm looking for somebody."

"I ain't working, bozo. Take a hike."

"His name is Ricky Arreola."

The woman made a face. "You see that sacka shit, you tell him I'm done with him. Fucker owes me twenty bucks, hasn't been around in a week."

"I take it you know him."

"I suck his cock once in a while. I guess that means I do."

"It sure does. You wouldn't happen to know where I can find him?"

"Why should I tell you?"

The woman took out a cigarette and lit up with

shaky hands.

"I'm a private investigator," Boff told her. "A client paid me to give him some money he was owed."

The woman's eyes narrowed. She blew smoke toward his face. He moved his head to avoid it.

"How much?" she asked.

"Enough to where I can give you twenty bucks out of it. Arreola owes it to you, anyway."

"Damn right he does. Do I look like the kinda girl who'd give free blowjobs?

"No, you certainly do not."

He pulled out his wallet, handed her a twenty and a ten. "The ten's a tip from Ricky. I believe in rewarding good service. I'm betting you give it."

She snatched the money and smiled. She had a front tooth missing and was ten years removed from her last dental cleaning. "You want your weenie sucked, mister?"

"I wish I could, but I suffer from erectile dysfunction."

"What's that?"

"Limp dick."

She stuck out a grotesquely long tongue. It was coated with grey-white fuzz. "The Snake can make a dead body stiff." She wiggled it.

"There's a pun in there somewhere," he said.

"Whatchew mean?"

"Never mind. You see the problem is if I failed to respond to Wonder Snake, it'd only make me more depressed about my condition. So how about I pay your twenty dollar fee—which I think is quite reasonable, considering the lavish tool you have to work with—and you tell me where Ricky lives." He took out another twenty. The woman tried to grab it. He closed his fist. "First tell me."

"You know where Las Vegas Boulevard is in the northeast section of town?"

"It's my second home."

"Stay on the boulevard past all the pawn shops and bodegas until you come to a buncha warehouses. Shit-for-brains has a mattress in an abandoned one. Place is fulla roaches an' mice, prob'ly rats. Ricky must feel right at home."

"How will I know which warehouse it is?"

"It's got a sign over the front door."

"What's it say?"

The woman suddenly stared blankly in front of her.

"Hello?" Boff said. "You still there?"

She came out of it and looked at him. "Who the hell are you? Whaddaya want? I ain't working!"

He waited for her to unscramble her brain.

"Oh," she said after a few moments, "you asked about the sign. It says, 'Wholesale Food Distributors.' Don't ask me to spell it. I failed spelling in school."

"I think I can manage." He gave her the twenty.

"You sure you don't want to have a go with the Snake?" she asked.

"Maybe I'll come back. You here every day?"

"Mostly. Sometimes I go to Sunset Park. It's a little classier there."

Boff got up to go.

"What's your name, mister?"
"Barack Obama."
"I heard of you."

Chapter 18

Finding the warehouse wasn't too hard. Getting in was another thing. All the windows were boarded up, and the front and side doors were bolted with heavy gauge steel. Boff walked to the rear of the facility, where the loading dock was, but the metal roll door was down. Arreola had to get in somehow. He looked around. A big window on the side of the dock appeared to have loose boards and nails missing. When he gave them a yank, they came off so quickly he lost his balance and tumbled onto his ass. Getting up, he stuck his head in the window. The place smelled incredibly musty. He climbed in through the window. Inside, he dusted off his hands and clothes and jumped back when a rat the size of a cat scurried by. He'd intended to search around and catch Arreola by surprise, but this stink hole was beyond the call of duty.

"Ricky Arreola! I have some money for you from Ellen Petrie!"

Nobody answered.

"She's been feeling really bad lately about losing your case. She sent me with some cash. Frank Boff. You remember me? I was on your team. We would've gotten you off with probation if the dumb broad had listened to me."

"That bitch ruined my life!"

Boff tried to identify where the voice was coming from, but it was too dark and the voice wasn't quite loud enough. "You got that right," he said. “Can I bring you the money?”

“Yeah, but I’ve got a gun if this is a scam.”

Boff started walking in the direction the voice had come from. “Keep talking so I can find you.”

“How much did she give you?”

“Fifty.”

“That all? Cheap bitch.”

“Considering all you’ve been through because of her,” Boff said, “I agree.” Rounding a corner, he saw the remains of what had once been the warehouse office. Its cracked windows were covered by yellowed newspaper and duct tape. The door was hanging on one hinge. On the floor lay a heavily-stained mattress.

“Tell you what, Ricky,” he said carefully. “I was paid twenty bucks by Petrie to deliver the money. You can have that, too.”

A skinny man in a soiled undershirt and filthy sweatpants appeared in the doorway. His hair was thin and matted with grime. He had a gun in one hand, the neck of a bottle of wine in the other. He took a long hit. Then, “Show me the money.”

Boff slid a fifty and a twenty out of his wallet. Arreola laid the gun down on the mattress.

“I can give you this and walk away, or you can make some more by helping me out.”

“Doing what?”

“I need some information about the fine upstanding cops you used to work with.”

“You ever hear of the fucking *Thin Blue Line*?”

“Yes I have, but it seems to me you’ve crossed over it long ago. I’m prepared to offer you a C-note for a little help."

"Make it a buck-fifty, you've got a deal."

What the hell, it was his client's money. "Okay." He put the twenty back in his wallet, took out a hundred. Arreola started to walk over.

"Stay where you are," Boff said. "First you give up the info. Then I turn over the cash."

"How do I know you'll live up to your end?" Arreola suddenly bent over. A spray of vomit spewed out of his mouth. He wiped his lips with his dirty shirt. "Fucking wine makes me sick. It's rotgut."

"I'll live up to my end because I wouldn't be able to do what I do if word got around I didn't pay my snitches. You were a cop. You know that."

Arreola took another hit of the wine. "What do you want to know?"

"You've heard of Yitzhak Soliman, right?"

"You can't work in Narcotics and not know that name."

"Well, I'm puzzled by something. Soliman sells his stuff in all these clubs, yet none of them ever get raided. He's never been arrested. How do you figure? Just good luck?"

Arreola laughed derisively. "Luck, my ass! He paid us off. Most cops never have enough money, you know how it is. Back then, I had a wife and two kids. They had needs I couldn't meet on my salary. So I put my neck on the line. Now the wife and kids hate me."

"I know the feeling."

"When I was in Narcotics, if you played ball

with Soliman, you made out pretty good because Harris took care of his people."

"That would be Lieutenant Harris, right?"

"He was sergeant then. Can't believe that crooked piece of shit got bumped up."

"Runs the bureau now."

"Then there's your answer."

"How deep was Harris in Soliman's pocket when you were there?"

Arreola hesitated. "I shouldn't be doing this."

"Why? You owe loyalty to Harris? Did he come to your trial and lend support or help with your legal expenses? Have you seen him once since you got out?"

Arreola took another hit on his wine. "Harris was bag man for Lieutenant Corcoran. He ran the bureau back then. We all got paid four hundred twice a month."

"To protect Soliman's clubs?"

"No, to wash his fucking cars. What the hell do you think we did?"

"I know what *I* think. I wanted to hear you say it."

"You wired?"

"Absolutely not."

Arreola frowned, then shook his head. "Aw, what the fuck. I don't owe that prick nothing, like you said. As far as Narcotics was concerned, Soliman's clubs were untouchable. Some of us even watched the places for him off-duty, just in case some eager-beaver detective from another department came snooping around. If Harris is in charge now, then Soliman's probably paying him plenty, and no one in Narcotics is going to rat him out or not go on the pad."

"You sure of that?"

"Trust me, pal. Let's just say Harris wouldn't be above fragging another cop. Don't ask me how I know. You won't get that from me. Now where's my money?"

Boff walked over to Arreola. The stench coming off him was worse than the redhead's. He held his breath and handed him the money, then gave him his business card and stepped back before taking a breath.

Arreola looked at the card. "What's this for?"

"I've got another deal for you."

Arreola looked wary. "What?"

"If you can get yourself into rehab and stick with it, I've got a buddy who runs a good-size private investigation firm. I can get you some kind of job there. But only if you're sober."

"Why would you do that for a piece of garbage like me?"

"Because I lost your case. Even if it wasn't my fault, it still bothers me. I should've pushed Petrie harder to have you plead out. Get sober. Clean yourself up. I'll do what I can."

Arreola looked at the card and laughed. *"When all else fails, see me*. That sure fits Ricky Arreola."

Boff turned to go.

"Hey, Frank. You were always square with me. I never blamed you. I hired the wrong lawyer."

Boff walked away fast. He was in bad need of

fresh air.

Chapter 19

Cullen stopped at Franny's and bought Gholston a meatloaf sandwich with gravy and onions. When he arrived at the station, the sergeant was on the phone. He motioned for Cullen to take a seat near Homer Sayson, a chubby Filipino in his mid-thirties who had recently transferred in from Vice.

"How do you like it here?" Cullen asked Sayson.

"It stinks. And I'm putting on weight. Pretty soon I'll look like Gholston. Then my wife will divorce me."

"So why'd you transfer?"

"They made me. I have to do six months of AA before they let me back in. Being sober sucks."

Gholston got off the phone. "What'd you bring me?"

"Franny's meatloaf."

"I'm not good enough for steak anymore?"

"If I brought steak you'd say, 'How about meatloaf for a change?'"

Gholston smirked and took the bag. Then he opened a deep desk drawer and brought out the box with Cullen's sneakers and the note.

"What did Forensics find?" Cullen asked him. Sayson pushed away a folder he had been working on and just observed.

"Zippo. Like I told you would happen. The only thing they noticed was a foul smell inside the sneakers. They suggested you start using Odor-

Eaters." Gholston began to unwrap the sandwich.

"So basically," Cullen said, "you're not going to do a thing about this and the van that rammed into me."

"That's correct."

"I've also been tailed by a blue Acura."

"Plate number?"

"I haven't gotten close enough to get it."

Gholston took a healthy bite out of his sandwich, then put it down and picked up a pad lying on his desk. "Now, moving on," he said with his mouth full, "these are my notes on the Pearce case. Did you look at them?"

"Your handwriting was impossible to read."

"I read it just fine. Anyway, I remembered something in the notes, so I took another look. What I forgot to tell you was Pearce had a gambling monkey. He was into Big Willie Barboni for a shitload and hadn't paid the vig in like six weeks. Apparently Pearce sensed it was time for a new zip code. He was preparing to skip town just before he got whacked."

"So you think his death had nothing to do with Julio?"

Gholston ignored the question. "Especially when you figure two nights before Pearce took a snooze in the dumpster, he got drunk and had a loud argument with Big Willie in a public place. Called him names unflattering to his Italian heritage. I couldn't find any hard evidence to tie Barboni to Pearce's murder, but I knew it was him. Like I told you from the beginning, Pearce didn't do Babbas.

He just pissed off the wrong guy."

"I agree," Sayson said. He'd been following the conversation. "Pearce's downfall was alcohol. Addiction clouds your reason."

Gholston threw him a look. "All day long, I have to hear this twelve-step crap. Tell me something, Homer. Back in the day, if you knew someone would break your fingers if you drank a whole free bottle of eighteen-year-old Glenfiddich, would you?"

"Tough question. I'll have to think about that."

Gholston picked up his sandwich again. "Looks like you'll have to find another bogeyman, Cullen. And bring steak next time. I hate meatloaf."

Before Cullen began his early evening sparring session, McAlary took him through the garage door leading into the kitchen. Kate was there. She didn't look happy. He got the feeling this wasn't going to be a friendly Gatorade break.

"Uh oh," he muttered. "Firing squad."

"Both of us," McAlary said, "are concerned about you."

"I'll beat this guy. Training's going great."

"You know that's not what's bothering us," Kate said.

"Listen to me good, Danny." McAlary tapped his arm. "Julio got killed for a reason. I don't know what it was. Maybe it was just God's decision. If you get killed, it'll be your own fault."

Kate stepped forward. "What you're doing is eventually going to attract the wrong kind of attention," she said. "Somebody's going to hurt you. And not in the ring."

"I know you're worried, but—"

"But nothing!" McAlary said. "It's been eight months. Kate and I loved Julio, too, but in Belfast where I came from, you learned to let go of the dead. A best buddy invited me out to a pub one night. I didn't go because I was in training for an amateur tournament. The IRA blew up the pub that night. Some things are beyond understanding. You don't fight life, you live it."

"What Ryan isn't saying," Kate said in a kinder voice, "is we couldn't stand to lose you, too. You're family."

"I feel the same about you guys. This is just something I have to do."

"Same thing my friends back home said before they got killed. Are you working with this Boff character?"

"Not really."

McAlary leaned toward him. "Are you or aren't you?"

"He broke into my apartment once. The only way I could get rid of him was to talk to him."

"Boff is trouble. He'll distract you."

"It's not like I invited him...."

"Why didn't you throw him out?"

Cullen hesitated. "I wanted to hear what he had to say."

McAlary's face reddened. "Back to the gym! We'll discuss this another time."

Chapter 20

Cullen was walking to his apartment carrying a bag of groceries when Boff's car pulled alongside. His Fifties music was blasting.

"Hop in," Boff called over the music. "I'll take you to dinner."

Cullen kept walking.

Boff kept up with him. "It'll be worth your while. I promise."

Cullen stopped and turned. "How?"

"You've got to get in if you want to find out."

"Go away."

Boff continued to follow him. This went on for a full block. Cullen could hear Boff's awful Fifties music still blasting. He stopped walking and turned to Boff again, practically shouting.

"I don't want you in my life. Can't you understand that?"

Boff smiled. "Sure. Most people don't. Especially indicted felons. But the scumbags are at least smart enough to know when they need me. Which you apparently aren't."

Cullen had reached another dead end with Pearce. His investigation was stalled, and he didn't have a clue how to jumpstart it. Maybe Boff was right. Maybe he was just spinning his wheels. He opened the car door.

"This better be good."

Boff turned the sound down as Cullen got in. The floor of the Malibu was littered with greasy brown bags and Styrofoam cups. Cullen kicked them aside and put his groceries down by his feet. Before Boff could even shift gears, Cullen said, "Okay, let's hear it."

"Wait until we get to the restaurant. Then we'll talk. I want to listen to this new CD. In case you're wondering, that's 'Mr. Lee' by the Bobbettes."

"More crap."

"How'd your hitman diversion turn out?" Boff asked.

"Pearce didn't kill Julio, but I do have one piece of news for you. A van rammed my rear end on purpose and spun me out of control. I almost hit a tree."

"How do you know it wasn't an accident?"

"Trust me, it wasn't."

"What color was it?"

"Gray. It had a tinted windshield. Do you know it?"

Boff shook his head. "I will now if I see it. Did you get the plates?"

"No. Do you think they were trying to kill me?"

"Maybe. Could've just been a bad driver. Next time you spot a tail, pull over and get the license plate when it passes by."

"What if they stop alongside and shoot at me?"

"Duck."

Boff took him to Aldo's Steakhouse, a pricey but informal place on Paradise Road. After they were seated at a table, Boff opened his menu, but Cullen left his lying unopened.

"I'm here," he said. "Now what's so

important?"

"What are you going to eat?" Boff asked him.

"Nothing until you tell me what's going on."

"The shrimp cocktail is excellent. I like the garden salad and any of the steaks. They even have buffalo sirloin, if you're the adventurous type."

"Stop playing games."

A waiter came over. "Hi, I'm Lawrence," he said. "Would you care for some wine or a cocktail?"

"Do you have Almaden Chablis in the box?" Boff asked.

The waiter made a face. "We don't stock the cheaper brands," he said in a supercilious tone, "but we have a fine selection of California chards. If you'd like to see the wine list…."

"That's okay. Just a cola with lime." Boff looked down at the menu again. "I'm going to have the jumbo shrimp cocktail, garden salad with ranch dressing, and a rib-eye. Medium well."

The waiter turned to Cullen. "And you sir?"

"If you have fat-free dressing, I'll take the garden salad and a T-bone, medium rare. Diet Coke."

The waiter picked up the menus and left.

"Now tell me," Cullen said.

"When you have a fight coming up, do you study tape of your opponent?"

"What does that have to do with anything?"

"It has everything to do with why you're here. Answer me."

"Yes, of course I watch tape."

"Why?"

"I want to know what I'm facing before I have to deal with it. I look for strengths and weaknesses."

"That's why you're here."

The waiter returned with their sodas, then left again without a word.

Cullen picked up his glass, started to take a drink, but instead put it down and glared at Boff. "Can't you ever tell me something straight without all the riddles and detours?"

"When you get paid by the hour, the shortest distance between two points is a zigzag." Boff took a pull on his Coke.

"I'm walking if you don't tell me!"

"You'd miss something important if you do. Not to mention a good meal."

As Cullen started to get up, Boff leaned back.

"Before you cut and run," he said, "ask yourself this. Does Frank Boff strike you as the type to waste good money on a fancy dinner when he could eat at home or McDonald's?"

Cullen sat down.

"My two favorite adages," said Boff, are 'appearances can be deceiving' and 'don't judge a book by its cover.'" He leaned forward again. "For example, if you met me and didn't know anything about me, what would you think by reading my face?"

"That you're an incredible pain in the ass who can't take no for an answer."

"That's only after you know me. Most people on first look would have a hard time pinning me down. The reason is, I've spent years trying to look as inconspicuous as possible because I'm very tall and easier to spot on a tail or surveillance. One glance at my face, people decide I'm not the threatening type." He smiled his blandest smile. "I've spent hours in the mirror perfecting this bland look."

The waiter bought Boff's shrimp cocktail. Boff speared one, dunked it in cocktail sauce and stuffed it down. "Want one?"

Cullen looked away.

Boff ate another one. "We once had a case in the DEA," he paused to swallow, "where we knew a great deal of Ecstasy was moving through London to New York. But we couldn't spot the carriers. I was at Heathrow one day looking for anyone suspicious, when I remembered basic DEA training. The best carriers don't look the part. Just at that moment, who should walk by but six young Hassidic Jews carrying identical leather suitcases. If it weren't for the suitcases, I never would've caught them. I mean that luggage cost good money, yet they were all dressed in hand-me downs and worn-out clothes."

Cullen shook his head. "I'm not listening."

Boff speared another shrimp. He looked like he enjoyed spearing shrimp. "Now take your Saint Julio. How long did you know him? I believe it was three years, during which time I'm sure you were very close and spent a lot of time together. Yet apparently there were things about him you didn't know."

Cullen still hadn't picked up his glass. "How

much longer do I have to endure this crap before you tell me why I needed to come here?"

"I estimate that around the time we get our dessert all will be revealed."

Boff kept yapping through dinner. When they finished their main course and ordered dessert, he asked for a calorie-loaded peanut butter and chocolate mini-pie. Cullen took a fruit salad. They were halfway through dessert when a man in a suit walked over to them.

"My friend asked if you gentlemen would join us for a drink." He pointed to a table where four other men in suits were seated.

"Thanks," Cullen said, "but we're getting ready to leave."

"We'd love to," Boff said.

"Good. We look forward to talking." The man went back across the restaurant.

"Why did you say that?" Cullen asked. "I'm not going to their table. I'm leaving now. I'm sick of your bullshit." He started to get up, but Boff clamped a strong hand on his arm.

"Don't stare directly at them," he said, lowering his voice just a little bit, "but turn your head a bit and look at the guy in the charcoal suit wearing sunglasses."

Cullen glanced over.

"Danny Cullen, meet Yitzhak Soliman."

After Boff had paid the bill, they walked over to Soliman's table, where a waiter slid another table over for them. Soliman took off his sunglasses and stared hard at Boff. Boff returned the look. Then the Israeli reached across the table and shook Cullen's hand.

"I'm Yitzhak Soliman."

The waiter brought over a bottle of Remy XO and snifters, set them down, and left without a word.

Soliman ignored the cognac and focused on Cullen. "I understand you're a fine fighter."

"I hold my own," Cullen said.

"You're modest. No one has beaten you. Your father was a great champion, and now you're to be showcased on TV."

"Are you a big fan of boxing, Mr. Soliman?" Boff asked.

Soliman gave him another stony look. "Of course," he said to Cullen, "fighting is second nature to Israelis. Did you know in my country, when a baby is born they wait for a rocket from Palestine to explode to make it cry? If none come in ten seconds, then they slap the bottom."

"When I was born," Boff said, "my father asked the doctor if he'd whack me in the back of my head. Dad thought it'd be a good lesson to prepare me for life."

This time Soliman was marginally interested. "Did the doctor do it?"

"He refused. My father was going to do it himself, but two male nurses escorted him out of the room."

"Good story," Soliman said. "I suspect you made it up. Perhaps one day I'll be able to teach you a lesson that'll stick."

"You're welcome to try."

They locked eyes again, and Soliman turned back to Cullen.

"Anyway," he said, "my point is Israelis grow up with conflict. Boxing reminds me of home. I especially enjoy the relentless attackers like you."

"Then you must've loved Julio Babbas," Cullen said.

If he was expecting to rattle Soliman, he was wrong. His expression never changed. "Yes. A remarkable fighter. Such a tragic ending to a brilliant career."

Cullen stared at the man who had probably killed Julio. Everything from the suave voice to the tailored suit and all-season tan said class. Only the dark fierce eyes hinted at the kind of lowlife he really was.

Soliman turned back to Boff. "And you, Mr. Boff, you're not a fighter. What do you do?"

"I sell vacuum cleaners."

"Do you? I think not. If I had to guess, I'd say you're someone very skilled at sticking his nose into other people's business."

"Nice guess. Of course it doesn't hurt that you already know who I am."

"Yes. You're a private investigator specializing in defending criminals—and quite good at it, I hear. Your job apparently has earned you powerful friends."

"Speaking of that," Boff said, "I'm curious how the guy with the funny colored eyes is doing?"

Soliman gave him another hard look. “He doesn’t work for me anymore.” With that, he signaled to one of his men to pour cognac around the table. Cullen put his hand over his glass.

“I’m looking forward to your fight,” Soliman told him. “I have front row seats. If you win, as I expect, I’d like to have dinner with you sometime.”

“Why?”

“There are things we might discuss.”

“Like what?”

Soliman raised his glass. “To Danny Cullen’s victory!”

The Israelis stayed ten more minutes, Soliman deftly dodging every question that might reveal something about him. Then he got up and glared at Boff again before leaving with his men.

Cullen watched them cross the room as if they owned it. “How did you know he’d be here?” he asked Boff.

“It doesn’t matter how. What’s important is now that you’ve come face-to-face with your opponent, what do you think of him?”

“Not an easy man to corner. The way he looked at you was downright scary.”

“That’s what you’re up against. I wanted you to know.”

Chapter 21

Eight days before his fight at the Paris Hotel & Casino, Cullen put all things Julio on hold. McAlary had drummed into him how important this fight was to his career, but now it had added significance: it could open a door to Soliman.

Boff called several times wanting to meet, but despite his curiosity, Cullen stayed away. He couldn't afford distractions now. There is no lonelier place in sports than being confined to a roped-in space with another man who wants to hurt you. You can't afford an off-night, like in basketball, baseball, or football because there are no teammates to protect you. Even though he was unbeaten, Cullen knew his opponents so far had been carefully chosen by Kate and McAlary to gradually move him up the ladder. Jesse Tucker was a significant step up.

When he left the gym three days before the fight, he saw Boff sitting in the Malibu. There was no music playing.

"Do you know a Lt. Harris in Narcotics?" Boff asked him.

"Yes. Why?"

"You're going to find this interesting."

"No. I can't do this until after the fight."

"Suit yourself." Boff put the car in gear.

"Wait!" Cullen got into the Malibu. "I can only spare ten minutes," he said. "Then I have to go."

"No problem. This won't take long." Boff let

the car idle. "What do you use as your Internet search engine?"

"What does that have to do with Harris?"

"Yahoo?"

"Google."

"I use the Dark Side. I find it the fastest way to get the kind of information I want. What I discovered surfing there is that Soliman has never been arrested, nor have any of the dance or strip clubs he uses to peddle his Ecstasy in been raided or shut down. That's highly unusual unless you have very good protection. The one name I kept hearing was Lt. Vince Harris."

"He's on Soliman's payroll?"

"I was given very reliable information that he is. So I went to a friend who's an information broker and a whiz on the computer. He hacked into the police department's computer system, got Harris' Social Security number, and did a financial workup on him." Boff took a folder off the dashboard and handed it to Cullen. "As even an untrained eye like yours can see, the lieutenant lives a life style beyond the means of a Las Vegas cop."

Cullen leafed through the file. Harris had two-bedroom condos in Las Vegas and Lake Tahoe, a new BMW, and a good size stock portfolio. He came to the financials. "Here's a deposit of twenty thousand to an off-shore account in Barbados three weeks before Julio was killed," he said. "It's much bigger than all his other deposits. Maybe Harris was paid to kill Julio. He's the same size and build as the guy in the ski mask."

Boff shook his head. "I wouldn't jump to that conclusion based on the money. It's possible his long-lost great aunt died and left him cash. Or he could've gotten lucky and hit the number or scored at blackjack."

"But if it looks like a duck and quacks like a duck—"

"It could still be a red herring. Let me look into this more while you prepare for your coming-out party on Showtime. By the way, I forgot to ask what you thought of Señor Arango."

Cullen blinked. "How do you know I met him?"

"I planted a bug of my own in your living room."

He remembered what Gholston had said about not trusting Boff. "You say appearances can be deceiving. How do I know your client really hired you to find Julio's killer? Maybe you were paid to steer me in the wrong direction."

"Son, you didn't need my help for that. You were doing a fine job on your own. I guess you're just going to have to trust me here."

Cullen looked out the window and mulled that over.

"I understand how you feel," Boff said. "In your place, Frank Boff would be the last person I'd want to trust. Unless I was facing jail time. So why don't you put faith in your instincts? What do they tell you?"

Cullen turned back to Boff. "That you're on the level. Well…as level as a person like you could be."

"There you go!"

"But I'm keeping my eyes open. The jury is still out on you."

"Good. I almost never lose when a case goes to jury."

Cullen closed the folder and put it on the dashboard.

"One more thing," Boff said. "Tell me again why you believe Soliman had Julio killed?"

"Because he was helping Arango cut into his business."

"I believe there's something more involved here," Boff said. "I've helped defend countless murderers. You'd be amazed at some of the crazy reasons people have to kill other people. But it's my experience that mobsters don't kill as impulsively as you see in the movies and on TV. And one thing they definitely try to steer clear of is whacking high-profile people, especially those as popular as Julio. Cops and prosecutors live for celebrity cases. The heat would be tremendous. So if Soliman did have Julio killed, he must've felt your friend was a much more serious threat than you think."

"What threat would that be?"

"I have a few theories. Let me work on them. I'll get back to you."

"After the fight."

"You got it."

When Cullen got home he called Detective Epps. "This is Danny," he said. "You get the tickets I sent you?"

Yes. Ringside. Thanks buddy.

"I need another favor."

In exchange I get?

"Ringside for my fight after this."

Okay.

"Is there any way you could find out what kind of gun Lt. Harris uses?"

Why do you want to know?

"I'd rather not say."

You're not going to do anything illegal with the information, are you?

"No."

Cullen could almost hear the cop making a decision. *Against my better judgment, I'll find out.*

Chapter 22

The fight card was billed as *Heirs to the Throne*. Two other young boxers whose fathers had been famous champions fought before Cullen got the call to come to the ring. Kate helped him slip into his black silk robe with gold trim and kissed him for luck, then they followed McAlary and cut man, Al Davies, out of the locker room. Cullen could feel the tension rising in him as they walked down a concrete corridor toward the arena. Entering it, he was so psyched up his senses were heightened and the intense white lights seemed impossibly bright. This was his first time on TV. He was eager to show everybody how good he was.

Approaching the ring, he saw Soliman in a front row seat. When the Israeli stood up and clapped, Cullen looked away to the opposite side of the ring. Boff was sitting there. They were, he couldn't help thinking, like bookends to his life right now. Once in the ring, he threw some combos and moved around to test how tight the canvas was and bounced off the ropes with his back a couple times to see how much give they had.

Now cheering came from the back of the arena as Tucker started heading for the ring. He was supposed to be a tough kid out of Detroit who'd cut his teeth at the famed Kronk Gym, home of many champions. Cullen didn't care where the hell the guy was from. He was sending him back home with a beat down.

Tucker entered the ring and his trainer took off his robe. He was cut with muscle and had a broad upper body like a light heavyweight. He tried to stare Cullen down, but in response, Cullen did something his father had liked to do. He circled the ropes, throwing combos as he went. Coming to his opponent, he stared into his eyes and smiled. It was meant to intimidate, but the truth was neither man would be rattled until the first time he got rocked by a punch.

Back in his corner, Cullen glanced again at Soliman, who nodded and gave him a thumbs up. He suddenly found himself wishing it was Soliman instead of Tucker in the ring with him. He'd love to punch that smug look off his face. He shut out the thought as the ring announcer took the mike.

"Ladies and gentlemen, our main event of the evening…."

Standing in his corner, he heard McAlary's voice as if speaking from far away.

"Stay balanced, keep your left up, get under his jab, and work inside."

Then the referee called them to the center of the ring and gave instructions. The two fighters touched gloves and went back to stand by their corners. When the bell rang, Cullen smacked his gloves together and moved in fast. From studying tape, he knew that Tucker liked to use his jab to keep the fight at a distance. He wasn't a good inside fighter. Cullen would've gladly battled it out in a phone booth.

Tucker's first two jabs lacked zip, so Cullen

slipped the next one and got close enough to throw two short punches to the ribs and a hard uppercut. Tucker immediately clinched, as Cullen knew he would every time he got inside. The ref separated them right away. That meant Tucker's clutch and grab tactics wouldn't be tolerated.

Next, Tucker snapped his jab again to try and keep him away, but Cullen changed angles and threw two quick right hands that landed hard. In the process, he dropped his left, and his feet were off balance when Tucker exploded with a right hook over his low left hand and caught Cullen flush on the chin. Down he went. He pounded his gloves in anger on the canvas and popped right back up.

The blow hadn't hurt him. If his feet had been set, he probably wouldn't have gone down, but Tucker didn't know this. He could see in Tucker's eyes that he was revved up by the knockdown. Tucker threw caution to the wind, apparently thinking he could take Cullen out fast, as he had most of his other opponents. As the Detroit fighter let loose with a flurry of punches, Cullen played along, backpedaling with gloves high by his head, as if trying to buy time to recover from the knockdown.

And Tucker fell right into the trap. He threw a wide, looping right that left his whole right side exposed, just like Raymond had done. Cullen fired a left hook at Tucker's liver. The shot just missed it, but the thudding blow to the ribs stung. Tucker clinched again. Through the remainder of the round, Cullen was content to work Tucker's body as often as he could, breaking him down.

Cullen's adrenaline was pumping when he went back to his corner.

"You okay, son?" McAlary said.

"He's shit! He ain't shit!"

"Maybe so, but show me good defense. Keep working the body. And be patient."

"First time I ever went down. Damn."

"New round. Move on."

Cullen nodded and sprang off the stool at the bell. Tucker had apparently realized Cullen was far from hurt and that he was dangerous, because he fought now with a high-glove defense, elbows tight to his ribs to protect them. But Tucker's shell defense was no match for Cullen's power. His punches exploded through Tucker's gloves and landed hard. Cullen kept pressing forward and succeeded in trapping Tucker on the ropes, where he unleashed a tremendous volley of punches, like in the popcorn drill. Tucker covered up until he was able to slip off the ropes. Then he tried to backpedal, but Cullen sprang right after him and nailed him with a lunging right to the jaw. As Tucker's knees started to buckle, Cullen went for broke, putting thunder in a right-left-right combo to the head. Suddenly Tucker wasn't standing in front of him. The referee pushed Cullen away, told him to go to a neutral corner, and began the count over the fallen fighter. Tucker managed to get to one knee, eyes glazed, struggling for breath.

"Get up!" Cullen called. "I got more for you!"

At seven Tucker tried to stand, but collapsed on

his ass. He was through. As the ref raised Cullen's hand in victory, McAlary and Kate leaped into the ring and hugged him.

"You did good, Danny boy!" McAlary said.

Flush with victory and hyped up, Cullen said, "I went down and got right back up! Just like you, Ryan!"

"I've never been down in my life, lad."

"Right. Forgot."

As McAlary lifted him up, Cullen raised both arms overhead, pumping them in triumph. The Showtime cameras were drinking it in. Dan Cullen's son could fight!

There were a bunch of fans waiting for Cullen when he walked out the side entrance with the McAlarys. He saw Boff standing quietly behind the crowd. If his father hadn't been a great champion, they wouldn't have been there, but Cullen patiently signed autographs.

When the last fan had left, Boff came over. "Not bad, Danny."

Kate stepped toward him. "I'm Kate, Danny's manager. You are?"

"Frank Boff."

McAlary stepped forward. "He's the snoop who's working with Danny on Julio's case and distracting my fighter."

"He looked pretty focused tonight," Boff replied.

They headed toward the sidewalk. A black limo with tinted windows was waiting at the curb. The back window came down. It was Soliman. The Israeli silently clapped his hands, then his driver took off.

McAlary watched the big car go down the street. "Do you know that man, Danny?" he asked.

Boff answered. "He was a big fan of Julio's."

"Is that so, Mr. Boff?"

"And he has other interests besides boxing."

"You mean drugs?"

Cullen looked surprised.

"Not much happens in this town I don't know about, Danny," McAlary said. "Did he have something to do with Julio's murder?"

"I think so," Cullen said.

"Then you believe Julio was involved with drugs?"

"Not using or dealing," Cullen said, then he told him about Julio's connection to Arango and how he'd been helping him meet club owners.

"Mr. Boff, is what Danny says true?"

"It appears so."

He turned back to Cullen. "And now it looks like Soliman is interested in recruiting you."

"Yes."

"Knowing you, you'll take up with him, like the fabled Trojan Horse of Ireland."

"Greece," Boff said.

"Whatever. Let me tell you something, Danny. I know a thing or two about playing with dynamite. I had friends lose arms or their eyesight, sometimes their life fixing a bomb. Do you get my drift?"

"Yes."

"But of course you'll do as you want."

"We're alike in that regard."

"There you're wrong," the trainer said. "Outside the ring, even I knew when to back off. It's why I'm here today training an undisciplined future champion, instead of pushing up daisies in a Shankill graveyard."

When Cullen entered his apartment later that night, he smelled the faint hint of a fart. He followed the odor trail to his office. A long white envelope was sticking out from between two books on his desk. A note inside read:

Julio would've been proud. Soliman has an interest in you. I've got your back. Arango.

Chapter 23

After taking a day off to chill out, Cullen returned to the gym and went through a light workout. Showtime had given him another date two months from now with Clifton Danielson, a former world champion on the downside. Opponents like him were good tests for young fighters.

Although Cullen was eager to get the ball rolling with Soliman, he didn't want the Israeli to think he was too eager. Instead, he decided to try and rattle Lt. Harris to see what he'd do. He called Boff and told him.

Even for you, said Boff, *that's a stupid idea. Stay away from Harris. He's dangerous.*

"What did you say, Boff? I can't hear you. You're breaking up. What? What?"

Cullen hung up. Let him get a taste of his own medicine.

***

Cullen spent his time outside the gym asking around about Harris in a very public way. He made a point of saying he suspected the lieutenant was on Soliman's payroll. All his sources agreed on one thing: Harris was not someone to mess with. Naturally, he had every intention of doing just that. He was determined to get a reaction and wasn't disappointed.

He was approaching his car in the rear lot of

Franny's after lunch, when a couple of well-built guys in loose-fitting suits came out from behind an eighteen-wheeler and blocked his path.

"You're in our way," the bigger one said.

"Whatever." Cullen tried to step around them.

The guy grabbed his arm. "You got an attitude."

"Screw you!" Cullen wrenched his arm free.

The thug pulled a pair of brass knuckles out of his pocket and slipped them on. "Let's see if we can get rid of that attitude."

He threw a big round-house right, but Cullen ducked under it easily and fired a jaw-rattling uppercut, temporarily immobilizing him. The other guy came forward with his right hand cocked and loaded with brass, but Cullen lunged at him before he could throw and punched him hard in his flabby stomach. The wind sailed out of the guy. Down he went on one knee, trying to catch his breath.

The first one came back for more. Not wanting to risk hurting his hands, Cullen threw a hard shot to the groin. When the guy grabbed his crotch and dropped to both knees, Cullen kicked him under the chin. The guy fell backwards, out cold. Seeing his partner down, the other one said, "To hell with this!" and hustled away.

Cullen pulled a wallet out of the fallen guy's pants and opened it, looking for ID. He got a bonus—a detective's gold shield. He pocketed the badge and headed for his car.

He couldn't resist telling Boff what he'd done, so he called and arranged to meet him that night at a

Dunkin' Donuts. Boff was already at a table when Cullen walked in. He pulled the gold shield out of his pocket.

"Look what I got."

"I'm guessing the badge belongs to somebody in Narcotics," Boff said.

"Yup. Guy named Fuller."

"Fuller and a couple other cops were indicted two years ago for allegedly taking kickbacks in Vice. He tried to hire me, but I was deep into another case, so I recommended one of the few private investigators I know who can tie his shoes without help. My buddy got the charges dismissed. Fuller landed on his feet. I'm sure Harris lobbied hard to get him transferred to Narcotics, where he could be of use."

"Why would Harris send two guys to rough me up if he didn't have something to do with Julio's murder?" Cullen asked as he sat down.

"Maybe he didn't. You might've just run into two cops in a foul mood looking for an outlet."

"Then how do you account for this? I found out from a detective I know that Harris uses a Smith & Wesson revolver. At the diner, you said the killer used a revolver."

"A lot of people do. Don't jump to any conclusion yet."

"I'm not," Cullen replied, "but it's hard to ignore the fact that Harris made a deposit of twenty thousand to his off-shore account three weeks before Julio was killed. And he also has the same build as the masked guy I saw and he uses a revolver."

Boff picked up his donut and gestured with it. "All good circumstantial evidence. I'm almost inclined to agree with you. Just not yet."

"Well, either way, I guess I showed you I'm not as clueless as you think."

"I'll wait to see if you live through the month before saying something like that."

"What do you mean?"

"If you're going to shake the tree of dangerous people—in this case, a bent cop with mob connections—then you'd better be prepared to dodge whatever falls out of it."

"I got rid of those two guys, didn't I?"

"Yes. But you're not streetwise enough to sense where the next shot is coming from, and, trust me, this is only the beginning. You upped the ante. That may not have been the smartest thing to do right now, considering what's going on between Soliman and Arango. You've just inserted yourself into the middle of a gang war."

"Don't worry about me. I can handle it."

Boff shook his head. "Now would be a great time for you to start being paranoid," he said. "Wherever you go, make a point of looking over your shoulder every so often. Don't go into your apartment if there's the slightest hint that rinky-dink lock you still haven't replaced has been tampered with. I also suggest that you vary your jogging route and don't go to the gym the same way every day. I'd tell you to buy a gun, but I know from experience that people like you only wind up shooting themselves. Finally, as painful as it may be, I want you to call me anytime you see anything out of the ordinary."

"You're asking me to play defense," Cullen said. "Isn't the best defense a good offense?"

"Maybe in football, yeah," Boff said. "But in real life, no offense I know will stop a bullet."

"Bottom line, the badge gives me a card to play."

"And how will you do that? Just walk up to Harris and deal it?"

"Sounds good to me."

Boff frowned. "If you were my client, this would be the point where I'd ask you to pay me two weeks in advance in case you got killed."

Cullen stood up. "Why are you always so pessimistic?"

"The last time I felt optimistic about life was when I was a little kid watching reruns of *The Andy Griffith Show*, the one where he's sheriff of Mayberry and everything turns out good in the end. I also loved *Father Knows Best* because it was comforting to know there was someone other than God who was always right, and I didn't have to go through the trouble of worshiping him."

As Cullen seemed to be thinking this over, Boff got up. "If you think a vehicle is tailing you," he said, "especially that gray van, what do you do?"

"Lose them."

"Brilliant. How?"

"Make a lot of turns?"

Boff shook his head. "Use the time-tested Boff

Method. Drive downtown. Some of the bigger parking garages have an entrance on one street, the exit on another. Go in one way, speed out the other."

"What if that doesn't work?"

"I've had nearly a one hundred per cent success rate with it." He headed for the door and then stopped and turned. "Do you have life insurance?"

"No. I'm only twenty-five."

"Get some."

Chapter 24

Cullen had trouble sleeping that night, so he finally went into the living room and put on a DVD of *Goodfellas*. A half hour into it, he found the violence was making him uncomfortable. If his life was in danger in real life, he wasn't in the mood to watch Pesci and De Niro stomp some guy to death in a movie. He popped the DVD and put in *Jerry Maguire*. The Tom Cruise character reminded him of himself: impetuous, fiercely determined, and reckless.

Around three in the morning, when his eyes were finally starting to close, he heard a tremendous explosion. It blew out his windows facing the street and sent glass flying all over his living room. He crawled under the coffee table in case there were more blasts and stayed there until he heard sirens coming. Within minutes, he saw flashing blue and red lights swirling through his broken windows. He grabbed a pair of sweat pants and sneakers from the couch, pulled them on, and crunched over broken glass to a window. Looking down, he saw firemen training their hoses on what was left of a flaming car. It was his.

He woke Boff up. Boff said to stay in his apartment until he got there, but Cullen went outside anyway. Other cars and apartment windows had suffered damage, and there was glass all over the street and sidewalk. A couple uniformed cops were standing outside the yellow tape perimeter. He headed toward them. One held his hand up.

"You have to keep back."

"That was my car."

The cops exchanged looks. One called to a burly man in plain clothes inside the perimeter.

"Detective Thornton!"

The detective turned around. "What?"

"This guy says the car belonged to him."

Thornton and another detective ducked under the tape and walked over. "Are you Danny Cullen?" Thornton said.

"Yes. How'd you know?"

"I ran the plates.

A third guy in plain clothes came up to Thornton with something in a tape-seal bag. "C-4," he said. "This was no accident."

Thornton looked at Cullen. "You have any idea who might've done this?"

"Not a clue. I'm a professional boxer. I mind my own business."

"Let me see some ID."

"Why? You ran my plates."

"I want to make sure you're who you say you are. For all I know, you set the bomb and came back to look at your handiwork."

That made sense. Cullen said, "I left my wallet upstairs. I can get it if you want."

"How about you and I go up to your place and you show it to me?"

"I'd rather you didn't come into my apartment."

"You got something to hide?" Thornton asked.

"No. I just don't see the need."

"I want to question you," the detective said.

"You can do that right here."

"I could get a search warrant. Then it'd be a lot more unpleasant for you."

Cullen was standing his ground. "So do it. You're not coming into my apartment without one. Any more questions, detective?"

"Not at this time."

"Then I'll be going."

Thornton put a restraining hand on his shoulder. "If you think of anything or find yourself in some kind of trouble, call me." He took a business card out of his breast pocket and handed it to Cullen, who headed for his apartment.

Twenty minutes later, he was looking out his window when Boff pulled up and parked. The fire had been put out, but there were still plenty of cops around. As Boff headed for the stairs to Cullen's building, Thornton slipped under the tape and hustled over.

"Sir!"

Boff turned around.

Thornton showed his badge. "Do you live here?" he asked Boff.

"No. My friend called me. His car was the one that blew up."

"You got ID?"

Boff opened his wallet to show his driver's license. His investigator's badge was visible on the other flap.

Thornton nodded. "You're a P.I., huh? Are you

working for him?"

"No. We're just friends."

"Must be real good friends to come out this time of the night. Do you have a business card I could keep?"

"Sure." He handed one to Thornton. "If any cops you know get in trouble," he said, "I'd be grateful if you have them call me. I can always use the business. Who knows, maybe one day even a brilliant detective like you might screw up and need my services."

Thornton sneered at him. "Did this kid have any enemies, the kind that would've done this?"

"I can't think of any. He's a very popular young boxer. Everybody likes him."

"Has somebody been harassing him?"

"Only me. I'm told I can be very irritating."

"Look," said Thornton, "I know you're feeding me a line of bullshit. I'm betting he hired you. Tell me what for."

"If he had hired me—which he didn't—I couldn't tell you anything. It's privileged information. I'm sure a smart officer like you knows that."

"I could make your life miserable and pull you in for questioning."

Boff smiled. "Go right ahead, Detective. I have a very good lawyer whom you really don't want to tangle with. He doesn't particularly like cops. He wouldn't hesitate to file a beef against you."

This made Thornton smirk. "I gather you don't like cops, either."

"On the contrary," Boff said, "I *love* cops. Every night, I go to bed and thank God I have police officers like you protecting me." He turned to leave, but stopped within a few steps as Thornton spoke again.

"Your name sounds familiar to me. Did you ever work for the D.A.'s office?"

"Not in this lifetime." Boff went up the stairs into the apartment.

"I was watching," Cullen said as a greeting.

"You're lucky you didn't get cut with all this glass," Boff said, looking around.

"What did detective Thornton say to you?"

"That he's heard of me and admires my work."

"I'll bet."

"He tried to harass me, so I did what I do best and busted his balls. If I have to be called out of bed at this time of night, I should at least have a little fun, right? Let's go into the kitchen and get some coffee."

Cullen took out a filter and put it in his Mr. Coffee. "I guess this is what you were worried about at Dunkin' Donuts," he said.

Boff shook his head. "No. This was meant only as a warning. One of us getting killed is what concerns me."

"You think Soliman did this?"

"Don't discount Arango."

Cullen poured tap water into the pot and then transferred it to the coffee maker. "If Arango was Julio's friend, why would he try to warn me off?"

"As much as I'm inclined to agree with you that

Soliman is behind this, there's still a possibility it's Arango."

Cullen flipped the switch on the Mr. Coffee. "I don't see it."

"That's what bothers me," Boff explained. "Soliman makes too much sense. Things in my world are rarely exactly as they seem. I can't think of a reason why Arango would've killed Julio, but he's supposed to have murdered an awful lot of people in Colombia. Even his own friends and gang members. A man like that is capable of anything. That's all I'm saying."

The coffee started brewing. Cullen sat down at the table with Boff. "I'm going to have to rent a car."

"Bring it home," Boff told him, "but don't drive it to the gym or anywhere else."

"Why not?"

"I need to do something to ensure that if your car or mine blows up, neither of us is in it."

"How're you going to do that?"

Boff got up, stuck a mug under the drip from the coffee maker, then slid the pot back in. "Get us some protection," he said, not turning around.

"What kind?"

"I'd rather not say right now."

Boff came back to the table, leaned close to Cullen, and whispered to him about the bugs. Then he said in a normal voice, "When you get the rental home, leave it here and take a cab to the gym. I'll come by McAlary's after your morning workout with a present."

Cullen stood up. “I’m not backing off, you know. This only makes me more determined to find Julio’s killer. I don’t scare easily.”

“You should be scared. I am. I have a wife and two kids to take care of. Getting killed would suck.”

“Look, why don’t you drop the case? I don’t have family, except for Ryan and Kate. You’ve got much more to lose.”

Boff put his mug down and stared at him. “Let me tell you something about me. I may be scared, but I’m also angry. Nobody pushes me around, not now, not ever. I intend to find whoever is responsible and punishing them.”

“You mean bring them to justice.”

“I said punish.”

Chapter 25

Later that morning, Cullen woke up in his bed and stared at the ceiling. He felt like more than his windows had been shattered. His sense of invincibility had taken a blow. He had always known there was an element of danger in his investigation, but now it had finally sunk into his thick head that he had to take his personal safety a little more seriously.

There was a knock on his front door. He slipped on his sneakers and crunched over the glass through the living room. Normally he would have just opened it without second thought. This morning, he decided it was time to be cautious.

"Who is it?"

"Juan Manuel."

It was the building superintendent. He let him in.

"The apartment underneath you looks the same way," the super said. "I'm glad you weren't hurt."

"By the way, it was my car that blew up."

"*Dios mio!* It's good you weren't in it."

"Is it okay if I replace my door lock?"

"Sure. A lot of tenants have done that. When they put up this building, they cut some corners, including installing cheapo locks."

The super recommended a locksmith, told Cullen he'd be back later to replace the glass, and left. First Cullen phoned the maid who cleaned his apartment twice a month and asked if she could come over right away. Then he looked up the locksmith's number and, following Boff's advice, asked to have a double cylinder deadbolt with keyholes on both sides installed. The locksmith said he was swamped today and tomorrow, but promised he'd be out the following day, first thing in the morning. A little later, Cullen walked to a nearby hardware store and bought a BEWARE OF DOG sign. It was probably a dumb thing to do, but until the new lock was put in, he felt slightly better having it on the door.

His last call that morning was the one he'd dreaded making.

"I'm going to be late for my workout."

"Why?" McAlary asked.

"I have to rent a car."

"What's wrong with yours?"

"Can I tell you later?"

"No."

He debated whether to lie, but McAlary would probably find out anyway. "It blew up."

"How'd it blow up?"

"Somebody planted a bomb under it."

"Get your ass over here as quickly as possible."

After renting a Corolla from Hertz, Cullen left it parked near his building and, again as instructed, took a cab to the gym. He was an hour late. McAlary was watching Trillo spar in the ring with a fighter from another gym. He pointed to a bench.

"Sit. How do you know it was a bomb?" he asked. "Maybe it caught on fire and the gas tank exploded."

Cullen shook his head. "The police said it was a bomb. They found C-4, which is used—"

"I know damn well what it's used for. Someone was trying to kill you."

"Well, not exactly. Boff said it was just a warning for me to stop looking for Julio's killer."

"Which you're going to do right now!"

Cullen looked away.

"Did you hear me?" McAlary asked.

When Cullen said nothing, McAlary walked over to the speed bag and smashed it so hard it came off its mooring and sailed across the gym. Trillo stopped sparring and stared.

"Get back to work!" McAlary walked over to the bench where Cullen was sitting. "If you don't drop this thing," he said in a measured tone, "I won't train you."

"Don't say that."

"Give me one reason why I shouldn't."

"When you were an amateur in Belfast and walked to the gym, were you ever in danger? Did bombs go off near you?"

"It's not the same thing."

"Why?"

"I didn't choose the Troubles, they chose me."

"And Julio chose me. He deserves more than just a gravestone with World Champion carved into it. I'm going to find out who murdered him."

"Even if it gets you killed."

"Yes."

McAlary shook his head. "Of all the talented young fighters I could've gotten, I wind up with one who thinks he's a battling Sherlock Holmes."

"Come on, Ryan. You want justice for Julio as much as I do."

"Not if it means losing you."

"If I have to go to another trainer, it won't change anything. I'll still look for Julio's killer."

"There isn't a trainer around who'd take you on, knowing the baggage you bring."

Cullen sensed McAlary was finally cooling down, so he said nothing. McAlary walked to the wall filled with pictures of Julio. "Julio," he said to one of them, "what do you think of all this?"

Cullen came over and pointed to a photo of a bloodied Julio having his arm raised in victory. A fighter lay flat on the canvas behind him. "Remember this one, Ryan? Julio got knocked down twice in round four and two more times in five."

"And he got up each time and eventually knocked the guy out."

"Yeah. Because Julio wasn't a quitter, and neither am I. Come on, Ryan. If Julio was alive, and I was the one who'd been killed, do you think he'd give up looking just because his life had been threatened?"

McAlary gave him a wry look. "You're a clever one, trying to manipulate me into keeping you on."

"I'm doing it because you're my friend and my trainer," Cullen said. "And I really need you. I don't want anybody else in my corner when I win my championship."

Without a word, McAlary retrieved the speed

bag, found a screw driver and began anchoring it back on the wood. “I’ll train you,” he said a couple minutes later, “but if you get yourself killed, don’t expect me to come to your damn funeral.”

“Fair deal.”

“Go wrap your hands. You’re going to spar with me.”

That was a surprise. McAlary rarely did that unless a partner failed to show.

“I am? Why?”

“I’ve got to take my anger out on somebody. You’re it. And if you drop that left hand, I’m going to hit you like you’ve never been hit before. Go change.”

Chapter 26

Boff drove to a Spy Shops franchise on West Charleston Boulevard operated by a cousin of Jenny's. Davie Akers was a former member of the New York and Las Vegas bomb squads who had been forced to retire after his partner was blown to bits in an explosion that cost Akers his right arm and right eye. Boff had called ahead to tell him what he was looking for. As he entered the store, his body triggered red laser beams. He threw his arms up in mock surrender, and Akers, who was standing behind one of his showcases cleaning the glass, turned the device off.

He looked up at Boff. "My latest toy. Scares off jittery burglars."

Akers was around fifty and looked like he stayed fit despite his disabilities. He wore a black eye patch with the word "BOOM!" imprinted on it.

"What happens if the burglar isn't the jittery type?" Boff asked.

"I'm working on equipping it with a high-pitched sound that is very painful to the ears." He reached over the case to shake hands with his left hand. "How's Jenny?" he asked.

"Lovely as always."

"When's she going to invite me and Lily over again for her braised pork roast? It was terrific."

"I'll mention it to her when I get home."

Akers took something out of the showcase that looked like an elongated cell phone. "This you'd like, Frank. It's a mobile phone voice-changer."

"Why would I want to disguise my voice? I'm not in the kidnapping or extortion business."

"Use it to scare Jenny or a friend. Here, try it."

Akers thrust it at him, but he didn't take it. "Not interested," he said. "Do you have what I'm looking for?"

Akers nodded and went into a back room and came back with three devices that looked like BlackBerrys. "Best bomb detector in the business," he said. "Uses radiation to detect explosive devices and displays the bomb's inner workings on the screen." He showed Boff how to work one of them.

"Simple, huh?"

"What's its detection rate?" Boff asked, examining the device more closely.

"Ninety-seven point seventy-five per cent."

"What happens if you fall into the small remaining bracket?"

Akers shrugged. "You get blown up. But don't think negatively. Life is about taking chances."

"How much will each of these run me?"

Akers showed him the price tag.

Boff frowned. "Ouch. Can you do better than that?"

"I'll cut twenty per cent off if you promise to get Jenny to invite us over for dinner."

"You got it."

"Can I ask what you need these for?"

"Sure," Boff said. "I always welcome questions."

"So?"

Boff just smiled.

"You keep your cards close to your vest," Akers told him.

"The best poker players do."

Akers ran his credit card, boxed the devices, and put them in a bag. Outside the shop, Boff took one of the devices out of the bag and tested it on his car. The warning light stayed green. He slipped the detector into his pocket, drove to the gym, and parked his car.

A half hour later, Cullen came out and got into the front seat of Boff's car. "Where's my present?" he asked.

"Bag on the floor by your feet."

Cullen took out one of the boxes out and opened it. "What is this?"

"Bomb detector."

"The other one's for you?"

"No. I have mine in my pocket. It's for my wife to use on her car. I'll show you how it works when we get to your place. I want you to keep it in your pocket or gym bag at all times. Make sure you remember to use it before you get in your car."

"What happens if they don't use a bomb? What if they just shoot me?"

"Then you're dead. But at least you'll have all your body parts for an open casket funeral so the very few friends you have can say a fond farewell."

"That's comforting."

Boff pulled over near Cullen's building. "Which one's your rental?" he asked.

"The gray Corolla."

They walked over to it and Boff took out his

own device. "See? You turn it on like this. Aim it at the car and press the button. If the light stays green, there's no bomb."

"What if it turns red?"

"Run like hell and call me."

Cullen checked for the green light, then opened the door to his rental.

"Where're you going?" Boff asked him.

"Pay a visit to Lt. Harris. I want to return the badge his man lost."

"Do you have a death wish?"

"Not that I know of."

"Then what do you expect to accomplish by giving the badge to Harris?"

"Piss him off," Cullen said.

"That's stupid."

"Maybe. But after what happened last night, it'll make me feel better."

Boff shook his head. "You, my friend, are a walking disaster. Pop the trunk."

"Why?"

"I want to see if there's anything in there that doesn't belong there."

After Cullen released the trunk lid, Boff took a GPS tracking device out of his pocket and planted it in the trunk. "You're clean," he said.

Cullen started his car. Boff was right, of course. It was dumb to confront Harris, but sometimes he just couldn't help himself. The shock from the explosion had worn off and had been replaced by an anger needing an outlet. He glanced in his mirror as he drove off. Boff was following, but for once he didn't mind. He had some backup in case things went south. Part of him hoped things would. Yeah, he'd get a lot of pleasure out of kicking that cop's ass.

Chapter 27

Cullen drove to police headquarters and parked where he had a view of the entrance but wouldn't be spotted. Boff pulled over half a block away. It was lunch hour. Cullen was hoping Harris left the precinct to eat, and, sure enough, at twelve-thirty, the lieutenant came out alone, got in an unmarked car, and drove to the El Burrito on Del Webb Boulevard. Cullen followed (and Boff followed him), then waited outside the restaurant ten minutes before going in. When he walked to a table where Harris was sitting with a pretty young woman, the cop's face flushed with anger.

"Cause trouble and I'll cuff you," Harris said.

Cullen dropped the badge in Harris' glass of water. "I just thought you might want this. Guess one of your men lost it."

Before Harris could react, Cullen turned and left the restaurant. Outside, he leaned against his car. Boff was standing by his. A couple minutes later, Harris came out and walked over. He poked a finger in Cullen's chest. Cullen batted it away.

"I'll say this once," Harris said. "Stay out of my way. You're in over your head. This ain't a boxing ring, pal."

"What are you gonna do?" Cullen asked him. "Kill me like you did Julio Babbas?"

Harris stared hard at him. "You wired, son?"

"Check me."

Harris gave him a rough pat down, searched his

pants pockets, and made him lift his shirt. “I didn’t kill Babbas,” he said. “I was a fan of his. End of story.”

“You’re not on Yitzhak Soliman’s payroll either, right?”

Harris looked like he was ready to lose it. He took one step forward. “Listen to me, son. I have a powerful friend on the Nevada Boxing Commission. It wouldn’t take much for me to find incriminating evidence in your home or your car indicating you’re involved in drugs. Then you can kiss your career goodbye. Do I make myself clear?”

“Crystal. Nice talking to you again, lieutenant.”

Cullen turned and started to open his door. Harris slammed it shut.

“Free advice,” he said. “Find a new jogging route. You’re too predictable.”

***

Jenny Boff rarely got angry, but when her husband showed her the device and told her what it was for, she lost her temper.

“That’s it! I want you off this case right now!”

He said nothing.

“Don’t give me that Frank Boff silence routine,” she said, getting right in his face. “I want to hear you say you’re going to stand down.”

Frank gave a tiny shrug. “I can’t.”

“Yes, you can! You’re not only putting yourself in danger, but me and the kids, too.”

“Dante’s men won’t let anything happen to you

or the kids."

She wasn't ready to let go. "If you won't drop it, then have Dante give *you* a bodyguard."

"I work better alone," he said.

"Dammit, Frank, can you for once not be so stubborn and just listen to me?"

"I always listen to you," he said in his most reasonable voice. "I just can't in this instance. If I backed off the case, it'd send a message that I can be intimidated. That would lead to more tactics like this in the future."

Jenny stormed into the kitchen. He followed her.

"What's for dinner?"

"Nothing! I'm taking the kids out to eat. And you're not invited!" She took a bottle of Stolichnaya out of the freezer and began fixing a screwdriver.

"Little early to be drinking, isn't it?" He tried to hug her, but she pushed him away.

"Okay, okay," he said. "You can hate me all you want, but at least let me show you how to work the bomb detector."

She sipped her drink.

"If you don't know how, you'll be putting yourself and the kids at risk."

Jenny slammed her glass down on the counter, grabbed the device out of his hand, left the kitchen, and went out the front door. He followed her to her Taurus.

"Turn it on like this," he said. "Point it at your car and press this button. See the green light? That means no bomb. If it starts blinking red, get far away and call me."

She shot him a dirty look and walked back into the house. Her husband followed at a distance.

Chapter 28

Cullen didn't alter his jogging route when he went out the next morning. He'd be damned, he told himself, if he'd let that slimeball Harris intimidate him. He knew he wasn't more courageous than other people, just more pig-headed. He did compromise a bit, however, by staying alert as he jogged, looking from side to side for potential trouble. Occasionally he glanced behind him. But after a couple miles of this, he found it too distracting and probably pointless. If there was a sniper on a roof, or a car suddenly swerved his way, he'd never spot it in time, so he put trouble out of his mind and kept going.

Around a mile from home, a black limo with tinted windows pulled alongside him and kept pace. Cullen's heart started racing. He was about to run off in another direction when the back window came down. It was Soliman.

"What time do you finish your evening workout?" the Israeli asked.

"Eight."

"I'll have a car pick you up at your apartment at nine. We'll have dinner at my house."

Soliman closed the window. After the limo drove off, Cullen stopped running and let out an anxious sigh. Then he walked the rest of the way home to think things out. If Harris was on Soliman's payroll, then the Israeli knew about their confrontation last night. It occurred to him that maybe he'd just gotten an invitation to his Last Supper, but something told him Soliman had other things in mind for now. There was only one way to find out.

When McAlary put him through another boot camp workout, Cullen got the feeling that until he stopped looking for Julio's killer—or actually found him—this was the way all his sessions were going to go. After the workout, McAlary led him to the den where Kate was waiting with DVDs of his next opponent's fights. They watched for a half hour, then Kate handed him one.

"Take this home and study it tonight," she said. "This is Danielson in his prime. He's years older now, of course, but with old champions you never know when they'll pull one out of their past. You want to be prepared for the best Danielson possible."

"I'll watch it soon as I get home."

He was lying, but that was better than telling them he was dining with Soliman.

On the drive home, he called Boff and told him about his dinner plans. There was only silence at the other end of the phone.

"Boff? You there?"

I was just wondering if I should shoot you myself and put you out of your misery or let Soliman do it.

Cullen went for humor. "There you go again, Boff. Being pessimistic."

Boff did not think anything was funny. *Well*, he

said, *I suppose there's a chance Soliman won't kill you. In which case you might learn something useful.*

"So you're okay with me going?"

Okay? No. Can I live with it? Yes. Especially because it's not my life on the line. In your place, I would've insisted he meet me in a restaurant. Obviously, it's too late for that.

Cullen pulled into a space near his apartment building. "I've got to take a shower and get changed," he told Boff. "I'll call you when I get back from Soliman's."

Cullen, if you're going into your apartment, do you remember what I told you?

"Check the lock." He bounded up the stairs.

First make sure the door isn't unlocked, Boff instructed him. *If it's locked, look closely at the key hole. See if there are any scratch marks.*

"Hold on," Cullen said. He bent down to peer at the lock. There's some scratches. But you broke into my apartment."

Son, when the Great Boffer picks a lock, it looks as shiny as the day it came off the assembly line.

"The Colombians were here, too."

True. Anyway, if Soliman was going to kill you, he'd probably do it in the safety of his home, not in your apartment. So you might as well go in.

"I'm having the new lock you recommended put in tomorrow."

Good.

He walked into the living room, his phone still at his ear.

Stand still and listen for sounds, Boff said softly.

He couldn't hear anything except cars on the street. Suddenly somebody shouted "Boo!" He yelped and nearly dropped the phone. Boff was laughing on the other end.

"Jesus Christ! That wasn't funny."

To me it was. Anyway, when Soliman greets you at his house—hopefully with a handshake, not a gun—you tell him right away you have to be home by midnight because McAlary has you scheduled for an early workout and sometimes does a bed check.

"You actually think that'd stop Soliman from killing me? For the Great Boffer, that's pretty lame."

I'm not done yet. Okay? I'll park my car three blocks from Soliman's house. At eleven-thirty, I'll call your cell phone. If you don't answer, then I'll go home and have a late snack because you'll obviously be dead.

"Great plan." He started slipping out of his grimy clothes.

Boff still wasn't finished. *However, if you do answer the phone*, he said, *act like it's McAlary on the other end saying you're in trouble for missing your bed check. Then I'm going to ask where you are. You tell me Soliman's house. Then I'll hang up.*

"What does that accomplish?" He turned on the shower.

If Soliman thinks McAlary knows where you are, he might feel it's too risky to kill you, at least tonight, anyway.

"Gotcha. When you call at eleven-thirty, I'm supposed to say, 'Hi Boff, what are you bothering me for?'"

This time Cullen was the one laughing. The phone went dead on the other end.

Chapter 29

Cullen was waiting on the sidewalk, wearing blue jeans and black T-shirt when the limo arrived at nine. He had thought about putting on the one suit he owned but nixed the idea. He wasn't dressing up for Soliman. The back door of the limo swung open. When nobody stepped out to greet him, he climbed in. There was a big thug in the back, two more up front. He got a flash of *The Godfather,* the scene where Clemenza has Paulie shot inside a car parked in a meadow.

"Leave the gun, take the cannoli," Cullen said.

None of the Israelis got it, or if they did, they didn't laugh. The driver put the car in gear, and they rode in silence. The radio was off. If they were trying to make him nervous, Cullen thought, they were doing a good job.

Soliman was sipping whiskey in a large room with a wood-beamed cathedral ceiling when the men brought Cullen in. There were three spotted Great Danes lying on the floor next to Soliman, and a pretty teenage girl was sitting across from him, drinking a can of Coke through a straw. The dogs stood stiffly at attention and growled as Cullen approached, but Soliman petted them and spoke a few words and they lay back down.

"My dogs are very protective of me," he said. Then he stood up and they shook hands. "Danny, this is my daughter, Rebecca. Next year she's going to Berkeley to study archaeology. The school offers summer field work in Israel and Egypt."

Rebecca smiled prettily. "Nice to meet you, Danny. What do you do?"

"I'm a boxer."

"Cool. I'm a mixed martial arts fan, but I also watch boxing. I wanted to train in kick-boxing, but Daddy wouldn't let me."

"So you went and did it anyway," Soliman said.

Rebecca frowned. "How did you know?"

Soliman smiled.

"I did it, Daddy, because Israel didn't survive all these years by backing down to bullies."

Soliman laughed. "Now I'm a bully?"

"You are sometimes." She got up and kissed him.

"Rebecca, I have some business to discuss with Danny."

"No problem. I need to study for an AP test on how to draw up a site plan for an archaeological excavation. Good luck with your career, Danny." She left the room.

"Rebecca also wanted to go to Israel and do the two-year army requirement for young women, instead of attending college right away," Soliman said. "That war I won." He looked off for a moment in the direction his daughter had gone.

Cullen decided it was stupid to tell him about the McAlary bed check, so he scrapped the idea.

Soliman turned back to him. "How was your workout?'

"Tough as always. My trainer likes to push me. After the session, I watched tape of my next opponent, Clifton Danielson."

Soliman nodded. "Good fighter in his day, which was yesterday. Today is yours. Sit down. Drink?"

"Sparkling water and lime."

One of Soliman's men fixed him the drink and brought it over. Then, on his boss's signal he left with the other men.

"If you want a candid conversation," Soliman began, "I have to ask you this: are you wearing a wire?"

"No. Do you want to search me?"

Soliman studied his face. "That won't be necessary. I hope you like lamb. My cook is preparing lamb-stuffed vine leaves."

"I'll try anything once."

"Even dining with the man you suspect killed your friend?"

Cullen said nothing to that.

"I understand how you feel about Julio's death. In my country, life can be gone in an instant. I lost my mother and younger brother while they were shopping for Passover at an open air market in Tel Aviv. A rocket fired from Palestine killed thirty shoppers. Your father died at forty-three, way too young. Life makes little sense sometimes, but if you accept that, then everything makes sense."

"So did you?"

"Kill Julio? Why would I do that?"

Same answer Soliman gave Gholston. "Maybe because he was helping the Colombians establish ties with club owners," Cullen said. "Also, I know

Harris made a big deposit in his off-shore account just before Julio was killed."

Soliman's eyes darkened a moment. "I see Mr. Boff has been doing his homework." He stood up and crossed the room to a bookcase. He slid out an embossed photo album, brought it back, and handed it to his guest.

"Open it, Danny."

Inside were fight programs and ticket stubs. Several were from Julio's bouts. There were also photos of Soliman taken with boxers. One shot showed Julio shaking hands with him in a restaurant. Cullen closed the album.

"As you can see," Soliman said, "I'm a big fan of boxing. Julio was one of my favorites."

Cullen nodded. "I'm sure that's true, but in your line of work, when business and pleasure are at odds, pleasure suffers…isn't that what they say?"

"Generally, that's true. But you have to realize the Colombians are just a nuisance, a *minor* nuisance. Of the Ecstasy trade in Las Vegas, they do maybe fifteen per cent. Tops. I handle the rest. My connections in Canada guarantee me as much product as I can move. When your Mr. Boff isn't interfering. The Colombians get their package from Mexico, where availability is sporadic." He paused, took a sip of his whiskey, and leaned slightly forward. "Do you understand what I'm saying?"

"To an extent. I just don't think you could afford to ignore a Colombian intrusion into what's considered your territory."

"True. Even though they're not a serious threat,

if I allowed them to take away a share of my market without making a statement, I'd lose respect and encourage others."

"Perfect reason to kill Julio."

Soliman took another sip of his whiskey. "Let me explain the politics of organized crime to you," he said, setting his glass on the end table. "Forget *The Sopranos*. Men like me don't kill without weighing very carefully the consequence it would have on my business. If you kill a drug dealer or a rival mobster, law enforcement doesn't break its back trying to solve the case. Kill a Julio Babbas, though, and they're all over it. If they catch the murderer, they get promotions and good publicity for the department. I'd have been stupid to kill him for the reason you gave."

It was the same thing Boff had said. Cullen nodded.

"Then," Soliman continued, "while I won't tell you specifics, let me just say I had a much bigger stake in seeing Julio alive than dead."

Cullen looked surprised. "I don't see how."

"Julio was performing an important service for me. Although he was not working directly for me. That's all I'll tell you. Perhaps you should look into that instead of wasting your time on me and Lt. Harris. If you persist in pursuing me—"

"You'll have me killed?"

"No, Danny, no. I have no interest in doing that. I have plans for you. What I was going to say is if you stay focused only on me, you'll never find Julio's killer."

"Did you blow up my car last night?"

Soliman shook his head. "Maybe it was Arango." He picked up his drink, then changed his mind and set it back down. "I don't like having my favorite boxers killed," he said. "Including you. If I find out who murdered Julio, I'll take my own action." He stood up. "Now let's eat. I want you to get home before Boff calls in the locals from his car three blocks away."

"How did you know—?"

Soliman laid an arm around Cullen's shoulders. "It's my business to know. Come, break bread with me. Then I have a proposition for you."

***

Boff was parked down the street from Cullen's building when the limo dropped him off. As soon as the limo was gone, Boff drove up and stopped. Cullen got in.

"Why didn't you answer your cell phone when I called?"

"I thought the whole idea stupid," Cullen said. "How come you didn't think I was dead and go home?"

"Knowing you, I figured you turned it off just to irritate me." He put the car in gear. "Let's go somewhere we're not easy targets." He drove downtown, frequently checking his mirror to see if he was being followed. Pulling into a garage, he parked on the basement level, well away from any other car.

“Okay, let’s hear what he had to say.”

Cullen told him everything, including the fact that Soliman knew Boff had parked near his house. “I’m surprised you let them spot you,” he finished. “That was sloppy.”

“Actually, I did it on purpose. That way, they’d know you weren’t isolated. Along with the fictitious McAlary call, I’d be a second person who knew where you were last seen alive.”

Suddenly they heard tires screeching not too far away. Boff started his engine, prepared to move. As the car sped off in another direction, he left the engine running.

“Soliman asking you to introduce his people to club owners, we expected that,” Boff said.

“I told him I’d think it over. What you and I didn’t expect was for him to make a pretty good case as to why he didn’t kill Julio.”

“Good case?” Boff shook his head. “I could crush that in court without working up a sweat. Which is not to say he lied to you. He may very well have been telling the truth, but what matters in court isn’t the truth. It’s which side presents the best illusion of truth. Soliman was unconvincing to me. The only interesting thing he said was that he wouldn’t have killed Julio because he was indirectly performing a service for him. It’s my experience a statement like that out of nowhere raises a red flag. Soliman could be bullshitting, but it might be worth looking into.”

“If we can figure that out—”

“Let’s start simple. What kind of service could

Julio do that Soliman would find valuable?"

"I can't think of anything."

"That's why you're fortunate to have me. Julio could've been spying on Arango."

"He never would've done that."

"Saint Julio, right?"

"Also, if Julio wasn't working directly for Soliman, then who was he doing it for?"

"A couple possibilities come to mind."

"Like what?"

Boff checked his watch. "It's late. I'm tired. Come around to my office tomorrow around noon. I'll explain things to you." He put the car in gear.

"Hey! You can't leave me hanging like this."

"What was it Hannibal Lector said? 'Good things come to those who wait.'"

Chapter 30

The locksmith was installing Cullen's new deadbolt in the morning when Boff called to say he couldn't meet that day.

"Why the hell not?" Cullen asked.

I have a busy schedule.

"Doing what?"

It's on a need-to-know basis only.

"Well, I fucking need to know!"

You don't have classified clearance.

"At least tell me who you think Julio was spying on Arango for. I can't wait another day."

You don't have much choice, do you?

***

Boff had a theory on Julio and needed to test it. He met DEA agent Ward in a cemetery in North Las Vegas. Ward was sitting on a bench working his BlackBerry.

"I've never understood the fascination with those things," Boff said as he sat down. "It'd drive me nuts typing with just my thumbs."

Ward looked up. "You're already nuts." He put the BlackBerry away.

"You picked a charming spot for a meeting," Boff said.

"Everybody minds their own business here."

Boff looked around at the headstones. "You ever think about dying?"

"I try not to."

"When my time comes, I'm going to cop a plea and get relocated to another live body."

"You think Death has a witness protection program?"

"I'm hoping. My wife, on the other hand, believes she's going to heaven."

Ward laughed. "Guess you'll miss her where you're sent to."

"She's trying to save me."

"Mother Theresa couldn't save you."

"Probably not. Anyway, what did Lasker do with the info I gave you?"

"First, he had to sit down to regain his composure," Ward said. "Then he refused to believe you'd ever do anything good for the agency, scumbag that you are. His word, not mine. After a while, though, he called the Royal Mounted. Given that Soliman knew you had the address, the Mounties moved in fast. They made a bust right that day. Can you imagine the DEA, FBI, or any federal enforcement agency acting so quickly?"

"My imagination is not that good."

"The lab was in the basement of a house in Toronto. The Mounties seized more than $40 million worth of drugs and paraphernalia. We hit the jackpot."

"Let me guess," Boff said. "Dickhead took all the credit."

"He got right on the horn to Washington to report his success. He did throw me a bone, though. He said he was acting on information dug up by

Bob Ward. Needless to say, the name Boff didn't come up in the conversation. I put in for a transfer to Miami, where the action is."

Two elderly Hispanic women walked by. Boff watched as they stopped at a nearby grave and laid flowers against the headstone. Then they made the sign of the cross.

"Think they're carrying?" he asked.

Ward hardly glanced at them. "Are you serious? They're harmless nice old farts. I mean ladies."

"Remind me to tell you sometime about a ninety-year-old fart who works for Dante Ferretti."

"Boff, I know you didn't come here to chat. What's the favor?"

"It's a very delicate matter. I need info. Because of the nature of the subject, I'm well aware there are limits on what you can tell me. I won't in any way compromise you."

"Okay, I'll do what I can. What is it?"

"Have you heard of Julio Babbas?"

"Boxer who got whacked a few months back."

"Hard as it is to believe, I've been hired to find his killer."

"You're right. That is hard to believe. Where do I figure in?"

"Not you, the DEA."

Ward frowned. "You know I can't reveal agency info on cases, old or new."

"Of course. So let's approach it like this. Hypothetically, would I be playing in the right ballpark if I said the agency knows the name Julio Babbas?"

Ward glanced at the two old ladies before answering. "Sounds like a good ballpark to me."

"Would I be swinging at a good pitch if I assumed not everyone in the agency who knows the name Julio Babbas is a boxing fan?"

"You could hit that pitch."

"Did Babbas ever bat in the same lineup as Humberto Arango?"

"If he did, it'd be a good one-two combo."

"Did Babbas sign a contract to play for the agency?"

Ward hesitated. He glanced at the old women again. "What I heard," his voice was a little softer, "he was already under contract to another team."

That puzzled Boff, but he'd have to think about that later. "Was the agency going to take action to void that contract?"

Ward stood up. "I'm just an assistant coach," he said. "They don't tell me everything. Game's over. Hit one out of the ballpark. It'll do your dark soul a world of good."

They walked through the cemetery toward their cars. Boff looked behind him a couple times to see if the old ladies were following. They weren't. As they approached Ward's car, Boff scanned the street out of habit. A gray van with a tinted windshield suddenly slowed down. Cullen had said the van that rammed his car was also gray with a tinted windshield. He yanked Ward down to the pavement just as a Hispanic man stuck an AK-47 out the passenger side window and started firing. The windows on Ward's car exploded and glass rained down on their hair and backs and the sidewalk. The van sped away before Boff could get its plates. He turned back to Ward. "You okay?"

"No, I'm fucking not okay!"

They both stood up and shook the glass out of their hair.

"Look at my goddamn car!" Ward shouted as he walked around it, inspecting the damage. "Thank God all they hit was the side windows, not the body. Why the hell were they trying to kill me?"

"They weren't," Boff told him. "I believe it was me they were after. You would've just been collateral damage. Lucky for you, I spotted the shooter."

"Yeah. Lucky me."

The two old Hispanic ladies came out of the cemetery and started down the street.

"Flash your badge at them," Boff said.

"I'm not going to bother those nice ladies," Ward said.

"Then play along with me and don't say anything." He took out his wallet, held up his old DEA badge so the old ladies could clearly see it, then quickly put it away. The women stopped and glanced at the damaged car.

"I need to call a tow truck," Boff said to them. "But I left my phone home. Do either of you happen to have a cell?"

"I do, officer," one of them said.

"Can I borrow it a second?"

She hesitated, then took a phone out of her purse and handed it to him. He walked off a few steps and turned his back to them so they couldn't see what he was doing. He punched in a few commands. After he found what he was looking for, he put the phone by his ear and spoke loudly. "Yes, I need a tow truck. I'm at—"

He turned to the women. "What's the name of this cemetery?"

"Vale."

"Vale Cemetery. How soon can you be here?" He closed the phone, walked back, and handed it to the woman. "Thanks," he said. "I appreciate it."

The woman said nothing, and she and her friend walked away quickly.

Ward frowned. "What the hell was that about? I have a cell phone, and I'm sure you do, too."

"Correct."

"Then what the fuck did you need her phone for?"

"Did you happen to notice the name on the gravestone these nice old Hispanic ladies put flowers at and made the sign of the cross over?"

"No."

"It was Seymour Hershkowitz." He let Ward think about that.

"You think they were spying on us?" the DEA agent asked after a minute.

"I believe it was something more sinister. That's why I wanted to see her phone. I checked her recent calls. She made one just after we started back for our cars."

"She alerted the shooter?"

Boff nodded.

"I assume you memorized the number."

"Yes." Boff took out his cell and called it. A recorded voice told him the phone was not in service.

"Well?"

"Out of service."

"Give me the number. When I get to the office, I'll try to find out who it belongs to."

"Waste of time," Boff said. "I'm guessing it was a TracFone and is lying smashed somewhere."

"Give it to me, anyway."

Boff took out a business card and a pen and wrote the number down for Ward.

"Who's trying to kill you, Frank?"

"Could be one of my ex-DEA partners. My first guess would've been you, except you're here."

Ward could only shake his head. "So how soon is the tow truck coming?"

"I didn't call a tow truck."

"Why the hell not? I can't drive this thing."

"Sure you can. Windshield and rear window didn't get hit. Just clear the glass off the front seat and drive it. Why waste money?"

Ward took out his cell, dialed information, and got the number for a towing service near the cemetery.

"Pretty exciting day, huh?" Boff said. "I bet this beats hell out of sitting in a stuffy office."

Ward flipped him the bird.

Chapter 31

Boff was steaming. He yanked open his car door, climbed in behind the wheel, and slammed the door closed. He was about to start the engine when he caught himself. He'd forgotten to check the car for a bomb.

He got out of the Malibu, moved a few feet away, and took out his device, then turned it on and pressed the button. The light remained green. Just to make sure, he turned it off and on again two more times. When he got the same result, he got back in the car. Even knowing the device said the car was clean, he held his breath as he turned the key.

The engine started. As he drove away, he kept his eyes peeled for a tail. They'd just tried to make Jenny a widow and his kids fatherless. That raised the stakes big time for him. He was even more determined now to nail down who was behind the killing of Julio and punish them. The shooter had been Hispanic. On the surface, that meant Arango, but it wouldn't have been hard for Soliman to find a Hispanic hitter to throw him off. He called his drug dealer pal.

"How's it going, Luis?"

Great, the dealer replied. *Panchito won his fight in about two minutes. First thing he did was bite out one of the other bull's eyes. The dog howled and backed away. Panchito took his sweet time killing him. He could've done it faster, just wanted to stretch it out to have some fun. What's up?*

"You're not mad at me for anything, are you?"

Me? I love you. Why are you asking?

"This Hispanic guy just tried to pull a drive-by on me."

It wasn't one of my men. Are you okay?

"Yes. Could you do me a favor? Have your people keep their ears to the street. They might hear something about the shooting."

No problemo.

"Thanks."

By the way, Panchito thanks you for giving him Kiko to play with.

"Sorry I missed seeing that."

I also beefed up my security, Luis said. *If Soliman thinks he's muscling in here, he's going to lose a lot of people. Thanks for the heads up.*

"Glad to be of service." Boff hung up. Next he called the gym. McAlary answered.

"This is Boff. I need to talk to Danny."

He's still working out.

"This is important. I just got shot at."

McAlary yelled for Cullen to come over.

"Who's on the phone?" Boff heard Cullen ask. McAlary told him.

What are you doing calling me in the middle of a workout? Cullen asked when he got on the phone.

"Somebody just tried to kill me."

Really? Wow. Was it a bomb?

"AK-47." Boff told him what had happened. "It was the same van that rammed your rear end," he finished.

You got the plate, I assume.

“Actually, no, I didn’t. I had an AK-47 pointed at me. By the time I got up from the sidewalk, the van was too far away. Do me a favor, Danny. Call Arango after your workout. Ask him why he’s trying to whack me if he didn’t kill Julio.”

You’re sure the gunman was Hispanic?

“Yes, I’m sure. Now listen. I want you to be extra careful when you leave the gym. They might make a try at you.”

Cullen seemed to be thinking about this. *Okay*, he finally said. *Will you tell me now who you think might’ve hired Julio to spy on Arango?*

“That’ll take too much time,” Boff said, “and you’ll piss McAlary off more than I assume he already is. Come by my office at eleven tomorrow morning. If you don’t have my card, look my address up in the phone book.”

When Cullen hung up the gym’s phone, McAlary, who had gone over to work with Trillo, came back and asked him what Boff had said.

“A Hispanic tried to shoot him from a moving car,” Cullen said. “He thinks it might’ve been someone Arango sent.”

“What else did he say?”

Cullen hesitated. “I should be extra careful because they might shoot at me.”

McAlary shook his head and walked away.

The day’s training over, Cullen walked to his rental car, a half block away. As he walked, he looked around for anyone suspicious sitting in a parked car. Then he used the device to check for a bomb. As he drove home, he kept looking in the rearview mirror to see if he was being followed. Blowing up his car as a warning was one thing, but shooting at Boff meant whoever killed Julio was prepared to take it to another level. He took out the card Arango had given him and picked up his cell phone.

"This is Danny Cullen. A Hispanic took shots today at a private investigator I'm working with. The investigator thinks it might've been someone you sent."

He's mistaken, Arango said. *Why would I kill this guy if he's helping find Julio's killer?*

Cullen didn't know. "I don't know."

Tell your friend to consider it was Soliman who hired a Latino.

"Somebody also blew up my car while it was parked outside my apartment."

This is not good. Arango gave it some thought. *Let me assign one of my men to guard you. I can send Francisco.*

"No, thanks. I still haven't gotten the smell out of my kitchen. Besides, it would make me look afraid if I had a bodyguard."

You should be afraid.

"If you show fear in the ring, your opponent gets bolder."

This is not boxing.

Cullen took a breath, let it out. "Okay, if things get worse, I'll take you up on the offer. Thanks." He closed the phone and looked in the mirror again.

In light of what had happened to Boff, Cullen

decided it was time to change his night jogging route, so he mapped out a new five-mile course. As he ran, he wondered why Boff suspected Julio might have been spying on Arango, and who for. It made no sense.

Turning a corner, he saw several police cars with lights spinning near a Mercedes sedan. He stopped running to look closer and saw that the cops had cuffed a man wearing a tuxedo and a woman in a black formal dress. The car's doors and trunk were wide open, and the police were searching inside with flashlights. He saw Lt. Harris, which meant drugs. A uniformed cop was standing by a barricade of yellow tape. He walked up to the uniform.

"Hi. I'm Danny Cullen of the *Review-Journal.* What happened here?"

The cop looked at him skeptically, probably never having seen a reporter show up at a crime scene in sweats. Then his eyes lit up. "Hey, you're the boxer. Showtime. Nice fight."

"Thanks. I've got another one in two months."

The cop shook his hand.

"Drug bust, huh?" Cullen asked.

"You should talk to the lieutenant."

"The lieutenant has taken a serious disliking to me."

The cop tried to suppress his grin. "That speaks well of you," he said. "Harris is a dick." He gestured toward the Mercedes. "They nabbed two mules humping a trunk full of H."

"They dress nice for mules. And I like their

ride."

"It makes for great cover. The old guys at the station tell me that back in the day, some of the biggest humpers were movie stars and singers."

Cullen thanked the cop and resumed running. Something about the drug bust nagged at him, though. He wished he could get a handle on it.

Chapter 32

Even though Cullen didn't have to be at the gym, he woke at seven the next morning out of habit. McAlary had cancelled workouts that day because an old friend from Ireland had died in a car accident and the funeral was in Lake Tahoe. With time on his hands before he was to meet with Boff, he visited Julio's grave, which was set on a hill under a shade tree. He had only been there a few minutes when a Mercedes pulled over on the street. Arango got out and walked up the hill toward him.

"You come here often?" Arango asked.

"As much as I can."

"Me, too."

"Quite a coincidence," Cullen said, "both of us being here at the same time."

"Yes."

"I think you're having me followed."

Arango brushed crusted dirt off the gravestone.

"Why are you following me?" Cullen asked.

Arango turned to face him. "To try and keep you from getting hurt. How did your dinner with Soliman go?"

Cullen didn't bother asking Arango how he knew. "He wants me to help him meet club owners. As you suspected."

"Good. You're in the door. What else did he say?"

"That he wouldn't have killed Julio because he was performing an important service for him."

Arango looked puzzled. "Julio working for Soliman? Not possible."

"I didn't say Julio was working *for* Soliman," Cullen replied. "Just doing something Soliman thought was valuable."

"Like what?"

"The investigator helping me thinks Julio might've been spying on you for somebody."

Arango turned to face the grave. "Julio, you hear this nonsense?"

"I don't believe it, either," Cullen said.

Arango turned back. "Good. Let me tell you something, my friend. Israel is about ten thousand square miles, roughly the size of your New Hampshire or Vermont. There are twenty-two Arab countries. They occupy over five million square miles. So how has this tiny country managed to survive? Through lies and deception. Israeli mobsters are second only to the Mossad in the use of deception."

Cullen gave that some thought. "My gut feeling is Soliman was telling the truth," he said, "even though it's pretty hard to believe. Then again, I've found out things about Julio I wouldn't have thought possible a month ago. So who knows?"

Arango threw his hands up. "What am I going to do with you?"

"Tell me the truth."

"What truth? I've already said Julio helped me out at the clubs. He was a visitor at my villa, and a couple times I stayed with him in his vacation home in Mexico. There's nothing more to tell."

Cullen touched the gloves carved into Julio's stone, then turned to go.

"I wish you'd let me assign one of my people to you," Arango said behind him.

Cullen kept going toward his car. "You're tailing me. That should keep me safe."

"My men can only do so much from a distance."

"It'll have to do for now." He stopped and looked back at Arango. "The Israelis aren't the only ones who've managed to stay alive in a hostile environment," he said. "Colombian drug lords have prospered a long time, too. Despite the best efforts of your government to eradicate them."

Arango nodded. "Not to mention the hundreds of millions of dollars the U.S. has given to Bogota to help in the effort. We're like the poppy fields. We keep growing back."

"Or the Israelis. Masters in the art of deception."

Arango shrugged. "That, too."

***

Boff's office was in a three-story building on East Charleston Boulevard. Cullen scanned the directory between the elevators. There were five lawyers, two accountants, six doctors of varying specialties, and Boff. He had a basement office. Cullen took the stairs down and walked along the corridor. The doors all had name plates. Boff's didn't. His office was the last one on the right and had just a number. An intercom was mounted on the door frame, and there were two surveillance cameras above the door; one covering the entrance to the office, the other aimed down the corridor. Cullen knocked.

"Who is it?" Boff said through the intercom.

"You know damn well who it is. You can see me."

"Identify yourself."

"Come on, don't screw around."

"I'm not. For all I know, you could be some hitman wearing one of those false faces like they use in the *Mission Impossible* movies."

Nevertheless, the door buzzed open.

"Welcome to my humble abode."

Boff was sitting behind his desk working on a computer. "Humble" didn't do justice to the place. It looked like a fly-by-night operation, with one desk, a couple cheap metal folding chairs, and a filing cabinet as old as Gholston's. The walls were empty except for a framed investigator's license, a cheap clock, and two Norman Rockwell prints, one of which hung behind Boff's desk. Cullen recognized the farmer with the pitchfork.

Boff barely looked up. "Pull up a chair."

"I gather you aren't big on luxury."

"Why waste money on expensive furniture? The people who come to me for help have nowhere else to go if they want what I can deliver. I could have an office in a broom closet and they'd still hire me."

Cullen sat down. "Can I ask why you took a place in a building loaded with doctors and lawyers?"

"Scumbag lawyers because I work for some of

them, doctors to irritate them by my presence. Every one of them hates me because I have a solid reputation for winning malpractice cases. Last year they tried to have me evicted. But they backed off when I hired the best defense attorney in town. Two years ago, this lawyer—with my help, of course—got alleged serial killer Travis Hill acquitted. That was one of my finest pieces of work."

"How the hell could you work for a serial killer?"

"His checks didn't bounce."

"What if he kills again?"

"I'd feel bad for the victim, glad for me if they arrest him. I could defend him again."

"You must've been born without a conscience."

"Not completely. I'm half Irish, half Jewish. The Jew tries to make me feel guilty, but the Irishman is a tough bastard and shuts him up." He pushed his keyboard aside. "Now tell me what Arango said."

"That it wasn't him, that he'd have no reason to shoot you since you're looking for Julio's killer. He said Soliman probably hired a Latino to throw you off track."

Boff nodded. "That's what I expected him to say. I just wanted you to ask to let him know I haven't ruled out the possibility he murdered Julio."

"Before I came here, I ran into Arango at Julio's grave. He has a tail on me."

"Good. They can provide some semblance of protection."

"Unless Arango killed Julio."

Boff suddenly stared at his computer screen.

"What is it?" Cullen asked.

"Take a look." He swiveled the screen so they both could see. On it was the corridor view. A heavyset man wearing a black sweat suit was walking toward Boff's office. He had one hand in his pants pocket.

"Did someone follow you?" Boff asked.

"Not that I know of. Except maybe Arango's men. Do you have a gun?"

"I haven't carried since the DEA."

When the man knocked on the door, Boff spoke into his intercom. "Who is it?"

"Jack Luzinski." They could see him looking up at the camera. "We talked on the phone yesterday about me hiring you."

"Your appointment is for tomorrow."

"I was in the neighborhood, so I thought I'd take a shot at seeing you sooner."

"Do me a favor," Boff said. "Take your hand out of your pocket."

Luzinski shrugged and complied.

"Is the pocket empty?"

"Yeah," Luzinski said. "What is this?"

"Pull the lining out and show me."

Luzinski complied again. "See? Nothing. Do you do this with all your clients?"

"Just the ones I don't know yet. Tell me again what you were charged with."

"Assault and battery."

Boff buzzed him in. Jack Luzinski looked to be in his mid-thirties. He also looked nervous.

"I hope this isn't a bad time," he said.

Boff put on his cordial face. "Always glad to see new clients," he said, "but I can only spare you a couple minutes today. Come back tomorrow at your appointed time. Then we can go into depth about your case. Did you bring your checkbook?"

"Yes."

"Here's what I charge."

"Before you start, I want you to know I'm innocent."

"It doesn't matter to me whether you're innocent or guilty, as long as your checks don't bounce."

"They won't," Luzinski said. "I have money."

"Good. You're going to need it. I charge one-fifty an hour. After four hours, it's considered a day and you don't have to pay anything for the extra time I might put in. You pay all my expenses, my mileage, any incidentals. Plus I require a five thousand dollar retainer."

"That's a bit pricey, isn't it?"

"Yes, it is. I'm sure you can find any number of investigators who'd only charge you half that. You'd save a lot of money, but you couldn't spend it in jail."

Luzinski wrote out the check, nodded at Cullen, shook hands with his new investigator, and left. They watched him walk back down the corridor.

"I didn't realize you charged so much," Cullen said.

"You want the best, you have to pay for it. Outside of guys like me, the vast majority of investigators make the bulk of their money working crappy divorce cases and doing boring surveillance for employers who suspect their workers are stealing from them. They rarely get involved in high profile cases, and unlike what you see in movies or read in books, one hundred percent of investigators do *not* take a case for free because they're noble and believe in truth, justice, and the American way."

Boff reached into the mini-refrigerator by his desk and brought out a can of generic cola and a Diet Coke. He tossed the Coke to Cullen.

"I bought that just for you," he said. "Now let's get down to work."

Cullen opened the can and aimed the metal pull-top toward a waste basket. He missed, but didn't bother to go and pick it up. "Any chance you might tell me now who hired you?"

"None whatsoever. Fill me in on what you've been doing."

"Just working out. Last night I watched Harris make a drug bust."

"Tell me about that."

Cullen gave him a quick rundown.

"I'm glad you saw that," Boff said.

"Why?"

"We'll get to that in a moment."

"How come you aren't taking notes?"

"I am." Boff punched a few buttons on a desk radio, and it started to play back their conversation. He clicked it off and pointed to the wall clock. "Video camera inside," he said. "Taped you from the moment you walked in." He typed something and swung his screen around. There was Cullen, walking into the office, every move and every word recorded.

“Isn’t it illegal to record someone without their permission?”

“The law states as long as one person consents—in this case, me—it’s legal. Anyway, based on what we know, I’ve come up with a theory.”

“Which is?”

“Your friend was a mule for Arango, got busted by the DEA, and was forced to inform on him.”

“Are you nuts? Even for you, that’s off the wall.”

Boff sighed. “An investigation is not just about finding hard evidence. A scientist often has to come up with a theory first and then try to prove it. My theory, as outlandish as it seems to you with the blinkers you wear on all things Julio, comes with help from a highly reliable source inside the DEA.”

Cullen thought that over a minute. “So give me one reason why a rich boxer like Julio would run drugs.”

“Because he could. If you follow sports besides boxing, then you know there’ve been many elite athletes who’ve gotten into trouble with the law for no rational reason. I’ve represented a couple. They have this mindset that because they’re so great at what they do, they’re untouchable and not bound by the same laws we mere mortals are.”

“Julio would never have risked his career like that.”

"Maybe he didn't see it as a risk."

"Humping drugs not a risk?"

"Danny, you just told me how surprised you were that the well-dressed man and woman with the Mercedes were mules. Why? They didn't look the part. That's the best kind of cover. Julio's would've been even better because it was real. I'd bet almost everybody at customs—especially on the Mexican side—would've known who he was. Instead of requesting that he open his suitcases, they'd have asked for his autograph. Plus, he had a reputation for being one of boxing's good guys. His risk would've been minimal. At least in his eyes."

Cullen thought that over. "So even if he didn't feel at risk, you still haven't given me a solid reason why he'd do it."

"I'll give you two. First, he was a macho guy. He might've wanted to show his powerful amigo he had *cajones*. He also might have done it just for the thrill. Most athletes in very physical sports get off on danger and risk. You, amigo, are a perfect example. There was absolutely no reason for you to confront Harris with the badge. It was a potentially dangerous thing to do, yet you did it anyway. Why? To piss him off. Great reason. Other examples: Who in his right mind would drive a car at nearly two hundred miles an hour in heavy traffic around a track? Or stand in the pocket and throw a football when a pair of three-hundred-pound monster lineman are charging him?"

Now Cullen recalled some of the things Julio had done as a street kid in Medellin. It wasn't like he was incapable of committing a crime. He'd robbed stores at gunpoint and mugged people. Still, that was when he needed money. When he became famous, money no longer had been an issue.

"I know this is hard for you to accept," Boff said. "Just try and keep an open mind. I'll walk you through it, okay? Remember, it's just a theory based on what I know."

"Okay."

"First," he stuck up one finger, "Julio had a house in Mexico. The Colombians move their product through Mexico. For the sake of argument, let's say Julio was a mule. For whatever reason. I don't dwell on reasons. Again contrary to what you see in movies, the DEA doesn't break cases with daring-do, high-tech equipment, or sheer brilliance. Which, considering the agents I worked with, would be an oxymoron."

"So how do they do it?"

"Stools and well-placed informants. A stool is the lowest form of life, even worse than doctors, lawyers, and FBI agents. You use stools and dispose of them the same way you would garbage. That's just the way it is. When I was in the DEA, we called stools 'crispy critters.'"

"Okay. I'll bite. Why?"

"Of the two we used in my first year on the job, both went out in a blaze of glory. One was tied to a chair, his eyeballs were scooped out, and his body doused in gasoline. They lit him up like a Christmas tree. The other was stuffed into a big office building furnace while he was still alive. Now, your friend was obviously not of the stool variety. That leaves DEA informant." A second finger.

"Because?"

"Let's say Julio got caught by Customs with false-bottom suitcases containing Ecstasy. The enforcement role of Customs is what's called interdiction, or intercepting the drugs as they're imported. They have no need to bring in the DEA, no interest in having an informant. They arrest the mule and hand him over to a federal prosecutor. End of job. Obviously, if Julio got caught, it wasn't by Customs."

Boff sipped some of his soda

"A more likely scenario is this." A third finger. "The DEA has a stool here in Las Vegas. Julio was known on the Dark Side to associate with Arango. That might've caught the stool's interest, so he told the DEA. They develop the info and stop him as soon as he steps on American soil. If they discover his suitcases have drugs in them, they have no obligation to tell Customs or the FBI or anyone else. They take a simple approach. You cooperate or you do the time, and the time on importation of any amount that constitutes possession with intent to distribute is the bell ringer. The judge's sentencing guidelines would be in the neighborhood of twenty to thirty years. There's no probation, no parole, only a possible fifteen percent reduction for good behavior. The get-out-of-jail-free card is cooperation. Agreeing to be an informant. It's called 'flipping.' Considering the length of the jail time, it's a very attractive incentive to squealing, even on your own mother. Ninety percent of the time they take the offer."

"Then what? Julio informs on Arango?"

"Yes. But it's a bit more complicated. If someone's been caught in a drug conspiracy and wants to cooperate, they have to make cases. It's called working off a nut. If you can't make a case or provide good information, they throw you in jail. The Feds don't give credit for effort. If they did, they'd be the biggest chumps in the world, because every scumbag out there would stroke them. Since Julio wasn't in jail, we can assume he was providing quality intel. Soliman said Julio was performing a service for him but not working directly for him. Spying for the DEA on his chief rival would fit that description perfectly."

"I see where you're heading," Cullen said. "Arango found out what Julio was doing and killed him."

"That's one possibility. Again, it's just a theory. We have to prove it." Boff set his can of cola on his desk. "While we're at it, for you own safety, I suggest you keep in mind that Harris and Soliman may have also killed Julio."

"Huh? How would Soliman have known Julio was a DEA informant?"

"Good question, my boy. One possibility is that the snitch who told the agency about Julio was working both sides of the street. Snitches have been known to do that. The reason is simple. They get paid for information. If the snitch told Harris, then that's how Soliman would've found out."

Cullen took a sip and then set his can down. "There's an awful lot of ifs in your theory."

"That often happens in a case. You just have to accept those ifs and move forward. If your theory proves wrong, you go in another direction. Now play along. Even if you don't think my theory holds water. How do we prove it?"

"You must still know plenty of agents in the DEA," Cullen said. "Couldn't you ask them about Julio?"

"Not directly."

"Why not?"

"No ex-Fed would ever think of asking an agent for specific info on an ongoing case, or even one where the informant was dead. It would put the active agent at serious risk. If what he told you ever got back to the agency, he'd not only lose his job, but he could be prosecuted for divulging classified information."

"How many years were you in the DEA again?"

"Ten. Each filled with fond memories."

"I can't believe that in all that time you didn't hook up with one agent who shared your disdain for scruples and would help you out here."

"Even if I had a friend like that in the DEA," Boff said, "it wouldn't matter. One needs access to info before they can provide it, and the way the system is structured, it would be next to impossible. All informant documents exist in an original copy only. No other copies are made. Once the informant is established, all subsequent reports refer only to what's known as a CI number. That stands for 'cooperating individual.' An undercover memo might state, 'On such-and-such a date, Special Agent Boff met with C1-06-0345 at Franny's Diner.' There's never an informant's name. So there's basically no way to learn anything concrete from an agent source." Boff shifted in his chair and glanced at the screen. "That being said, there's always office scuttlebutt, and sometimes agents drink too much and say things they shouldn't. What I found out from my DEA source was undoubtedly of this nature. Helpful information. But not a slam dunk."

"So how *do* we find out if Julio was a mule?"

"We build on the info I got by checking his credit card and phone records. Look for patterns in his bank accounts. I want you to get his Social Security number from his wife and ask her if he kept a date book. It'd help if we knew who he was meeting with and when."

Boff got up. "Let's take a drive now."

"Where?"

"To the Dark Side."

Chapter 33

Cullen followed Boff to northeast Las Vegas. On the way, he called Cassandra to ask for Julio's Social Security number. She didn't want to give it to him, but she finally coughed it up after he nagged her for ten minutes. He didn't press his luck about the datebook. That could wait for later.

Boff parked by a bodega in a seedy neighborhood. The store was attached to an abandoned building with faded sign, Donnie's Auto Body. Its front entrance had been sealed with cement blocks and the windows bricked up.

Cullen looked at the store. "This is the Dark Side? A bodega?"

"On the Dark Side," Boff replied, "things aren't always what they appear to be." Before he opened the door, he stopped to glance around the street.

"What are you waiting for?" Cullen asked him.

"Making sure we weren't followed."

After a minute or so, Boff was satisfied there wasn't a tail, and they went inside. The place was stocked with a mix of American junk food and Mexican groceries. He went over to a counter where a clerk was labeling bottles of Chihuahua hot sauce.

"Tell him Frank Boff is here," he said.

The clerk nodded, picked up a phone, and turned his back on them. He mumbled a few words, then hung up. Turning back to his customers, he said, "You can go back."

They walked down an aisle filled with snack

foods to a door in the rear, where Boff pressed a buzzer. The door clicked open. Cullen was surprised at how heavy it was when he pulled it. Going in, he saw why. The wood was backed by steel. It also had slots to slide a bar through.

The room was about twenty feet by thirty and had been built in what used to be Donnie's Auto Body. There were wall-to-wall carpeting, a refrigerator, an electric wok, and shelves stocked with food. It was also extremely neat. Sitting in front of one of four computers arranged along a large, L-shaped desk was a very broad-shouldered man with long black hair pulled into a pony tail. His back was to them as he typed without stopping. Not your typical computer geek.

"Take a seat," the man said. "Be right with you."

They sat on a leather couch. In one corner of the room was a bed, to its right, a bathroom. Finally, the man swiveled around in his chair and stood up. He was enormous, taller than Boff, about 250 pounds of well-proportioned muscle. He had on a button-down shirt, designer jeans, and yellow tinted glasses. The guy looked familiar, Cullen thought, but he couldn't quite place him. Boff led him over and Cullen stuck out his hand.

"I'm Danny—"

The man raised a hand. "No names, please. Pull up chairs."

As they rolled two chairs across the room, he sat back down. On his desk were a six-pack of Red Bull and several different land-line and cell phones.

Three of them were ringing, but he didn't pick up.

"Tell me what you need."

Boff explained what he was looking for and gave him a slip of paper with Julio's Social Security number.

"No problem."

Cullen suddenly realized who the man was. "Javier Vasquez! The San Diego Chargers defensive end!"

The man smiled. "Back in the day," he said. "Now I tackle things with computers."

"I didn't recognize you right away, dressed like that and with the sunglasses. Dumb question—how does an All-Pro football player like you wind up," he glanced around the office again, "here?"

"Let's just say I pissed away my money, then did a little jail time." Vasquez smiled again. "The question you really wanted to ask is how a big jock like me can be a computer genius."

"Yeah. The thought crossed my mind."

"Long story short, I attended Cal-Berkeley, where I majored in computer science and dabbled in football because I liked hitting people. Guess I was too good for my own good. I ended up in the NFL. Now I'm where I belong."

"You looked pretty comfortable on a football field, too."

"It was fun while it lasted. Picked up some bad habits, though. Like coke, Vicodin, uppers and downers, HGH, steroids. But I'm clean now and a health food fanatic without any vices. Unless you consider this little business of mine a vice."

"You could get busted."

Vasquez looked at Boff. "Tell him."

"First, it would take over a minute to knock down that steel door," Boff said. "They could get through the bricked up windows a little faster, but either way, it wouldn't matter. Every machine in here is wired to melt down its hard drive within seconds of a breach. Javier's filing cabinets would also flame out."

"But then he'd lose everything."

"Not really," Vasquez said. "First and foremost, I'd retain my ability to do things on computers other people can't. It would be an inconvenience to set up shop somewhere else, yeah, but my client list is good. I'd be back up in no time. As for the data in my files, I have it all stored and encrypted somewhere the police would never find it. I have several email accounts in other names on sites like Yahoo!, Gmail, and EarthLink. Everything is stored there. It's better than saving to disc because discs aren't indestructible. They can be lost, stolen, or confiscated and used as evidence. Anyway, let me get to work on your problem. Come back in a couple days."

They got up to go.

"I recognized you, too," Vasquez said. "I saw you on Showtime. You're not as good as your father yet, but you give fans their money's worth."

"If you ever need tickets, I can get them."

"When I need tickets, I print them."

Chapter 34

McAlary and Kate had flown directly from the funeral to California, where Trillo had a fight scheduled at the Home Depot Center in Carson outside Los Angeles. Cullen could have taken the day off, but he hadn't worked out the day before and was something of a gym rat.

Even though the gym was in a safe neighborhood, he locked the door. To get his blood pumping, he shadowboxed awhile; then did strength and conditioning drills. He was doing one-handed pushups when the door knob rattled. He quickly slid the weights off a dumbbell and carried the steel bar over to the door.

"Who is it?"

"Boff."

He unlocked the door.

"What were you going to use the bar for?" Boff asked, pushing it easily aside and walking in.

"Protection."

"If somebody had a gun, they'd shoot you before you could even swing it."

"Yeah, well, I felt better holding it. If you don't mind."

Boff sniffed the air and made a face. "How do you stand the smell in here?"

"What smell?"

"And why don't you turn on the air conditioning? It's stifling."

"This is an old world gym," Cullen said. "No air

conditioning. High heat makes boxers sweat more, so it's easier to lose weight."

Boff looked around. "I hope there's a toilet. I have to pee something fierce."

"Behind the partition."

Boff disappeared into the locker area and emerged a minute later zipping up his fly. "Ahh, I feel like a new man. How'd you like my friend?"

Cullen laid the bar down on the floor. "Why didn't you tell me we were going to meet Javier Vasquez?

"He asks me not to use his name. Which is absurd because most people recognize him."

Boff was starting to sweat profusely in the near one-hundred-degree heat. When he pulled off his T shirt, Cullen saw that he had a big upper body that had probably been muscular once, but had now turned to flab. Cullen grabbed a twelve-pound medicine ball off a rack and set it on the floor. He stood with feet parallel, knees slightly bent, and lifted the ball. When he got it behind his head, he threw it down hard on the floor. It bounced up, he grabbed it, and repeated the drill five times.

Boff watched with medium interest. "What does that do?"

"Gives me more power. Strengthens my thighs. Want to try?"

"Lifting that thing would give me a hernia. The only time I play with a ball is when I shoot hoops with my son in the driveway."

Cullen threw the ball toward Boff's pudgy belly anyway. Boff caught it, but it hit his stomach hard and he winced. When he hurled it back at Cullen's head, the fighter ducked, and the ball sailed across the gym.

"You need some exercise, my man," Cullen said.

"Getting out of bed in the morning is strenuous enough."

Cullen let fly with a flurry of punches into the air to show off his hand speed. "Pretty fast, huh?"

"Not bad."

"Now take out your car keys."

"Why?"

"Just do it."

Boff pulled his keys out of his pocket.

"Hold them out in front of you at waist level," Cullen said. "Now let them drop."

Boff released the keys. Cullen's right hand shot out, and he caught them before they could hit the floor.

"I'm impressed," Boff admitted. "With that kind of hand speed, if you crap out as a boxer, you can always make a living as a pick pocket."

Cullen tossed the keys back and began shadowboxing around Boff. "What did you do today?" he asked.

"I went to see some defense lawyers who handle a lot of drug cases."

"Why?"

"If Julio got busted, he might've called a lawyer. But nobody seems to have heard anything about it."

More shadowboxing, then, "How come you left

the DEA?"

"Whoa. Where did that question come from?"

"Just curious."

"You really want to know?"

"I've got nothing but time."

"First off, I wasn't canned as you suggested at the diner. I quit."

"Why?"

Boff stepped back out of range of the punching. "I had worked for a year on a case in which this fine, upstanding heart surgeon in Houston was moonlighting as an importer of large quantities of high-grade cocaine, which he dealt to doctor friends and important politicos. My team was all set to bust him, when suddenly our supervisor ordered us to back off. Why? The good doctor was close friends with the governor of Texas. The governor made some phone calls. The end result was a year of my work down the drain."

"And that's why you lost your respect for law enforcement?"

"Yes. It wasn't the first time that'd happened to me. A police officer or federal agent doesn't just battle bad guys. He or she is up against department bureaucrats with their own agendas, also powerful politicians and people rich enough to override the rules. The whole system is corrupt. After Texas, let's just say, I started seeing things differently."

"I bet you were pissed at your supervisor."

"I punched him out."

"That's pretty pissed. I'm surprised you weren't fired."

"They did worse. They put me in charge of the Rubber Gun Squad."

Cullen bounced forward, landed a couple quick shots in Boff's gut, then danced away. "What's the Rubber Gun Squad"?

"Whackos too screwed up to wear guns unless issued for a specific bust. But not screwed up enough to be drummed out. One guy was a kleptomaniac. He always stole stuff during raids. Another had this annoying habit of quacking like Donald Duck when he got nervous, which really was a problem when he testified in court. Judges do not like federal agents quacking at them."

"You're making this shit up."

Boff shook his head. "I also had a porn addict. If we raided a place where there was a *Penthouse* or a *Playboy*, he'd go in the bathroom and whack off. Then there was Hugo **Kieniewicz**. Bad enough, I could never spell his name. If we made a bust, he'd line the cuffed perps up against a wall, make them stick out their tongues, and put a thin wafer on each. Then he'd say, 'First guy whose wafer melts, I'm shooting.'"

Cullen stopped punching. "What finally made you quit?"

"My wife got very angry at me during dinner one night because I was quacking at the table. I didn't even realize it." While Cullen was deciding whether or not to laugh, Boff checked his watch. "Anyway, I've got some errands to run for her. She's talking to me again."

"She stopped speaking to you? Why did she

stop speaking to you?"

"She asked me to quit the case. I refused. When she cooled off, she saw things my way, more or less. She's punishing me by making me go food shopping. I hate shopping. Tonight I'm going to play poker with a bunch of mob friends. I'll put Julio on the table to see what I can learn."

Cullen threw another punch. "If you win, I want half for having to put up with you."

"No problem. Half of nothing is nothing. I never win. Not because I'm not a great card player, which I am. It just makes them happy to take money from an ex-fed. When can you find out if Julio had a datebook?"

"Tonight."

"Good. We'll go see Vasquez tomorrow afternoon. I have to spend the morning in court. Some tree huggers are fighting a construction company that wants to build a housing development near a protected forest. Guess which side I'm representing."

Boff grabbed a clean towel, wiped the sweat off his face, chest, and arm pits, then slipped his shirt on. After he was gone Cullen relocked the door and went back to his workout.

Chapter 35

That night, Cullen went to see Cassandra to find out if Julio had kept a datebook. Her three-year-old daughter Lila let him in the front door. A pretty teenage baby sitter he had seen before was on the couch watching a reality TV show.

"Mommy's got a date," Lila said. "Don't tell her I told you."

He headed toward the kitchen, where Cassandra was mixing an Absolut and cranberry juice. She was wearing a sleeveless black cocktail dress and lots of jewelry and apparently had been to a hair stylist for highlights. Seeing him, she blushed. He hadn't called to tell her he was coming because she would've asked why and made a stink.

"It's none of your business," she said before he could utter a word.

"What? I didn't say anything."

"You figure I have a date."

He stopped at the door. "Lila squealed. But I would've guessed anyway from the clothes you're wearing."

"So what if I have a date? It's been eight months. Don't judge me."

"Slow down," he said. "I'm happy for you."

"You are?"

"I want you to have a social life again."

Cassandra let out an anxious sigh. "Danny, I'm so nervous. This is my second drink. He's coming to pick me up in fifteen minutes."

"Who is he?"

"His name's Marco Morales. He books lounge acts for the MGM Grand. I met him through Julio." She fussed with her hair. "How do I look?"

"Hot tamale."

"But not too much heat, right? Marco is sort of a conservative type."

He smiled at her "You look terrific. Any man would go for you."

"I've been wound up all day. You came just to see me?"

"Well, not quite. Did Julio keep a datebook with a schedule of things he had to do?"

Cassandra frowned and swallowed half of her drink. "You never quit, do you."

"I'm a fighter. Losing is never an option."

"Okay, Julio had a big book, like a photo album. In it he wrote down training schedules and meetings."

"Is it here?"

"Nothing of his is here. I couldn't deal with seeing it. I rented a storage unit at one of those big facilities."

Cullen stepped forward. "Can I have the key?"

"No. I'm not going to encourage you."

"If you don't give me the key, I'll stay until you're date arrives and tell him I'm your live-in lover."

"You wouldn't!"

"Wanna bet?"

"You are such a jerk." She walked over to a sugar jar, took a key out of it, and flipped it to him.

"Thanks."

"You're not welcome. Julio's stuff is in a U-Haul Self Storage on Las Vegas Boulevard."

"I know where that is." He pocketed the key. "When I get in the unit, where should I look?"

"I put the book with some other personal papers in an empty case of Don Eduardo tequila. The name's right on the box."

The doorbell rang.

Cassandra drained her glass and put it in the sink. "Back door! Quick! I don't want him to see you!"

"You sure you don't want me to stay and check him out? I can tell him I'm your brother."

"No! No! Go!" She hustled him out the door and all but slammed it behind him.

He waited a few minutes in the back yard, then walked around to the front of the house and looked in the living room window. The guy was good-looking and dressed well. Cullen tapped on the window. When Cassandra looked up and saw him, he gave her the thumbs up. She glared back and took her date into the kitchen.

Cassandra had rented one of the larger storage units in the rear of the facility. As he parked his car, Cullen didn't see any other vehicles or people around. It was spooky, though. He got out of his car and stood there a moment, listening for sounds. Hearing nothing, he went over to the rolled-down metal door. The lock was the same kind McAlary used to secure the gym, a MAX Armored Discus, which he said was virtually burglar proof.

Cullen used the key and pulled up the door. A wave of overheated stale air hit him, so he waited a few moments for it to clear before going in. He had brought a flashlight, but there was a light switch near the entrance. He flipped it on and put the flashlight on the floor near a trunk. The room, which was about ten feet wide and twenty deep, was only three quarters full, leaving him room to maneuver. Most of the space was taken up by metal closets, numerous boxes, and trunks. Cullen shook his head. A great champion's life left in U-Haul Storage. It didn't seem right. He was about to start his search when he thought he heard a noise outside. He hurried out and looked around. He didn't see anybody. He noticed again that it was quiet. Way too quiet. He hoped Arango's men were watching his back.

He searched the garage until he found the Don Eduardo box toward the rear, behind six of Julio's leather suitcases. Before checking the box, he opened each suitcase to see if it had a false bottom. Three of them did. Damn. There could have been an innocent reason Julio had one suitcase with a false bottom, but three? Why was Boff always right? As he knelt down to take the datebook out of the box, he felt a sudden explosion in his head.

When he came to, all he could feel was the fierce pain in his head. He opened his eyes. The light was out, the metal door closed. The heat was suffocating. He had no idea how long he'd been unconscious. Feeling along the top of his head for the source of the pain, he found a lump, then his fingers came away sticky. Injured and locked in a storage facility with nobody around. Way to go.

Getting to his feet, he walked carefully toward where he sensed the door was. His foot kicked something metal and it rolled along the floor. Probably a pipe that had taken him down, he thought. He reached the door, found the light switch, and flipped it on. No light. He felt along the door for the handle and yanked. It didn't budge. Don't panic, he told himself. He bent down and felt along the floor for the pipe. When he found it, he began banging it on the door and yelling for help.

After about thirty seconds of this, he stopped. The unit was probably too far from the office for him to be heard. He hadn't seen anybody in the parking lot, but he was already wondering if the Colombians were out there somewhere, and how long would it take before they thought to investigate. Then again, maybe they were the ones who had clocked him. If he could see, he might be able to figure out a way out of there. The flashlight! He had put in on the floor not far from the light switch. He took a few steps and bumped into a trunk. He bent down and searched the floor until he found it and switched it on. It didn't feel so claustrophobic now.

He banged the pipe against the door some more, then gave up. If he had a gun, he thought, maybe he could shoot out the lock. Julio had guns and had liked to go to shooting ranges. Once in a while Julio had taken him out to the desert and given him a Beretta so they could pop tin cans. No way, he knew, would Cassandra have kept the guns in the house. Either she sold them or…. He moved the flashlight beam around, looking for a likely place he might find them. A trunk seemed to be the best bet.

Cullen opened the one closest to him. It was filled with sweaters. There were three more trunks a few feet away. He searched inside the first one and found more clothes. The next one was locked. He retrieved the pipe and whacked the lock until it broke. The first thing he saw was the pair of boxing gloves he had bought Julio when they had come to Las Vegas from Venezuela. Under them was Julio's championship belt. Memories started flooding his mind, but he forced himself to shake them off and searched under the piles of clothes until he found a wooden box. It was heavy. Yess! Inside were the Beretta and a Magnum .44 caliber Desert Eagle, which Julio had said was among the most powerful pistols in the world. He hoped it was powerful enough to blast through the door lock. Picking up the gun, he ejected its clip. It had a full nine rounds. He slapped it back in. Knowing Julio always kept his guns cleaned and oiled, he felt highly confident that it would shoot.

He held the gun a few inches from the lock and fired point blank, then suddenly felt an instant piercing pain in his left thigh. Dropping the gun, he fell to the floor. The lock was intact, but one side of his jeans was ripped and bloody. "Ricochet," he said aloud, slamming his hand on the door. "Bloody genius." He ripped the tear in his pants open and trained the flashlight on his leg. The bullet seemed to have only clipped the outside of his thigh, not entered it. "Flesh wound," he muttered. But it was bleeding pretty bad and stung like hell.

He picked up the gun, managed to get to his feet, and inspected the lock more closely. There was some damage. "Try it again," he told himself. This time he backed six feet away and shielded his body behind one of the metal closets. He fired and missed the lock by a foot. He was about to pull the trigger again when someone shouted.

"Don't shoot! I'll get you out!

Boff! Praise Jesus! "Can you open the lock?" Cullen called.

"You dare ask that of the Great Boffer?"

Within minutes, he heard a buzzing noise. The door started vibrating, then the noise stopped and Cullen saw a hand pulling the door up. Boff was standing outside holding some sort of device in his hand.

"State-of-the-art lock pick," he said. "A burglar I got acquitted gave it to me as a present."

All Cullen could do was shake his head in relief. "How did you find me?"

"I put a tracking device in your trunk when you went to give Harris the badge. After the poker game broke up, I checked for your location. Thought I'd drop by and see what you were up to. How did you manage to lock yourself in?"

"Somebody whacked me on the head with a pipe."

Boff glanced at Cullen's head, then looked more closely at his bleeding leg. "I see you handle a gun about as well as I thought."

"I think it's just a flesh wound."

Boff took the Desert Eagle, ejected the clip, and looked at it. "Three hundred-grain, jacketed, hollow point. Would've punched a hole through you the size of my fist," he said. "You're lucky it didn't hit you in the balls, or I'd have to start calling you Danielle." Boff was sweating profusely. "This place's as hot as your gym. I hope you lost some weight for your efforts."

Cullen ignored the remark. "I found the datebook."

He hobbled over to the Don Eduardo case and brought the book back. "I need to go to a hospital."

Boff stepped forward. "I can fix you up good as new."

"I'd prefer—"

"Hospitals are required to report gunshot wounds to the police. You want them asking you questions? Dr. Boff can handle this." He went out and opened the trunk of his car, then came back with a first aid kit.

"Sit down."

Cullen parked himself on one of the trunks.

"Might sting a bit," Boff said. "You want some Vicodin?"

"You got it?"

Boff reached in his kit and tossed him a tin of Bayer aspirin. "Here, crybaby."

Cullen swallowed three dry while Boff went to

work cleaning and bandaging the wound.

"Three of Julio's suitcases had false bottoms," Cullen said.

"Does that surprise you?"

"At this point nothing surprises me."

Boff finished patching up the wound. "There you go. You owe me Chinese takeout for saving you a hospital bill."

They left the garage and closed the door.

Cullen's head still hurt. "Who do you think hit me on the head?"

"Not sure. The intriguing thing is whoever it was didn't kill you. What does that tell you—besides the fact that your head is made of cement?"

"They wanted me alive."

"That's obvious. What's not is why."

"You tell me."

"Well," said Boff, "in Soliman's case, he claims he has plans for you. Maybe he sent Harris to remind you you're only alive at his convenience."

Cullen considered this, then said, "Could've been the Colombians, too."

"Yes, it could. Or it's possible some lunatic escaped from an asylum and mistook you for his abusive father. Instead of standing here jerking off, I suggest we go to your place and check out the datebook.

Cullen opened the door to his car.

"Wait!" said Boff. "Use your device."

"Shit. I forgot." He took it out, aimed it at the car. "Still green."

Boff got in the Malibu and followed him.

Chapter 36

On the way to Cullen's apartment, they made a pit stop at a Chinese restaurant, where Cullen paid for the takeout. At Cullen's building, Boff stood on the sidewalk and looked up and down the street.

"What are you looking at?" Cullen asked him.

"Check out the parked Crown Vic." He nodded toward the car on the opposite side of the street, about thirty feet away. There were two men inside.

"What do you think?" Cullen said.

"We should get our asses up the stairs. You go first. I'll be right up."

Cullen kept the lights off and walked over to a window, where he looked down at the car. A minute later, Boff came in, carrying binoculars, a grease-stained bag of Chinese food, and a rectangular device with holes arranged in a circular pattern on the front. He put the device and the Chinese food down on the coffee table, then joined Cullen at the window and trained binoculars on the Crown Victoria below.

"One's a cop," Boff said after a few seconds. "Detective Thornton. He was here the night your car blew up."

"Lemme see." Cullen grabbed the binoculars. "The other guy's his partner," he said. He gave the binoculars back to Boff. "What are they doing here?"

"Surveillance. Or they might have an agenda."

"Like what?"

"Maybe they were paid to kill you."

"What should we do?"

Boff put the binoculars down on an end table, scrolled through his cell phone's directory for a number, then picked up Cullen's land line on the table.

"This is Danny Cullen," Boff said. "I live at 457 Carter Street. There are two men sitting in a parked car by my building. My own car was blown up the other night by an explosive device. I'm a little worried. I think I recognize one of the men as a Detective Thornton, just not sure…yes I'll hold on."

"What are you doing?" Cullen asked.

Boff didn't answer. A moment later, the person on the other end of the line apparently came back on. "I see," he replied. "I feel much better. Sorry to have bothered you." He hung up and turned to Cullen.

"They're on surveillance. The desk sergeant checked with the detective bureau. Thornton and his partner signed out for this address. You can hit the lights now." Boff picked up his binoculars, went back to the window and trained it on the Crown Vic. Then he dialed information and asked for a Pizza Hut nearby.

"Hi," he said. "Do you have vegetarian pizza? What kinds of toppings are available?" He listened, then said, "Okay, I'll take the Veggie Lovers Pizza with banana peppers, pineapple, jalapeños, and lots of anchovies." He paused, then, "You wouldn't happen to have any marshmallows around, would you? … That's okay. I'd like it delivered to two friends sitting in a Crown Victoria near 457 Carter Street, license plate 326NEB. Throw in a couple large Mountain Dews and attach a note saying the pizza is compliments of Frank Boff. Yes, I'll pay by credit card." He read his Visa number, then hung up.

"What does that accomplish?" Cullen asked.

"I want Thornton to know he needs to do a little more work on his covert surveillance technique."

"That was one ugly pizza you put together. Nobody in his right mind would eat that."

"That's the point."

Cullen grinned. "Does a day go by when you don't bust somebody's balls?"

"I'm sure that happens from time to time. I just can't recall any. Let's go into the kitchen." Boff picked up the bag of Chinese, sat down at the table, and pulled out the food.

"Aren't we going to look at the datebook?" Cullen rubbed his head again. It was still sore.

"After we eat. I'm starving."

"You're always hungry."

"I'm a growing boy."

As Boff dug into the shrimp and pork chow mein, Cullen went to the bathroom and washed the blood off the bump on his head, then used a wad of toilet paper to dab hydrogen peroxide on it. Then he changed his jeans, leaving the ripped and bloody pair on the bedroom floor, and went back into the kitchen, where he sat down to eat his shrimp and steamed vegetables. Boff was already working his way through two soggy-looking egg rolls and the spareribs.

"Do you have any ketchup?" Boff asked.

"Yes. What for?"

"Just get it."

Cullen went to the refrigerator and brought back a plastic bottle of Heinz, which Boff spanked over his spareribs.

Cullen made a face. "How the hell can you put that on spareribs?"

Boff gave the ketchup bottle another shake. "I love ketchup and I love spareribs. Why not marry them?"

"And chow mein is like McDonald's junk food."

"So? I like junk food. Want some? I've got plenty." He lifted a big forkful of it and held it out.

Cullen backed away. "Get that crap away from me."

"Your loss." Boff shoveled it into his mouth. "Needs a little seasoning." He opened several packages of duck sauce, hot mustard, and soy sauce and soaked the chow mein, then he crumpled two fortune cookies in the mixture. Taking in a big mouthful, he smacked his lips. "Ahh, that's better."

As Cullen frowned and shook his head, Boff picked up the fortunes.

"This one is obviously mine. *Your greatest fortune is the large number of friends you have.* This is yours. *He who throws dirt is losing ground.*"

Fortune-telling completed, Boff dove back into his food. He ate so fast, you'd think it was his first meal in a week. All Cullen could do was push his carton of cooling steamed vegetables away.

Boff looked up. "What's the matter? You're not hungry?"

Cullen didn't answer.

"Then I'll eat yours when I'm done with mine. You know what would really go great with this? My boxed Almaden Chablis."

"What kind of crap is that, anyway?"

"Tasty economical wine. Why pay twenty bucks or more for a fancy bottle when you can get a five-liter box of Almaden for sixteen? That being said, I do like a good Russian River Chardonnay or French Bordeaux. But only when the client is paying."

It took Boff fifteen minutes to polish off his food, then Cullen's shrimp and vegetables. While he ate, Cullen sat there fuming, not saying a word. He wasn't going to give Boff the satisfaction of knowing he had gotten under his skin again.

Boff finally looked up. "God, I love Chinese food." He belched loudly.

"Is there anything you *don't* like to eat?"

"Brains. I eat enough of those in court."

Boff laughed. Cullen didn't.

"Let's do some work," Cullen said. "I'll put music on."

"Not necessary. Let's go into the living room." Boff went over to the coffee table and picked up the rectangular device.

"What's that for?" Cullen asked.

"I couldn't stand hearing that awful music of yours, so I bought this at a spy shop."

"What does it do?"

Boff fiddled with it a moment. "There, it's on. This is an audio jammer. It emits a random masking sound which defeats any listening device within a hundred and fifty square feet. The bugs won't pick up a thing now. Even if they had a parabolic mike in the next apartment, it wouldn't hear our conversation."

Now Cullen was moderately impressed. "You're big on gadgets."

"I operate on the theory that no matter how stupid and incompetent I think my opponent is, I assume he may be using the best devices money can buy. So I stay one step ahead. Okay, now let's check out the datebook."

They sat down on the couch, and Boff opened the book and started to leaf through it.

"This guy did a lot of training," he said as he scanned the pages. "Do all boxers have two-a-day sessions?"

"Some. Most only do it when they have a fight scheduled. Me, I basically never stop training. There's still too much to learn, and it's easier to make weight if I keep active."

"You need some fun in your life, my friend."

"I've *been* having fun. It's not often I get attacked by two cops, have my car blown up, get clubbed on the head, and then shoot myself in the leg while locked in a storage facility." He turned to face Boff. "What do you do for fun?"

"I like spending time with my wife. I'm a homebody."

Cullen just shook his head. A homebody? The

man was mass of contradictions. Well, he thought, with Boff, anything was possible.

Boff turned another page. "Dinner with Arango," he read out loud. "Beginning in September two years ago, almost every six weeks he had dinner with Arango. Does that mean anything? I don't know, but it does raise a little red flag because the time interval was constant." He turned pages back and forth. "Beyond the obvious boxing bullshit, there are lunches with Sal, Nat, Sammy, Jack, and Lou." He looked up. Know them?"

Cullen frowned. "No."

"Sal could be Sally, Nat, Natalie. Sammy could be short for Samantha, Jack for Jackie, Lou for Louise. Did you get confirmation on what that boxer told you about Julio having trouble keeping his pecker in his pants?"

"Yes. From Arango."

Boff turned more pages and let out a whistle. "Lover boy must have really had the hots for Lou. Starting in February of last year, he had lunch with her every three weeks." He looked off for a moment. "The DEA guy I met with told me the agency hadn't signed Julio because he was under contract to another team. I didn't understand what he meant then, but now I think I do. Lou could also be short for lieutenant. In cop speak, lieutenants are often called Loo."

"Harris?"

"Could be. Three weeks is the usual time frame for an informant to report to his handler."

"Harris as handler? That would mean—"

Boff finished the thought. "—he busted him. Not the DEA."

"How would Harris have known Julio was running drugs for Arango?"

"Same way the DEA could have. Harris is head of Narcotics. He's got snitches all over the streets. Because he's local, it'd be easier for him than the agency to hear about a big-time athlete mixed up with the Colombians. Harris gets Soliman to assign some of his men to watch your friend. They see he goes to Mexico every six weeks or so, and maybe when he comes back he doesn't drive right home."

"He goes to Arango's?"

"And Arango's men take out of Julio's trunk the three suitcases with false bottoms you found in the storage garage."

"How much could just three suitcases of Ecstasy be worth?" Cullen asked. "Doesn't seem like a big enough delivery for the risk."

"Three suitcases could easily hold forty pounds," Boff said. "Roughly one hundred-seventy thousand pills. Street value is about four-point five million."

"Wow."

"So…Julio comes out of Arango's place later carrying the same three suitcases. To Soliman's men that seems suspicious. The next trip Julio makes to Mexico—"

"—Harris pulls him over on the way home from the airport for speeding. Easy to do because Julio drove like he fought, pedal to the metal."

Boff nodded. “Harris would be alone in an unmarked so he doesn’t have to tell a partner why he isn’t taking Julio to the station. Julio would’ve been no use to him booked. Harris reads him the riot act, a no-brainer. Spy on Arango for Soliman or Harris will bust him.”

Cullen gave this a minute’s thought. “If so, then Soliman was lying when he said Julio wasn’t directly performing a service for him.”

“Shocking isn’t it. A mobster who lies.”

“Fucking Soliman!”

“Don’t get your balls in an uproar yet,” Boff said. “This is all conjecture. Let’s wait to see what Vasquez turns up, but I like this more than the DEA scenario.”

“Why?”

“The DEA is a little better at protecting its key informants. A little. Not much.” He put the book down. “I’ll pick you up after your morning workout. What are you going to tell McAlary about your leg?”

“Anything but the truth.”

Chapter 37

Cullen pulled up to McAlary's house at the same time as Trillo the next morning. Nodding at each other, the two fighters got out of their cars and walked toward the gym. Trillo's right eye was puffy and purplish.

"How'd the fight go?" Cullen asked him.

"Knock-out in three."

"Great."

"Not so great. I was the one knocked out."

"Sorry."

"Ryan told me what I did wrong. I'll bounce back."

McAlary was skipping rope when they entered the gym. "Danny," he said, "get dressed quick. Wrap your hands. I want to work you hard on the mitts. We lost two days while I was away. Miguel, you do your shadowboxing."

Cullen kept his back to Trillo while they both changed so he couldn't see his bandaged leg. He put on sweat pants instead of shorts. After wrapping hands, he tapped his fist on Julio's locker and hustled into the gym. McAlary helped him on with the gloves and they climbed into the ring.

"Show me some pop," the trainer said. "Pump up the volume."

Cullen had only been hitting the mitts a minute when McAlary stopped him. "What's wrong with your left leg?"

"Nothing."

"Don't tell me nothing. You're favoring it."

"I cut myself with a knife while cooking," Cullen said. "It's too stupid to even talk about. The cut is nothing."

"Let me see."

Cullen backed up a step. "Ryan…."

"You heard me."

Cullen slowly pulled down his sweat pants.

"Take off the bandage," McAlary said.

"Really, I'm fine."

"Do it!"

Cullen took Boff's bandage half way off. "See, it's not bad."

McAlary gave it a close look. "No knife did that. I've seen enough gunshot wounds to know one. Somebody shot you."

"Uh, not exactly."

"Then what?"

"It's a long story."

McAlary looked his boxer straight in the eye. "Tell it. You aren't training until I hear."

Cullen put the bandage back in place, then they sat on a bench. McAlary didn't say a word as Cullen told him everything, but his face kept getting redder.

"And that's it. I'm sorry," was all Cullen could think to say.

McAlary got up, walked back over to the ring, and sat on the apron.

"Dammit, Danny! I can make you a champion, but not if you're dead! First your car, now this. What's next? They blow *you* up?"

"Not likely," Cullen protested. "Boff bought me a bomb detector to use on my car before I drive it. I should be safe." He could tell McAlary was straining hard to control his anger.

"The next time I see outside activities are hurting you too much in the gym," the trainer finally sputtered, "I cancel this fight. We clear on that?"

"Yes."

"Get back in the ring. And do yourself a favor. Never tell Kate what you just told me. She'd rip your head off. She's a lot tougher than I am."

***

Cullen left his car at the gym and drove with Boff to the bodega to meet with Vasquez again.

"What we have here," Vasquez said, handing them printouts, "is a pattern of deposits roughly six weeks apart with a few longer intervals, I assume while he was training for a fight. The money was placed in a bank in the Caymans owned by a Colombian drug dealer named Humberto Arango. Arango uses the bank to launder his money."

"Plastic?" Boff said.

Vasquez handed them another printout. "Nothing unusual in his Las Vegas charges. What's curious is when he went to his home in Mexico every six weeks or so, there generally were very few charges."

"He wasn't there to sightsee," Boff said.

"The airline charges indicate he'd go down and

back within a couple days," Vasquez said. "But there were exceptions. Two or three times a year, he stayed for a couple weeks and charged plenty. Many of them were at women's boutiques, hair salons, and jewelers."

"He took his wife on vacation," Cullen said.

"Or a girlfriend."

As Cullen shot Boff a dirty look, Vasquez picked up a box of cranberry/orange granola, poured some in a bowl, and started eating it dry with his fingers.

"There's other stuff," he said. "Frank, you'll pick it up. Basically, I'd say this is an individual with something to hide."

On the drive back to the gym, Boff put all the pieces together.

"Julio was apparently making a drop to Arango every six weeks," he began, "which coincided with the deposits to his off shore account. Every three weeks he met with Lou, which is consistent with the time frame for reporting to a handler. It's hard to dismiss these as coincidences."

Cullen hated to agree, but it looked like Boff was right. When they'd met at Franny's Diner, Boff had said Julio must have lived a secret life. He'd scoffed at the idea then, but now? Now he didn't. But how could he have missed the signs? Probably because he'd created a Julio Babbas in his father's image and it had blinded him.

Boff put a Little Richard CD in and turned up the volume.

"Turn that down," Cullen said.

"Why? I had to listen to your classical crap."

"That's because of the bugs. What's your excuse for this stuff?"

"I enjoy it. Jerry Lee Lewis is up next. 'Whole Lotta Shakin' Goin' On.'"

Ignoring Boff, Cullen turned the sound down so low they could barely hear it.

"You want to hear Beethoven?" Boff said.

"Like you'd have him in your collection."

"As a matter of fact I do." He hit eject, took a CD out of his leather case, slid it in, and turned up the volume again. As Cullen gave him a dirty look, he said, "Chuck Berry's 'Roll Over Beethoven.' One of my favorites."

Cullen ejected the CD.

"You take life much too seriously, my man," Boff said.

"Is that so? How should I take it?"

"You want the Boff Theory on How to Get Through Life?"

"Do I have a choice?"

Boff smiled. "I start with two basic assumptions. One, all people suck. Two, they're out to screw you. If you accept these two basic assumptions, you aren't aggravated when it happens. The bonus is when you meet someone who doesn't suck or try to screw you, like my wife, then you feel blessed and never complain about them. Even when they do something you don't like."

Cullen shook his head. "Most people go under

the assumption human beings are basically good."

"That's because a lot of them listen to their priests. Which is comical, considering that penguins are among the most perverse human beings on earth. And I'm not just talking about the child molesters. I mean, what kind of man chooses never to have sex with a woman? That's sick."

"They call it devotion to God."

"Why would God want priests to keep their peckers in their pants? Give me one good reason. Fact is, God wants people to get laid because that's how the human species propagates. Ministers claim to have channels to God, yet they marry and lead relatively normal lives. So do rabbis. It makes no sense that God would tell only priests not to get their dicks wet. Bottom line? If there is a God, he's the only one more clever and diabolical than me."

"You know you'll never get into heaven with that attitude."

"Is that where you think you'll be going?"

"I like to think so."

Boff gave a short laugh as they turned a corner. "You love to box, right? Do you think they have boxing in heaven? What are you going to do up there to kill time? Play the harp? From what I've observed, you have no outside interests. Everything is boxing for you. Well, heaven is a pipe dream. If it wasn't, how come nobody in the history of man has gone through the Pearly Gates and come back and given us the skinny on what they do up there all day without sex, sports, movies, and all the other things we love down here on earth. This life is The Big

Show, so enjoy it before the final curtain comes down." He glanced over at Cullen, who was still frowning. "That's why I tell you not to take things so seriously. If there was a trial to prove the existence of heaven and twelve priests were on the jury, I guarantee you I could convince them there isn't any evidentiary way to show beyond a reasonable doubt there is such a place. Face it, my boy. When you die, the only place you're going is into the ground or an urn."

Boff stopped talking. His usually bland face was flushed with emotion.

Cullen turned to him. "Did you ever tell your wife what you just said to me?"

"Are you fucking crazy? My wife draws comfort from believing in God. As big an asshole as you think I am, I'd never do or say anything that'd cause her pain."

Cullen considered this and nodded his head. Then, "Do I suck?"

"Not sure yet. You're on the borderline between those that suck and those that don't. Could go either way."

"When I first met you, I thought you sucked."

"Didn't you just say you go under the assumption people are basically good?"

"I did. Until you came along. When God made you, he obviously threw away the mold."

This made Boff smile in spite of himself. "That's because he was so disgusted with what he'd done, he didn't want to create any more like me. Now can we get off this airy-fairy talk and get back to the problem at hand?"

"Okay. What do we do next?"

"I'd like to see Julio's case file."

"You haven't done that yet? I would've thought it would be the first thing you'd do."

"As I've told you many times, I have a very low opinion of the investigative powers of cops. If this case went cold, that didn't mean it couldn't be cracked. All it proved was incompetent people who don't like to work hard or think outside the box had failed."

"So why do you want to look at the file now?"

"With the information we've gathered, there might be some basic facts that could lead me in directions the cops weren't able to see."

"It's files, by the way. Plural. One from Homicide, one by Gholston. I've been over the Homicide file a zillion times. There's nothing there."

"We'll see about that. Besides, it gives me a chance to say hello to my friend Lew."

Chapter 38

Hearing the door open, Gholston looked up from his cheese crackers. "There goes my day."

"Good to see you, too, Lew," Boff said.

Gholston turned to Detective Sayson. "Homer, take an inventory of everything not bolted down. Cullen, why'd you bring him here?"

"You're the one who put him on the case."

All Gholston could do was shake his head. "I did that hoping it would keep you out of my hair. Stupid me. Okay, so where's my bribe?"

Boff tossed a McDonald's bag at him, but Gholston fumbled it and the bag hit the floor. Shooting Boff a dirty look, the detective picked it up.

"McDonald's? You gotta be shitting me."

"Double cheeseburger, jumbo fries, and plenty of ketchup," Boff said. "You don't want it, I'll eat it."

Gholston opened the bag. He took out the fries and stuffed a few in his mouth. "Where's the salt?"

"Salt's not good for your blood pressure," Boff said. "Which I suspect shot up very high when you saw me."

Cullen saw it was time for him to intervene. "Boff wants to look at Julio's Homicide file," he said.

"What for? Even Darth Vader here won't find anything."

"Only one way to know," Boff said.

Gholston sighed and put the fries down. Then he went over to a file cabinet, pulled the drawer out until it got stuck, banged it open, and found the folder, which he handed to Boff.

"Can I make a copy of this on your Xerox?" Boff asked.

"Over my dead body."

"No harm in asking." Boff sat down at an unoccupied desk and began reading.

Gholston picked up the double cheeseburger and took a huge bite. "Danny," he said through the meat and cheese, "do you remember Avery Haymon? He was the assistant D.A. here who got whacked. They never found his killer.

Cullen shook his head. "What year was that?"

"Nineteen ninety-three."

"Christ, I was six years old!"

Gholston took another bite. "My kid read newspapers when he was six. That's why he went to UCLA and is an orthopedic surgeon, while you run around in short pants punching people for a living. I closed the case yesterday. Schneider was murdered while preparing to indict—"

"Lew, I don't care. I'm happy for you, but the guy's still dead."

"So is Julio."

"And you're disturbing Boff's concentration."

Boff looked up. "Let him talk. I never pay attention to anything a cop says."

Twenty minutes later, he closed the file.

"So?" Cullen asked.

"A few things look promising."

"Bullshit," Gholston said. "Name one."

"I wouldn't want to embarrass you in front of your partner."

"You didn't find squat."

Boff handed the folder to Gholston. "Let's go, Danny."

Gholston stood up and stepped toward Boff. "Not before you give me back the piece of paper you swiped from the file."

"Paper? Oh, you mean this." Boff took a folded sheet out of his pocket. "Sometimes I take things without realizing."

Gholston snatched it. "This is from the CSI report. How the fuck could you steal something that important?"

"*Borrow*, not steal. I would've returned it. Besides, it's your fault because you wouldn't let me use your copier."

"Cullen, get him out of here before I really do have a stroke!"

"So," Cullen said as they walked up the basement stairs to the first floor, "what did you find out?

"Nothing. But rather than make it a wasted trip, I got some enjoyment out of busting Gholston's balls."

"Nothing? I thought you were the Great Boffer."

"Let's talk to the lieutenant who ran the investigation."

The minute they entered Homicide, the three detectives on duty reached for pencils and made crosses, which they held up as if they were warding off either vampires or the devil.

"Nice to see you guys, too," Boff said.

"Please tell me you're not working on my Anderson case," a young detective said. "I put three months into this thing."

"Relax," Boff told him. "Anderson's going to prison. Now if he'd hired me…."

One of the other detectives said, "I'm surprised that primo sleazeball didn't."

"Actually, he tried," Boff said, "but he didn't have the money for my retainer. The only thing worse than being an indicted felon is being an indicted felon short on cash."

The joke fell flat.

"We've got nothing to say to you, Boff," the third detective, an older Hispanic man, said.

"No problem," Boff said in a more cordial voice. "I'm here to see Lt. Wilhelm."

"First door on the left. And don't steal anything. I'm going to frisk you on your way out."

Lt. Wilhelm's door was wide open. He was on the phone. Seeing Boff, he frowned and swiveled his chair so his back was to them.

"Not many people here seem to like you," Cullen remarked.

"As I've told you before," Boff said calmly, "the more cops hate me, the better the job I'm doing."

They waited a couple minutes until Wilhelm finished his phone call and swiveled back to them. He looked at Boff. "Why me? I was having a good day."

"Because you were in charge of investigating the Babbas murder," Boff said.

"We didn't have a suspect then. Don't have one now. Go see the bone collector, Gholston. Who the hell are you defending?"

"Actually, I'm working for the good guys."

Wilhelm shook his head. "That'll be the day."

"He's helping me find Julio's killer," Cullen said.

"Lots of luck. Babbas' case is colder than my grandma's tit."

"How would you know your grandmother's tit was cold unless you've touched it?" Boff asked. "Shame on you, Herman."

Wilhelm sighed. "Okay. Let's make this as painless as possible. What do you want to know?"

Boff asked questions. Wilhelm gave short answers. "Only thing I found suspicious was that three of Babbas' suitcases had false bottoms," he said.

"Let me guess," Boff said. "You discovered an Ecstasy tab or two."

Wilhelm hesitated. "How would you know that?"

"I'm Frank Boff."

Cullen spoke up. "Why wasn't that in your report?"

"It *was* in the report."

"No. I've been over that folder countless times. There's no mention of the suitcases or Ecstasy."

Wilhelm frowned. "I had my detectives looking

into the drug angle. They found out Babbas took trips to Panama to the estate of a Colombian mobster named Arango. I assume you know who he is. They go back a long way."

"Did you talk to Arango?" Cullen asked.

Wilhelm shook his head. "He wouldn't see me. One of my people suspected Babbas might've been humping Ecstasy for Arango, but that went nowhere. It was pretty farfetched to think a wealthy boxer like him with his solid-citizen reputation was a mule. And, yes, I put all that in the report."

"It wasn't there," Cullen insisted.

Wilhelm picked up the phone and punched three digits. "Gholston, have someone bring the Babbas folder to my office … Yes, they're here—no, it's not for them. *I* want to see it." He hung up and looked at his visitors. "Now if you're done, I'd like to get back to work."

"As always, Lieutenant, it was a pleasure talking to you." Boff nodded his head and started toward the door.

Wilhelm opened a desk drawer and brought out a can of air freshener and sprayed.

Boff sniffed the air. "Lilac. My favorite scent."

"You thinking what I'm thinking?" Cullen said as they entered the parking lot.

"Harris signed out the folder from Homicide," Boff said, "and when he heard it was going to Gholston, he did a little creative editing."

Boff used the bomb detector on his car, then they got in and started back to the gym for Cullen's next workout session.

It felt to Cullen like they were crawling.

"Do you think you can go faster than friggin' thirty-five?" he said. "McAlary is already pissed at me about the gunshot wound. If I'm late, he's going to grind my ass into the ground."

"I never break the law," Boff said, "even when I'm driving."

"So go forty. No cop is going to stop you for that."

Boff pushed it up to exactly forty. Cullen still felt like they were moving in slow motion.

"Here's the situation," Boff said. "It's almost certain Harris busted and flipped Julio. The most obvious reason Julio ended up dead is Arango found out and killed him."

"That's what I think."

"By now you know what I'm going to say next."

"On the Dark Side," Cullen said, "things aren't always what they appear to be. So we still can't rule out that for some reason Soliman killed Julio."

"Correct."

"Why would Soliman kill Julio when he was an asset?"

Boff shrugged his shoulders. "Maybe he stopped being an asset and became a liability."

"How?"

"I have a theory. I'm not ready to air it yet, though. I want to see what I can turn up on the Dark Side first."

Boff said nothing more the rest of the way to the gym. Cullen dashed in with three minutes to spare, dressed fast, and reported to McAlary.

Chapter 39

After Cullen went six hard rounds with Julio's former sparring partner, Emilio Rojas, he invited him out to lunch because he wanted to ask him some questions about Julio. Rojas walked around to the passenger side of Cullen's car and opened the door.

"Wait!" said Cullen. "Don't get in yet."

"Why not?"

Cullen took out his device and checked the car. The light stayed green. "Okay," he said, "you can get in now."

Rojas looked at the device. "What's that in your hand?"

"Bomb detector. Somebody blew up my Camry."

"Jesus! What are you into?"

Cullen got in the car and started it. "I'd rather not say."

At the Torrey Pines Pub, they both ordered the charbroiled chicken salad and diet sodas. After minimal chitchat about boxing and diets, Cullen decided to get down to business.

"Did you notice anything different about Julio in the time leading up to when he was killed?" he asked.

Rojas put his fork down. "Yeah. As a matter of fact, I did. Why?"

"What was it?"

"Well, about two months before he got shot, he

started acting strange in the gym. You know, edgy. Short-tempered. It wasn't like him. He even cussed me out for not hitting him harder." Rojas shook his head. "I told him if I did, I'd be out a job, but he kept insisting I try to rough him up. It was almost like he wanted me to punish him. Yeah, yeah, I know, I ain't a shrink, but it was so out of character. I asked him if he was having trouble with Cassandra, but he said no, it was just, well, he had a big decision to make and couldn't tell me about it. Then, like a month before he got killed, he suddenly seemed back to normal. I asked him if his problem had been solved. He said yes. I still remember exactly what he said. 'Like in boxing, when you're pinned on the ropes you have to fight your way off.'"

"What do you think he meant?"

"Not a clue. You think it had something to do with his murder?"

Remembering the troubled look he'd seen on Julio's face before the masked guy shot him, Cullen shook his head and looked down at his food. "Who knows?"

Rojas laughed. "Danny, you were never a good liar. Neither was Julio. If you don't want to tell me, fine. I mind my own business. Just don't get yourself killed like Julio, okay? I could use a steady paycheck as your sparring partner."

When Cullen got home that afternoon, he found a message from Boff on his answering machine inviting him to his house for dinner and to discuss the case. He was eager to tell Boff what Rojas had said. He was also curious to find out if Boff really was the suburban Joe he claimed to be. He called Boff and asked for directions.

Right away, when Cullen pulled into Boff's driveway, he spotted two men in a Cadillac parked in front of the house. He called Boff on his cell phone and told him.

"They're friends of mine," Boff replied. "Come on in. I'll explain."

Sidestepping a skateboard on the sidewalk, Cullen headed for the house. Before he could even ring the doorbell, he was met at the door by an attractive woman about Boff's age.

"Hi," she said. "Come on in. I'm Jenny, Frank's wife. Glad you could come. It'll just be the four of us. Our daughter Sharon went out to eat with her friends."

She led him through a living room, where he saw the clear plastic covers on the couch and into the dining room, where he saw the same plastic on the chairs. Sliding doors connected the dining room to a wooden deck. Darth Vader had exchanged his black cloak for a white apron with 'What Would Julia Child Do?' printed on it. Big, Bad Boff was grilling steaks.

Jenny went over and kissed him on the cheek. Turning, she said, "Danny, would you like something to drink?"

"Bottled water if you got it."

Boff looked at him for the first time. "I bought a

fresh box of Almaden in case you want to get adventurous and imbibe."

"Frank, don't be obnoxious," Jenny said in a voice Cullen recognized as one that he'd heard coming from his own mother. She turned to him. "I have no idea how he drinks that dreadful stuff, Danny, but then you don't 'figure out' my husband. You just learn to live with him." She went into the kitchen to get the bottled water.

"So," Cullen said when she was out of hearing, "why are those guys sitting in the Caddy in front of your house?"

"Somebody threatened my family."

"About this case?"

"Yes."

"And you hired bodyguards?"

"Something like that. You take your steak medium rare, right?"

"Yes. Boff, I want to tell you what Julio's sparring partner said to me this afternoon. I have a feeling it has something to do with his murder."

Boff shook his head and used his fork to point toward the kitchen. "Wait until after dinner when we're alone."

At this point, Steven walked onto the deck, and Boff introduced him to Cullen.

"So," the boy said, "what were you indicted for?"

"He isn't accused of a crime, wise guy. Danny's a professional boxer. I'm helping him find the guy who killed his friend."

"You're a boxer? Cool! Hey Boff, could I take

boxing lessons?"

"No, you cannot. You're a basketball player. With the grades you've been getting, you don't need another distraction."

Steven dismissed his father's remark with a wave of his hand. "Look who's talking," he said. "Grandma told me you weren't such a hot student, either. She said you majored in basketball at that dinky little college you went to. With a minor in goofing off."

Ignoring his son, Boff buttered raw ears of corn, wrapped them in tinfoil, and put them on the grill. Then he replied. "Your mother tells me you're been calling your bodyguard Butt-head."

"That's because Sharon named hers Beavis."

"I want that to stop. These men are doing me a big favor. I don't want you disrespecting them. Do you understand?"

"Then can we call them Frodo and Gollum?"

"What you can do is ask them their names. Any more disrespect, and I'll cut off your allowance."

Steven waved off his father's comment again and stared at the backyard.

It seemed fitting to Cullen that Boff had fathered a son who took pleasure in busting his balls.

Jenny returned carrying a tray with a pint of Poland Springs, a can of Sprite and a bottle of Saint Emilion, plus three glasses.

"Where's my Almaden?" Boff asked in an aggrieved voice.

"We have company," she said. "Just pretend

you're civilized and drink it."

"Give me a big kiss, and I might consider it."

Jenny kissed him on the lips; then looked at Cullen. "Don't you just love this guy?"

Hiding his smile, he said, "I think I need more time to get to know him better before I could say that."

Boff laughed. "He thinks I'm a big pain in the ass."

"Well you are," Jenny said, "but a lovable one."

Steven looked at Cullen. "My mother has mental problems."

"Steven!" Jenny said. "Don't say something stupid like that to Danny."

"Well, you must be mental if you think Boff's lovable."

"That's it! You can eat in your room. I don't want you at the table tonight."

"No problem." He picked up his Sprite and went into the house. "Hey, Boff," he called back. "Don't overcook my steak."

Dinner went pleasantly enough thanks to Jenny, who did most of the talking. She was a kindergarten teacher, Cullen learned, which no doubt explained how she had developed the patience of a saint to deal with her husband.

"I know you two big guys want to be alone," she said as she cleared the table. "I need to grade some papers." She put dessert plates in the dish washer and left.

"Is she a great wife, or what?"

"Better than you deserve," Cullen said.

Boff dumped the good French wine he hadn't drunk into the sink and returned to the dining room with a clean glass and his chilled box of Almaden. He poured from the plastic spout, held the glass with his pinky finger raised, made a show of swirling the wine in the glass, and sniffing it before sipping. His little act over, he said, "So what did this boxer say that you found so interesting?"

Cullen told him about what Rojas had said about the way Julio had been acting in the gym. "The main thing Rojas said was Julio told him he had to make a big decision and then did something to take the pressure off him a few weeks before he was killed. What could that mean?"

Boff gave this a minute's thought. "Well, it would tie in with this theory I've been working on about why Julio might've gone from an asset to a liability. One possibility is Julio decided to tell Harris he was through informing. Not smart, but who knows."

"Why not smart?"

"Because there's no way Harris lets him walk. Julio was too useful to Soliman, and Harris undoubtedly was rewarded handsomely for giving him the asset."

"But what could Harris do to Julio? He had sat on the evidence, so it was too late to arrest him. Harris would be guilty of obstruction of justice or something, right?"

"Correct. So what Harris tells him is, if he stops informing, he'll get word to Arango he has a rat in his house."

"Why would Arango believe Harris?"

"Harris would make sure Arango was given information only Julio could've supplied. From what you've told me, your friend was a street kid. He would've known better than to try and quit cold."

Cullen considered this, then said, "Julio told Rojas, 'It's like in boxing. When you're pinned on the ropes you must fight your way off.' Maybe he threatened to go public about Harris being on Soliman's payroll."

"Another bad move," Boff said. "In order to be credible, at some point he'd probably have to reveal he was humping drugs for Arango. That would mean the end of his boxing career and leave him open to criminal charges, too. Also, faced with a threat like that, Soliman would've whacked him. Again, I think if your friend was streetwise, he'd know that."

"Okay, then…why *did* he say his problem was solved?"

Boff took another drink. "My theory is Julio taped his conversations with Harris over a period of time. All he had to do was pop a simple old microcassette recorder in his pocket, then turn up the volume and leave it running. At some point, then, Julio would've played one of the tapes for Harris and offered to turn over all the others if they let him stop spying on Arango."

"That'd work."

"Yes. It might. Of course, me being a cynic, I

find it hard to believe Soliman would tolerate having Julio as a constant threat hanging over their heads. They'd figure he had backup copies. What we also know is he's dead. Which means he may have thought he solved his problem. But didn't."

"Yeah. I understand why Harris would see the tapes as a threat. But what could they charge Soliman with?"

"For starters, try bribery of a police officer and conspiracy to distribute illegal drugs. That's only for starters. Then there's numerous tax and wage law violations—assuming payments to Harris were in cash—some of which could be very serious. Also aiding and abetting official misconduct. There's a bunch of creative ways to indict a guy."

"So you think…."

"If your boy did record his meetings and showed Harris he had tapes, there's a good chance that's why he was killed."

Cullen nodded. Now it was making sense. "If we could find the tapes—"

Boff raised one hand like a traffic cop. "Slow down, junior. Assuming the tapes existed in the first place, they might not still be around."

"I don't care. Let's look for them. What do we have to lose? How about the storage facility?"

"Harris would've gone there."

"Julio's house?"

"Another obvious place. It could be something as simple as a train station locker, in which case we're probably screwed."

"No," said Cullen. "Julio couldn't walk into a

public place like that without attracting attention. Maybe he put them in a safety deposit box?"

"I doubt it. Julio would worry that Harris had the influence and Soliman the money to bribe bankers."

As Boff poured more wine into his glass, Cullen leaned forward. "Please don't do that swirling and sniffing routine again," he said. "It's really annoying."

"So sorry." Boff took a drink. "Anyway, Julio was your amigo, you know how he thought. Where do you think he would've put the alleged tapes?"

Something Julio had once told him suddenly came to mind. "'Hide in plain sight,' Julio always said. That's how he survived in Colombia. He said he'd always be very visible, and the cops got comfortable seeing him around, so when he did commit a crime, they'd look at the guys who stayed in the shadows. That's what he told me."

"That's a wonderful stroll down memory lane, but—?"

"Maybe it *is* as simple as a locker! But not in a train station. His locker at McAlary's. It's got a cheap combination lock. I'm sure Harris wouldn't bother looking in a place so insecure."

"Actually, my friend, the first thing a good investigator does is check out places like that to eliminate them." Boff finished off the glass. "Then again, I'm smarter than everybody else, so maybe Harris didn't. Who knows? It's probably a colossal waste of time, but my client is paying. Let's look at that locker."

Chapter 40

The lights were still on in the gym because McAlary liked to work out every night after he was done with his fighters and house chores. He was hitting the speed bag when Boff and Cullen walked in. They waited until he was done before walking over. McAlary didn't look pleased to see them.

"It's late, Danny. You should be getting ready for bed. Did you run tonight?"

"I didn't have a chance," Cullen said. "I'll do extra miles tomorrow."

McAlary looked at Boff with obvious hostility. "First time you came here," he said, his tone hostile, "I thought I'd seen your face somewhere. Then I remembered. It was on TV. You were defending a serial killer."

"An *alleged* serial killer."

"You do that a lot, do you?"

Boff nodded. "Most of my practice is involved with individuals indicted for felony crimes."

"You get many off?"

"I have a very good acquittal rate."

McAlary was getting more hostile. "Proud of yourself, are you?"

Cullen interceded. "Boff is helping me find Julio's killer. We're getting close. He's a very good investigator."

That seemed to appease McAlary. He grabbed a towel and wiped his face. "So, Mr. Boff, what is it you think I can help you with?"

Boff pointed at Cullen. "It was his idea to come."

"What for, Danny? You know I don't like having my workout interrupted."

"It's important."

McAlary picked up a rope and started jumping. "Too important to wait until morning?"

"We want to look in Julio's locker."

He stopped jumping. "You do, do you? I've kept that locked since the night he died. Why should I open it now?"

"There might be tapes in there," Cullen said, "that could help us find Julio's killer."

McAlary draped the rope around his neck and led them to the locker area. They stopped in front of Julio's locker. "Two, eighteen, five. Go ahead. Open it." He crossed his arms and stared at Boff.

Cullen spun the combination and took off the lock, but then he hesitated. If the tapes were inside, they had cracked the case. If not, it would be yet another depressing dead end. He opened the door. Inside were a pair of Julio's trunks, his boxing shoes, two rolls of adhesive tape, and a bottle of Advil. No cassettes.

McAlary stepped closer. "Can I close it now?" Cullen nodded. "Now, if you great detectives don't mind, I'd like to get back to my workout."

"Sorry about interrupting you for nothing," Cullen said in a quiet voice.

McAlary crossed the gym and started jumping rope again. Boff knelt down by the elevated ring. He looked under it a moment. "Nothing taped to the underside," he said. He looked around the gym. "The water heater and washer-dryer don't look promising." After one more look, he said, "Okay, let's go."

As they were starting to get into their cars, McAlary came running outside.

"Wait!" he called. "Follow me." He led them to the door connecting the gym to his house. "Now don't be making any noise," he whispered. "The wee one's sleeping and Kate's doing our taxes on the computer."

They followed him into the den. McAlary moved a big lounge chair aside and pulled back a throw rug, exposing a floor safe. He punched a five-digit code and opened it. Reaching inside, he lifted out a small metal box.

"This would be what you're looking for."

Cullen opened it. Inside were six mini-cassettes.

"The day after Julio was killed," the trainer said, "I checked his locker to see if there was anything of value his wife might want. I had no idea what these tapes were, so I brought them in the house and played 'em. Needless to say, I was stunned…and more than a little hurt and angry, too. My first impulse was to turn them over to the cops. Maybe with the tapes they might've found his killer." He shrugged his shoulders. "But maybe not. Only thing for sure is Julio's reputation woulda been ruined. I kept the box in the safe for a couple days while I thought some more about it. I didn't tell Kate, never have to this day. I didn't want her to know what Julio had done. In the end, I decided even if they were able to catch Julio's killer, it wouldn't bring him back, just hurt his reputation. Julio was a great boxer and good man. That's the way I wanted him remembered."

"Did the cops come around?" Boff asked.

"Three days after I made my decision, a detective named Fuller came by. He had a search warrant."

"Did you read it?"

"Glanced at it. Looked official enough. He checked under the ring like you did, then asked to see Julio's locker. So I opened it. He looked disappointed, like he was expecting to find something. Then he left."

"You weren't tempted to give him the tapes?" Boff said.

"Nay. I had already made up my mind. I don't usually change it, as Danny well knows." He managed a small grin. "Plus I didn't like the guy. He seemed more criminal than cop. Not sure why I felt that way."

"You have good instincts," Cullen said. "But why are you giving the tapes to me now?"

"Let's go back out to the gym before Kate walks in."

In the gym, they stood beside the ring and McAlary continued. "When you came here tonight, it made me realize I was guilty of what I preach against. Not letting go of the dead. That comes with…well, my background." Cullen and Boff both nodded. "As long as I kept Julio's secret, I was tethered to him as sure as if he was alive. Julio was what he was. No matter what happens now, true fight fans will remember him for all he gave them in the ring. My biggest fear now is by giving you these tapes it will put you in more danger than you already are." McAlary looked at Boff. "If you're as good as Danny seems to think," he said in a level voice, "you keep my boy safe."

"Count on it," Boff said. "Dead, my client might stop paying me."

McAlary frowned.

"Ignore him," Cullen said, stepping between them. "He always talks like that. It's an act. At home, he's putty in his wife's hands. A regular wuss."

"Well then, we have one thing in common, Mr. Boff."

"Kate wears the pants in the family," Cullen said. "She was even his manager."

"Yours, too, Danny boy, and I don't hear you giving her no guff."

McAlary went back to his training routine.

Chapter 41

As Boff drove up to the roof of a parking garage downtown, he saw only a few other cars in widely separated spaces. He parked in a space distant from every other car.

"This way," he said to Cullen, "nobody can sneak up on us."

Then he took a tape player out of his glove compartment. Julio's recordings were labeled by date. Boff popped in the one from a month before his murder. Cullen was startled to hear Julio's voice again.

Lt. Harris, he was saying, *I can't spy on Arango anymore for you and Soliman.*

They must've been at an outdoor café. There was traffic noise in the background.

Why not? Harris asked.

It's eating me up. My training is suffering. Arango is my friend. I want out.

A new voice interrupted. *Hey, Julio Babbas! Can I get an autograph, champ?*

Sure. What's your name, my friend?

Juan Alvarez. You're a true Mexican warrior. For a Colombian.

There you go.

The man evidently took his autograph and walked away as Harris spoke again.

You want out? He sounded angry. *Well, let me explain something here. There is no out! I busted you I own you.*

What are you going to do, put me in jail? How would you explain not arresting me before?

Boff hit the stop button. "Julio's smart," he said. "He's getting all the key names and facts on tape." He turned the tape back on. Harris was speaking.

Screw jail! If you back out, I'll get word to Arango you've been informing on him. What would your life be worth then?

There was a pause in the tape. All they could hear was traffic. Finally Julio spoke again.

How much longer do I have to do this?

For as long as it takes Soliman and me to run Arango out of town.

Another pause. *Next time we meet, I'll give you my decision.*

There was the sound of a chair scraping. Apparently Harris left, because they could still hear traffic noises. Then the recording stopped.

"At the next meeting," Cullen said slowly, "he probably played one of his tapes…."

"Given the time frame," Boff replied, "that sounds about right."

"You still think it wasn't Harris who shot Julio?"

"With all we know now, I guess not."

Boff put the car in gear. "Well," he said, "you have two choices."

"Which are?"

Boff pulled forward and turned into the aisle. "Let's grab a bite first. My sweet tooth is killing me. Then we'll talk."

As they pulled up in front of Franny's Diner, Boff took something the size of a fifty-cent piece out of his glove compartment and put it in his pocket. It was well past the dinner hour, and only a few truckers were eating at the counter. They took a booth far enough away that they couldn't be overheard. Boff ordered a double serving of key lime pie with whipped cream, Cullen, just coffee.

"So here's the deal," Boff said. "One option would be take the tapes to the D.A. and hope he'd have enough to make a case."

"Would he?"

"He could probably get an indictment. Maybe a conviction. Although I have to tell you, if I was defending these guys, I could get them acquitted."

Cullen nodded. "Second option?"

"Get corroborating evidence."

"Such as?"

Boff wolfed down what was left of the first piece of pie, started on the second. "This really is terrific."

"Such as?" Cullen repeated. He hadn't touched his coffee.

"You meet with Harris and let him know you have the tapes."

"Are you crazy? He'll kill me like he did Julio."

"Not with the Big Boffer running the op."

"Okay, what purpose does it serve for me to tell Harris?"

"After you tape your conversation with him, you'll have corroborating evidence."

"Oh, sure. Like he isn't going to search me for a

wire."

"You won't be wearing a wire."

"What then?"

Boff took the device from the glove compartment out of his pocket and laid it on the table. "Tiniest transmitter on the market. You're going to hide this inside your shoe. It has a powerful receiver that'll pick up every word, even from inside a shoe. The device can transmit up to fifty feet, so you park your car within range of Harris. We also stash a recorder in your car that'll pick up the conversation."

"What if he makes me take off my shoes?"

"In my long experience, I've never known a law officer at a spot meeting to search that deeply. In jail, sure. Not a public place. Also—and don't take this the wrong way—he wouldn't think you were smart enough to have such a sophisticated device, assuming he even knew one existed. Which I doubt."

"So after I get him on tape, then what? We go to the D.A.?"

"You could do that if you want to," Boff said. "But you know I have very little faith in the judicial system."

"Then what the hell is the alternative?"

"You can punish him yourself."

"What? You want me to shoot him? Feed him poison? Get real. I'm a boxer, not a hitman."

Boff gave a wide smile. "Little old ladies, even midgets, have made fine hitmen. One time, this skinny, old broad tried to knife me in the heart.

Luckily, I was wearing Kevlar. I punched her out."

"You did that to an old lady?"

"Danny, if somebody ever tries to stab you, we'll revisit this conversation. Meanwhile, let's not get too far ahead of ourselves. Part one, we set up the meeting. If you don't live through that, there's no need to worry about part two."

Cullen wasn't quite ready for all this. "Why don't you meet with Harris?"

"It would be unethical."

"Since when have ethics stopped you from doing anything?"

"When it would constitute grounds for revoking my license," Boff said evenly. "They could prosecute me on a number of things, beginning with extortion."

"But we're not asking for money."

Boff said nothing to that. When the waitress came by, he picked up the check as if to pay, then handed it to Cullen. "My son will take care of this," he told her.

Cullen put down some bills. "You didn't answer my question about money."

"All will soon be revealed."

Chapter 42

Because his mind was on the tapes and Harris, Cullen put in a half-hearted morning session. But McAlary didn't make a federal case out of it. They had almost two months to get ready for his next fight.

"What are you going to do with the tapes?" McAlary asked during a short break.

"Boff's working on a plan. I don't know all of it yet. I'll tell you when I do."

From the gym, Cullen drove to the police station as Boff had instructed and walked into Harris' office without knocking. The lieutenant was doing paperwork. There were a couple other detectives in the room.

Harris looked up. "What the fuck are you doing here?"

Cullen set a copy of Julio's tape on the lieutenant's desk. "This is something you'll want to listen to. I suggest you do it when you're alone."

Harris tossed the tape in his waste basket. "Get out!"

"After you listen to it," Cullen said, "call me on my cell. Here's my card." He put it on the desk. Harris crumbled it and threw it in the basket, too.

"I'm looking forward to hearing from you."

Harris called at three in the afternoon. "Five o'clock, Sapphire Strip Club," he said before Cullen could say a word. “Don’t be late.” He hung up.

Boff was eating Mexican takeout at Cullen’s kitchen table. His audio jammer was on so they could talk safely. Cullen told Boff what Harris had said.

“Okay,” Boff said, setting his burrito aside for a minute, “first thing you’ve got to know is once you get to the strip club, be prepared for him to take you somewhere else. That’s standard procedure so you can’t set him up. He’ll want you to go in his car. For obvious reasons, you can’t. Tell him there’s no way you’re driving off alone with him. Say you’ll follow in your car, and if you’re the least bit uneasy about the place he takes you to, like the desert or an abandoned warehouse, tell him you’re going to split. Insist it be a public place.”

“Will he go for it?”

“Absolutely. He’ll want to hear what you have to say. If you do feel okay about where he takes you, park within fifty feet of his car. Don’t get into his car right away. Make him turn off the engine and throw his keys out the window first.”

“Why?”

“So he can’t drive you away to a more isolated spot.”

“Got it,” said Cullen. “Public place keeps him from shooting me in the car.”

“Wrong. But shooting you wouldn’t be his first option, anyway. He’ll want to know about the status of the other tapes. And the deal you’re offering. And after what you tell him, he won’t be inclined to shoot. Also let him know that in the event of your death or disappearance, someone will open an envelope containing the tapes. Nine times out of ten, that cliché actually works."

"The one time it doesn't?"

"He pops you in the head. But let's not be pessimistic." Boff picked up the burrito again.

"Easy to say when it's not your life on the line."

"The last time I risked my life, I was in the DEA and very patriotic. I've matured."

"Like rotten fruit."

Boff ignored this. "Another reason you want a public place is he won't risk searching you outside the car, where he might attract attention. He'll have to frisk you in the car, which is awkward to do and will likely discourage him from searching up your ass with his finger. Nobody likes to smell shit inside a car. I tried it once. Never again."

"The transmitter won't be up my butt, so what's the difference?"

"You ever had a proctologic exam?"

"What's that?"

"Trust me, it hurts, and you can bet Harris wouldn't be gentle."

"This whole idea sucks."

"You have a better one?"

Cullen shook his head. "I'm not a private investigator."

"That's why we do it my way. Or it's the highway." No reaction from Cullen, so Boff merely said, "Now I'm going to coach you on what you have to say to Harris."

Boff knew his stuff. From the strip club, Cullen wound up following Harris to a Wal-Mart on East Tropicana Avenue. Harris chose a spot away from most of the cars. Cullen parked his car fifteen feet from Harris and only got into the lieutenant's car after he had tossed his keys out the window.

"Take off your shirt," Harris said.

Cullen removed his tee. Harris made him turn around so he could see his back. Then he searched inside his sweatpants pockets before making Cullen slide them down to his ankles. He felt inside his socks, but didn't ask him to take off his shoes.

"Underpants."

Cullen pulled them down.

"Okay. Get dressed and start talking."

"I have all of Julio's tapes," Cullen said. "And a safety net should you decide to kill me."

"How many tapes?"

"Five."

Harris nodded. "The fact that you're here and not at the D.A.'s office tells me you have a deal in mind." He paused. "I'm listening."

"First, I want some answers."

"Like what?"

"Why did you kill Julio?"

"I didn't kill Babbas."

"Bullshit."

Harris smiled. "Let's just say you'll never prove I killed Babbas. Leave it at that."

"I figure Soliman ordered you to do it."

"Why do you think Soliman ordered me to do it?"

"Because even with the tapes in your possession, Soliman would assume Julio had copies. He wouldn't want Julio hanging over him as a constant threat."

His voice carefully noncommittal, Harris said, "Okay, let's hear the deal."

Cullen recited what Boff had told him to say. "I've spent months trying to find out who killed my friend. Now I know. I also know it might be hard to get a conviction based on the tapes. Maybe they nail you on a lesser charge. You get five to ten years, you're back on the street in seven. Julio is dead. I can't bring him back, and seven years is not justice."

"So what do you want?"

"I'm an undefeated prospect. One day I might become a champion and make millions, but like every top prospect, I'm only one or two defeats away from being just another talented guy who never made it. I want two million in old bills. Then you get all the tapes. Half the money I'll keep. The rest goes to Julio's wife and daughter."

Harris's laugh was a short bark. "And you think Soliman will give me the money?"

"Let him hear the tape I gave you. He'll pay.

"I choose the drop."

"No," Cullen said. "I do."

"I'm not walking into a trap, pal. No fucking way."

"Why would I want you arrested? Even if you get indicted, I still wouldn't be sure they could prove you killed Julio. I'd also have to give up the two million. I want something tangible to have come from Julio's death. Money for his wife, his daughter, and me. And by keeping the money, I wouldn't be a threat to you anymore because I could be indicted for extortion."

Harris shook his head. "Soliman is hot-tempered. His first reaction will be to kill you."

"Sure. But he knows I have more tapes in safe hands. He's got a multi-million-dollar business to worry about. I'm small potatoes. So is two million. There are people who know I've been trying to find Julio's killer and suspect it was Soliman. Two murdered boxers linked together should be cause enough for the FBI to enter. The heat wouldn't be good for his business."

Harris gave this some thought. "Okay, I'll get back to you."

After Cullen got out of the car, Harris retrieved his keys and drove off. Cullen walked over to his car. There was a pile of clothes on the passenger side floor. He picked them up. The recorder was under them. The numbers were still turning.

Chapter 43

Cullen left his car outside his apartment and rode with Boff to see Vasquez again. Boff gave Vasquez the tape and told him what he wanted done.

"When do you need it?" Vasquez asked.

"I know this is rushing it," Boff said, "but do you think you can have it by noon tomorrow?"

"It'll cost you a little extra."

"That's fine."

After Boff drove Cullen back home, they sat in the car a few minutes without saying anything.

Finally Boff tapped the steering wheel a couple times, then said. "You okay with everything so far?"

Cullen was staring at the glove compartment door. "Yes."

"Now it gets more difficult. You sure you're up for it?"

"Stop friggin' asking me that. I told you I'm all in."

"Your church-indoctrinated morality is not going to cause this operation any problems?"

"You worry about holding up your end."

When Boff outlined the rest of the plan, Cullen was stunned, though he kept his face from showing it.

"Still okay now?" Boff asked him.

"Yes."

"If you're the slightest bit hesitant, tell me now. Before we get in too deep."

Cullen still wasn't looking at him. "I can handle it."

"If at any point I detect you can't, I'll pull the plug."

"You won't have to."

Cullen got out of the car and headed for the stairs. No, he sure as hell wasn't morally comfortable with this, but he'd reached the end of the road in his search for Julio's killer, so there was no stopping now. He went into his apartment and plopped down on the couch, still deep in thought. In no mood to do roadwork, he decided to skip it. Boff's plan clearly placed him on the Dark Side. If there was an alternative, he'd take it. That was the problem, he told himself. There was no alternative. Besides, he just wanted it over. He'd paid a price for his obsessive investigation. Julio was not the man he'd thought he was. What hurt most was that Julio hadn't trusted him with his secret or come to him for advice before making his fatal decision.

It was fully dark outside when he finally stood up. When this was done, he promised himself, he would have to let Julio rest in peace and move on with his life. It was long overdue.

The next morning, he made a quick stop at Julio's grave, told him what he was about to do, and asked him to pray for him. Then he went to the gym.

"I know the whole plan now," he told McAlary.

"Let's hear it."

They sat on a bench, and he filled McAlary in on what had gone down so far. When he said what Boff's plan was for the rest of the way, McAlary looked surprised.

"Son, are you sure you want to do something like that? Boff didn't force you into it?"

"Yes, I'm sure. And it was my decision."

"You're aware this could blow up in your face?"

"Yes."

"Let me ask you this. Would your father have done what you're about to do?"

Cullen shook his head. "No. He believed things would run their course if you let the professionals handle it."

"Yet you are…."

Cullen stared hard at McAlary. "I'm not my father."

"About time you realized that."

Cullen nodded and stared off a moment. *I'm not my father.* It felt good to finally say that. He repeated it out loud.

"As for the path you've chosen," McAlary said, "many a time in Belfast I felt like taking the same road. Only my love for boxing kept me from doing it. Danny, I'll say it again. Julio is dead. This won't bring him back. And you're going to have to live with it the rest of your life."

"But this isn't just about Julio," Cullen replied. "It's about *me*. I need closure on him. And my father, too. When I was young, I was always my father's son. After he died, I didn't know who I was until Julio came along. Then I was Julio's friend and mentor. I'm boxing now because of Julio. I don't feel like a boxer, not in the way you and he did. It's your identity. Maybe it'll be mine when this is over." He clenched his hands together. "Or maybe I'll become something else. What's important is that for the first time *I just want to be Danny Cullen.* Whoever that is. Can you understand?"

"Someday I'll tell you about me and my da." McAlary slapped him on the back. "Now let's get some work in."

Boff was sitting in his car when Cullen arrived home. Cullen parked and got in the Malibu.

"I picked up the tape from Vasquez," Boff told him.

"And?"

"Listen for yourself." Boff took out his recorder and popped the tape in. He fast forwarded it a bit and then hit play. Cullen heard his own voice.

I have all of Julio's tapes and a safety net should you decide to kill me.

How many tapes?

Five."

The fact that you're here and not at the D.A.'s office tells me you have a deal in mind. I'm listening.

First, I want some answers.

Like what?

Why did you kill Julio?

Let's just say I killed Babbas. Leave it at that.

Soliman ordered me to do it.

Boff stopped the recorder.

"Wow," said Cullen. "Vasquez made it sound like Harris admitted to killing Julio. Saying Soliman ordered him nails them both."

"As long as you've got the key words on tape, they can be used any way you want."

"If we have this tape, why don't we just take it to the D.A.?"

"Because, genius, as good as Vasquez is, an expert would detect the changes." Boff studied Cullen's face.

"What are you friggin' staring at me for?" Cullen said.

"Just trying to make sure you're as committed as you say you are."

"I already told you I'm not quitting. It's just, well, I never thought I'd be doing something like *this*."

"That's because of your hang-up about justice," Boff said calmly. "Was it just that your father died at forty-three? Or that your boxer friend got cut down in his prime? Is it just that seventy percent of the indicted felons I get acquitted are guilty as sin? What does that tell you?"

Cullen didn't answer.

Boff went on. "Justice is a word politicians use when they're picking your pocket. It's a word people in law enforcement exploit to further their careers, even when they know they're probably sending someone that isn't guilty to prison. It's a lousy world, Danny. Justice is where you find it."

He held up the recorder. "This is your justice for Julio. You either take it or the chance slips away. And let me admit to something painful. I'm rooting for you to go through with this because I want to see the right side win for a change. But don't bother telling anyone I said that, I'll deny it to my grave."

"Let's do it."

Chapter 44

That night, Cullen parked in Soliman's driveway and got out of his car. The same three goons who had picked him up in the limo for dinner were waiting outside the front door. They escorted him into the house and to a bathroom off the kitchen. When they shut the door, he felt his stomach tighten.

"Get undressed."

Boff had told him to expect this, but that didn't make it any easier. Stripping in front of mobsters was not his idea of a good time. He took off his shoes and set them down. One of the guys looked inside them with a pen light, then tossed them away. His sweatpants came next, then his T-shirt. The guy grabbed the sweats, searched in the pockets and flung them aside. They weren't playing nice. He figured they were trying to intimidate him. It wasn't necessary. He already was.

"Underpants!" said one of the other guys. "Let's go!"

This was the hardest part. He picked a spot on the wall in front of him and kept his eyes on it and then slid his underpants down to his knees.

"Bend over."

He cringed. This wasn't Harris on a spot search. They were going to look up his butt. He bent over. One of the men put on a surgical glove and moved behind him. When he felt a finger poking at the crack of his ass, he flinched and clenched his cheeks.

"Loosen the fuck up. It'll be less painful for you."

Cullen couldn't relax. The glove man struggled to insert his finger.

"Shit. Get me some lubricant."

One of the others went to a medicine cabinet and came back with a tube of K-Y Jelly. All of a sudden, Cullen felt a cold, wet finger plunge deep into his ass. He yelped. Then the finger hit a spot that was excruciatingly painful. The head of his dick felt like it would explode and a drop of white pus came out the tip. The man withdrew his finger.

"Get dressed."

Cullen's butt was still hurting. As he put his clothes back on, he told himself he understood now why Boff had wanted to spare him a proctologic exam from Harris. The bodyguards took him into Soliman's study.

The Israeli was at his desk watching a black and white fight DVD on his plasma TV. "Salvador Sanchez and Wilfredo Gomez, 1981," he said. "Awesome fight. Sanchez was as talented as Ali and Robinson."

"Sanchez died in a car crash when he was twenty-three," Cullen said.

Soliman turned off the fight. "Yes. Sudden death in his prime. Something you know more than a little about." His voice was cordial with an undertone of threat. "Take a seat, my boy. You guys can go."

The bodyguards left, and Cullen sat down. His

composure was coming back. "You talked to Harris?" he said.

"Yes, and you're right. I'll pay the two million."

"I don't want two million."

Soliman frowned. He got up and poured himself some Chivas Regal from the bar behind his desk. Then he sat back down. "You're upping the price?"

"No. I want my payment in another way."

"What might that be?"

Cullen took out the tape Vasquez had doctored and put it and Boff's tape recorder on Soliman's desk.

"This tape Julio didn't make. I did."

Soliman sipped his drink, then put in the tape and played it. His face went from curious to angry when he heard Harris saying, "*Soliman ordered me to do it.*" When the tape ended, Soliman said nothing. Cullen guessed he was digesting what he had just listened to.

"Harris was very sloppy," Soliman finally said. "I assume you have copies of this in someone else's hands."

"Yes."

"You don't want money. So…you plan to go the D.A. with this? You think putting me in jail is a form of payment?"

"No. Sending you to jail would probably end up being a death sentence for me."

"Yes, it would."

"And I want to live to become a champion like my father and Julio."

Soliman leaned forward. "Then I'm puzzled.

What kind of payment do you want?"

As Cullen laid it out the way Boff had told him, Soliman first looked surprised, then he smiled. "I wouldn't have expected this of you," he said. Cullen heard approval in his voice.

"It solves your problem and mine at the same time," was all he replied.

"If we do this, of course, then I'll have something to hold over your head."

"Not after you erase the recording you just made of this conversation." More Boff.

Soliman reached under the top drawer of his desk and brought out a digital recorder.

Cullen watched carefully as he deleted the file. "Turn it off," he said, "and leave it on the desk where I can see it."

"I wouldn't have used it anyway," Soliman said. "I like watching you box. You fight like an Israeli."

"Israelis don't box."

"But they fight."

"Then you won't mind giving me your backup."

This brought a smile to Soliman's face. "I see Mr. Boff has schooled you well." He picked up the phone, said something in Hebrew, and then hung up. Turning back to Cullen, he said, "So we have a deal?"

"It would seem."

A bodyguard entered and handed another recorder to Soliman, who deleted what was on it. When Cullen stood up, so did Soliman.

"You can keep the tape," Cullen said. "Listen to it again if you need inspiration."

"Inspiration will not be a problem." Soliman extended his hand.

Cullen didn't want to shake with the fucker, but he had to close their deal. They shook. When he tried to withdraw his hand, Soliman didn't let go. The Israeli's eyes went stone cold.

"Never lose track of who I am or what I'm capable of."

Cullen yanked his hand free. He felt like breaking Soliman's face. "Tell me why they kicked you out of Israel."

"They thought the country would be better off without me."

"So would Las Vegas."

Chapter 45

The next day Cullen felt like doing anything but train. After he called Harris and set up the exchange for that night, he felt the hours weighing heavily on him as he mechanically worked the double-end bag.

"You're distracted," McAlary said. "I can't train you when you're like this."

Cullen stood still and lowered his hands. "After tonight," he said wearily, "it's over. Either I walk in the gym tomorrow a hundred and ten percent committed to being a champion, or—"

"Or you'll be dead." McAlary rubbed the stress from his face. "Go home, Danny. Get done with your business." He looked off a moment. "In Belfast during the Troubles, I never let myself get involved in the risky things my friends were doing. But if you need me tonight, I'm with you."

Cullen shook his head. "It's bad enough *I'm* doing this. I don't want you at risk, too."

In answer, McAlary walked over to Julio's wall. "He was so much like me. A kid who came from nothing and saw too much violence on the streets. He was a warrior who'd die in the ring if he had to. Know what I'll never forget?"

"The night he won the championship?"

"The day you brought me this ragamuffin you found in Venezuela, fat and out of shape."

"And you had to spar with him to see what he had before you'd agree to train him."

"Yes. That's what I'll long remember. Sparring

with Julio on that day."

"Why?"

McAlary smiled. "When you warned him you'd send him back to the streets of Colombia if he didn't keep throwing punches, and he got angry and came at me with his eyes full of demon fire, it scared the living bejesus out of me. First and only time I ever felt fear in a ring." He dabbed at moist eyes.

That was probably hard for him to admit, Cullen thought.

"You come back to me tomorrow, Danny Cullen! You hear? You come back!"

He did a lot of thinking about the night ahead as he drove home. He wished his father were still alive. Dan Cullen would've talked him out of what he was about to do. But relying on his father had been his big problem as a kid. Now he had to make decisions like this for himself. He wondered if Boff had manipulated him over to the Dark Side to help punish Harris and Soliman. Well, he said to himself, it didn't really matter if he did. This was the way he wanted to do it, too. It was out of character for him, but…well, maybe not. He thought of himself as a decent person who obeyed the rules and treated others with respect. Yet the minute he stepped into the ring, he was an animal with a killer's instinct, and winning was never enough. His father had always said victory was more satisfying when you took their heart. He was like him in that regard.

Parking his car, he thought about how in boxing

they say every great fighter needs a great opponent to help define him. Like Ali and Frazier. Leonard and Hearns. Tonight was going to be Danny Cullen's defining moment. When it was over, if he was still alive, he'd never be the same.

Chapter 46

The only lights on inside the MGM Grand Arena were those shining down on the ring from directly above. Cullen stood there alone, leaning against one corner. There was a brown paper bag at his feet. Light spilling off the ring faintly touched the first few rows of seats. Beyond, the seventeen-thousand-seat arena was black. He checked his watch. It was two a.m.

He heard footsteps coming from the direction of a hallway leading into the arena. The footsteps stopped a moment in the dark, perhaps the walker was checking out the terrain. There was nothing to see except Cullen and the bag. The footsteps continued until out of the darkness came Harris. He was carrying a suitcase.

"What is this?" Harris asked. "You're going to fight me for the money?"

"Another time," Cullen said. "Come into the ring."

Harris shrugged and climbed through the ropes without letting go of the suitcase. He stood in the opposite corner from Cullen.

"This is where Julio fought his last fight," Cullen said.

"So you told me. I'm moved to tears. You got the tapes?"

Cullen picked up the bag. "My money?"

Harris tapped the suitcase. When Cullen tossed the bag into the center of the ring, Harris walked over, picked it up, and looked inside. "These better not be blank," he said, "or you'll be hearing from me."

"They're real." Cullen didn't move.

Harris left the suitcase in the center of the ring. He was heading for the ropes to leave when he heard his own voice coming from somewhere.

The fact that you're here and not at the D.A.'s office tells me you have a deal in mind. I'm listening.

First I want some answers.

Like what?

Why did you kill Julio?

Let's just say I killed Babbas. Leave it at that. Soliman ordered me to do it.

The sound stopped.

Harris looked up, then around. "What the fuck! I never said that!"

They heard another set of footsteps coming down an aisle toward the ring. Harris looked in that direction. Cullen didn't have to. He knew who it was. Soliman walked into the light. He was holding a recorder in one hand. His other hand was in his suit jacket pocket.

Harris stood still. "Yitzhak. What are you doing here? I can handle this."

Soliman walked to the ring and climbed in. Then he hit a button on the recorder, and it rewound. He pushed play.

Why did you kill Julio?

Let's just say I killed Babbas. Leave it at that. Soliman ordered me to do it.

Harris raised both hands in front of him, as if pushing something away. "I never said you ordered me to do it. The tape's a phony. It's doctored."

"You always were a risk," Soliman replied. "A necessary one, as it were. But there are other cops to buy."

"I swear to you that tape's a phony."

"What do you think, Danny?"

"He's lying."

Soliman nodded. "I think you're right. Either way, it doesn't really matter. It was time to rid myself of him, anyway." His hand came out of his pocket. It was holding a pistol with a silencer. Harris dropped the bag and went for his holster, but Soliman shot him twice in the chest before he could even draw. Harris went down.

Suddenly every light in the arena flashed on!

"POLICE. DROP THE GUN AND LIE FACE DOWN ON THE FLOOR."

Soliman turned to see Gholston and five detectives running down the aisle from the locker rooms. He aimed his gun at Cullen and quickly moved closer to him.

"Stop. Or I'll shoot him."

"I wouldn't do that if I were you." Now it was Boff walking down another aisle toward the ring. "Check out the catwalks," he said.

Soliman looked up toward catwalks that formed a square about two hundred feet above the ring. What he saw were SWAT snipers pointing scoped rifles down at the ring. A matrix of red laser lines suddenly crisscrossed the canvas.

Gholston yelled up to the shooters. "If he doesn't drop the gun, take him."

Soliman lowered his gun as if to let it go, then suddenly grabbed Cullen in a headlock with his other arm and dug the barrel into his temple. "Looks like we have a standoff," he said.

Boff was almost at the ring. He glanced at Harris, who was bleeding out and barely conscious. "It doesn't look like you're going to beat the count, lieutenant." Then he climbed into the ring.

"What the hell are you doing?" Soliman asked.

"Consider me the referee. I want a clean fight. That means you have to break that clinch." Boff took a step toward Soliman.

"Stop or I'll kill him!"

"I don't think so. He's your only way out of here."

As Boff took another step, Soliman removed the gun from Cullen's head and started to point it at Boff. In the split second it took him to do this, Cullen grabbed Soliman's wrist and wrenched it down as hard as he could. As the Israeli cried out in pain and the gun fell from his hand, Cullen let go of his wrist and threw a vicious shot that cracked Soliman's nose with an audible snap. As the Israeli staggered backwards, Cullen sprang after him and pumped four more punches into his face, driving him into the ropes. Voices seemed to be screaming at him, but he couldn't hear what they were saying, he was so full of rage. He kept pounding. Soon Soliman's face was little more than pulp, just like the opponents his father had finished off. But then a pair of strong arms wrapped around him. He tried to get free, but Boff was a big man and held on tight.

"Let me go! I'm not done with him!"

"It's over, son. It's done."

Cullen struggled a moment, then, deflated, let out a sigh. Yes, it was finally over.

Gholston and the other detectives climbed into the ring. One went immediately to check on Harris. Soliman was lying on the canvas, unconscious. A second cop bagged his gun, and a third cuffed him.

Boff let Cullen go. He didn't feel like he had the strength to move, but he walked over to Soliman and stared down at what was left of his face. And spit on it.

Gholston came up to him. "You okay, Danny?" he asked. His voice was surprisingly gentle.

"Yes. No. Not at all."

"You mind telling me what the hell you were trying to do?"

"Kill him."

"But we had this all worked out."

He gave Gholston a hard look. "Sometimes in the ring you have to go to Plan B."

Boff turned to Gholston, "Lew, I guess Soliman shooting Harris caught you off guard."

Gholston locked eyes with him, then a hint of a smile creased his face before he turned to his detectives. "How's Harris?" he asked.

"DOA."

"No loss."

Soliman had come to. The detectives yanked him roughly to his feet. His face was barely recognizable.

"YOU'RE A FUCKING DEAD MAN," Soliman said. Bloody spittle sprayed out of his mouth in Cullen's direction.

As the detectives started to take him away, Boff said, "Wait!"

Gholston held up a hand for them to stop.

Boff walked over to Soliman. "You probably think you're a smart man," he said, "so I'm sure you'll understand this. While it's true that mobsters are generally not the brightest people, they usually have brains enough to know when to jump ship. As soon as word gets out that you've been arrested, your men will be on planes scattered from here to tomorrow."

Soliman tried to speak, but Boff overrode him.

"Even in the remote chance they don't leave, even if they try to keep your drug trade going, the last thing they'd want to do is kill Cullen and bring even more heat on themselves. Now, as for me, if by some miracle you don't get the death penalty and wind up in the general population of whatever hellhole they send you to, I promise I'll get word to my jailed friends who are members of the Aryan Nation that you like taking skinheads out to the desert and using them for target practice." He smiled. "Harris was luckier than you. He died fast."

Now Boff turned back to Gholston. "Take this sack of shit away."

Then he walked over to Cullen. "Risking my life is not something I've ever done for a client," he said. "Nor will I do it again."

Cullen blinked. “But you said I had the hand speed to stop him from shooting you if this happened.”

“Yes, I did. What I didn’t say was there was only a fifty-fifty chance you could pull it off. Maybe forty-sixty. Which is why I wore this.” He undid a few buttons on his shirt to reveal a Kevlar vest. As Cullen gaped, he said, “This was the stupidest thing I’ve ever done in my life. I’m going to make sure I get a large bonus from my client.”

“Will you tell me now who that client is?”

Boff shook his head. “Let’s just say you should give two dozen roses to Cassandra Babbas next time you see her.”

It had been her, after all.

“One question,” Cullen said. “If Soliman offered you a truckload of money to help defend him, would you?”

“Not a chance. Even I have scruples, few though they may be. If you ever need me again, you know where to find me. See you around, champ.” Boff started to go. Then he looked across the ring at Gholston. “We square, Lew?”

“Yup. So, Frank, how did it feel working the right side of the street again?”

“Like being in the twilight zone. Thankfully, I have a new client coming to my office tomorrow. He’s accused of racketeering and various other bogus charges, which should keep me busy racking up the hours.” And with that, Boff left the ring and headed for the exit.

“Strange man,” Gholston said. “Meanwhile, I

just want to thank you, Danny, for bringing me in on this. I'll get a promotion."

"So was it worth it then? Putting up with me nagging you all this time?"

"Well, if I factor in forcing Boff to work with you on a righteous case, plus the steak and meat loaf sandwiches, plus the promotion, well, yes, then on the whole, I'd have to say…*no*."

With a smirk, Gholston went to join crime scene personnel.

Chapter 47

On his way home, Cullen called McAlary, who answered on first ring. He didn't sound sleepy.

"So it's over?" he asked.

Cullen sighed. "Yes."

"And you're okay?"

"Physically. I've got some other things to work out."

"You want the day off tomorrow?"

"No. I might be a little late, but I'll be there."

First thing in the morning, Cullen drove to the cemetery and sat down by Julio's grave. He stared at the boxing gloves carved into Julio's headstone and the words *World Champion* and touched them with his right hand. No matter what he had learned about Julio's other life, this was what his friend would always be. A champion.

"It's done, *Perro*. The man who killed you is dead. The one who gave the orders is in jail. You won the rematch by knockout."

He stared off a few moments. He was having a hard time finding the right words.

"I helped kill a man. He was a murderer, but that doesn't make it any easier for me to deal with. All I can say is, well, it was the only way to get justice for you. Maybe now I understand better the things you did in Colombia. You cast a big shadow over me, *Amigo*. It's gone now. I can walk side by side with your spirit and feel like I deserve to."

He got up and headed for his car. A Mercedes pulled over on the street. Arango got out. Cullen walked over to him.

"If you ever need a favor," the Colombian said, "no matter what it is, call me. I blame myself for Julio's death. I never should've allowed him to do what he did for me. Of all the things I've done, this one will follow me to the grave."

Cullen nodded and walked away.

McAlary was holding the heavy bag for Trillo when Cullen entered the gym. "Miguel," he said, "take a break. There's Gatorade in the fridge."

McAlary waited until Trillo was across the room, then turned to Cullen. "Bruised your knuckles, I see. Was it worth it?"

"Absolutely."

They sat on the apron of the ring, and Cullen told him everything, leaving nothing out. Well, almost nothing. Then he reached into his gym bag, pulled out the metal box McAlary had stored the tapes in, and handed it to him.

"You could've thrown out the box," McAlary said. "I don't need it."

McAlary opened it. There were tapes inside. "I thought the cops took them in the bag."

"Blanks."

"You stole evidence, lad."

"These tapes were never at the crime scene."

McAlary took the metal box and put it on the floor. "Be right back," he said.

He went into the house and returned with a box

of stick matches. He lit three and dropped them on the tapes. They started to burn. “Best this way,” he said. “Julio was a great champion. That’s how he’ll be remembered. So what about you? How will you be remembered?”

It was the question Cullen had been wrestling with all day. He thought of the Dempsey quote taped to Julio’s locker. *A champion is someone who gets up when he can’t.* Over the course of his investigation he’d proven he could get up. He looked around the gym with fresh eyes. Everything here was part of him, and he was part of it. This was where he belonged. He turned to McAlary. They stared at each other a moment. Then Cullen smiled.

“Let’s get to work. I’ve got a fight to win.”

ACKNOWLEDGEMENTS

This novel was inspired by Fred Boff.

Many others contributed with their time and insight including Barbara Selwyn, Annette Jones, Winifred Golden, Larry Patten and Jen Estes.

Special thanks to my editor, Barbara Ardinger, who taught me so much and William Trillo, who designed my wonderful cover and created my book trailer.

ABOUT THE AUTHOR

Nathan Gottlieb is a former sportswriter and author of two previous books, *Stinger* and *The Zukovka Experiment.* He currently writes about boxing for HBO's website and is working on a sequel to The *Hurting Game*.